I0726421

# The Elemental Coven

## Witch's Ambitions Trilogy Book Two

Kayla Frederick

The Elemental Coven



Nacogdoches, Texas



Cover by betibup 33

Edited by Beth Agejew

ISBN: 978-1-950530-48-9

Library of Congress Control Number: 2025905478

Second Edition January 2026

https://authorkaylafrederick.com

# The Witch's Ambitions Trilogy

**Book One:** The Council
**Book Two:** The Elemental Coven

# Chapter One
## The Battle of Ignis

AS A LITTLE girl, I had an idea of what my life would be like after graduation. I'd have my own home, maybe something with my two best friends, Clio and Helena, where we could live in harmony and do our part to keep our Coven running.

War had never been part of that.

But plans change.

When I see Ambrossi, our Coven Healer's, den on fire, a thousand thoughts go through me. Ambrossi's been a part of my life for as long as I can remember. An injury during the early years of my childhood had disabled one of my legs, and Ambrossi was the one who dedicated himself to trying to fix it. I can't remember the Healer Ignis had before him, and I don't want to imagine someone else in his place.

"Ambrossi!" I holler and rush toward the opening as if I could save him if he *is* still inside.

Clio throws out an arm, halting me. "Don't, Li. It's too dangerous." His green eyes twinkle in the firelight. He's right, but he's not happy to be. "We'll have to find another way," he mutters, glancing toward the rear of the building.

I follow close as we circle the scorched exterior, searching for an entrance that isn't engulfed in flame. But the fire has already leapt to the building next door, its greedy fingers climbing walls and swallowing windows whole. Smoke curls around us.

I rack my brain for a way to put it out or at least soothe the blaze long enough to get Ambrossi out. But water is scarce in Ignis.

A scream rings out in the distance, and a sickening feeling washes over me. The Elementals are near. Rogue witches of the Land of Five, dangerous, unpredictable, and for some reason, they've taken an interest in me.

"There's too much fire," I start to say, but Clio's no longer at my side.

Panic flares. Did they take him? Did he charge ahead anyway, into the inferno to reach Ambrossi?

"Clio!" I shout, again and again, until my throat burns worse than the smoke. No answer.

Where is he?

Another shriek sounds in the distance, closer this time.

What do I do?

Tarj and Crowe, my allies from the Council, are somewhere in Ignis, but we split up hours ago. They could be deep in the chaos by now, or worse.

I cast one final glance toward Ambrossi's burning den. Still no sign of movement. Gritting my teeth, I run in the direction they traveled earlier, hoping that when I arrive, I'll find some clue as to what I should do next. The heat of the fire gives way to the cooling evening desert air as I sprint beyond the last flaming rooftop and out into the cracked, dry earth that makes up the rest of the Coven.

"Lilith! Over here!" a hushed whisper floats from behind a boulder.

I almost ignore it, positive it's in my head, until I spot Tarj crouched in the shadows. Two weeks ago, he'd been Ignis' representative in the Council. To see him cowering in fear goes to show how bad this situation is.

I rush over to him, falling to my hands and knees. If a former councilmember is taking shelter, something big is happening. Something I'm not ready to face.

"What's going on?" I ask. My heart pounds so hard that the words are punctuated with breaths.

"The Elementals are here," he says, peering over the top of the boulder, toward Ignis' heart where the worst of the noises seem to originate.

"Ambrossi's den is on fire," I tell him.

"They planned this," Tarj says. "Someone drained the oasis."

My jaw hangs open, and I struggle to process his words. Ignis witches are known for their fire gifts. Putting them out is a separate issue. The oasis is the only water source in the Coven. The rest comes from the Council. Without either available, there isn't a thing we can do to stop the fire.

"Where's Crowe?" I demand.

Tarj shifts, jaw tight. "We saw two Elementals on the way to find you. He went after them."

"Alone?" I stare hard at the side of his face, the urge to ignite something crawling just under my skin. If I had any real control over fire yet, he'd be singed. "Why would you let him go alone?"

He huffs. "Wasn't like I could stop him."

Of course not. That's why he's hiding now behind vague excuses and half-measures. Once a Council member. Now...

nothing. He'd been dismissed, quietly, after freezing up during an attack at the Dedication Ceremony. Cowardice. I, a fledging witch, had saved him once. Seems I'll have to do it again.

"I came to find you," he adds, as if that makes it better.

I can't speak. Can't even move. I'm too stunned by how backwards this all is. Tarj, who'd spent years in the Council's inner circle, should be the one leading now. He should have strategies, spells, contingency plans and know exactly what to do. But instead, he's here, chasing after someone who barely understands her powers.

"Which way did he go?" I ask, climbing to my feet. If I can find Crowe, maybe he'll know what to do.

"You can't go," Tarj says, reaching out as if to grab me.

It's a weak attempt. I dodge him and scurry away. I don't stop or look back as I rush through the fading sunlight. Wails fill the air, mixed with more troubling sounds, energy blasts, as more witches find their way to the fight. This isn't a typical skirmish over Coven boundaries. This is what we'd hoped to prevent with Chastity's execution. Instead, it was the fuse that detonated this entire bomb.

Some of the voices sound familiar, and I can only imagine how many of my UnEquipped loved ones are caught in the middle of this, powerless and unable to defend themselves. I loop through paved stones at the center of the Coven and end up on the other side. I'm almost to my childhood home when I see smoke. Then I see *them*—my adopted parents, Raya and Haze, tucked into a nook behind a few sparse shrubs. Raya's on her knees, clutching Haze's hand tight to her chest, half of his limp body draped over her lap.

My first instinct should be to run to them, but I don't know which side of this fight they're on. They took me from my real parents, and I still don't know why. Our last interaction burns at the front of my mind, a fight all on its own. The smell of blood is sharp and coppery as I approach. Haze's shirt is soaked in it from a laceration across his abdomen. Raya is covered in blood as well, but as far as I can tell, none of it's hers.

Her eyes are wide and glassy, fixed on nothing like the world isn't real. And maybe, right now, it isn't.

My father is dead.

The last time I'd seen him, I'd been arguing with him, and now he's *dead*, and the weight of all the words I didn't say is crushing.

Another shout in the distance jolts me back to the situation at hand. I'll have to process my grief later. "We have to go," I tell Raya. "It's not safe here."

She's so deep in her grief, my voice startles her, and she looks up with watery eyes. "B-but…"

"He's gone," I snap, probably harsher than I should, but I have no patience to spare. Incoming footsteps have me on high alert. Time is short. My priority right now is finding a good place for Raya to wait out the fight. Dragging a corpse with us will only slow our progress.

Raya doesn't move. Her gaze goes back to Haze as if she can fix everything if she stares hard enough.

"We have to go," I repeat, pulling her hand from his. She's in shock, which means I'll have to put more effort into saving her life.

With an ugly snort, she sniffles and finally slides out from under the weight of her husband's body. As soon as we emerge from the rocks, a figure in a red robe appears, blasting us with a wave of fire. I lift a hand, blocking the attack with telekinesis. Using the same blast, I throw the witch far enough away to give us the opportunity to run.

I glance left, then right, scanning the smoke-choked horizon for any hint of safety. Ash swirls in from every direction, transforming the world into a shifting gray maze. Our only hope is to get as far from the heart of Ignis as we can. Judging by the settled soil, the fight hasn't gotten this far yet.

"Come on," I murmur, guiding Raya toward a dense cluster of undergrowth. I crouch and press her into the bramble, shielding her with my body for a moment before stepping back to assess. Through the tangled green, she's barely visible.

"This should be far enough away," I say, taking a quick survey of the land.

"Wait… where are you going?" she asks, her voice trembling. It's soft and scared, like a child's. She's always been the gentler of my two parents. Never a warrior. That had been my father. And now he's gone.

I kneel beside her, my tone firm. "Whatever you do, don't leave. This place should keep you safe until it's over."

"I-I—" she stammers, but I cut her off, urgency rising in my chest like a wave about to break.

"Stay here until it's over," I repeat, starting to run when her fingers clamp around my arm.

"Don't go," she whispers. Her grip is trembling, but strong. Her eyes lock onto mine, wide with fear and something deeper. "Please."

"I have to," I say, thinking of everyone who could be in the line of fire while I'm here, wasting time. Ambrossi, Helena, Clio, Angel. They're all still out there, in the fray.

I pull free, ready to dash away, when her voice stops me. "Haze wasn't always UnEquipped."

I've tried so hard to get the truth from my parents that it seems unreal for her to let it go now.

"Your parents, your *real* parents, were Elementals. When we took you in, we didn't want to do what we did, but we had to. That was the only way we could hide the truth. If the Council had known who you were, they would have destroyed you."

"Who did it?" I ask, straining to get the words out of my dry throat.

"Your father."

That's the assumption I'd made, but I let those words sink in before I ask, "If Haze had powers, why didn't he fight?" His lifeless eyes come to me again. Toward the end of my time with my adopted parents, his eyes had been filled with only anger each time he looked at me. Especially when I asked about my accident. Now they'll never show emotion again.

"He *used* to have powers," Raya clarifies. "Before he was stripped of magic."

Everything goes blank as I try to understand what she's telling me. *Always expect the unexpected,* Misty's speech from my final day of school comes back to me. I manage to ask, "Who could do such a thing?"

Raya opens her mouth, but instead of words, a horrid, strangled sound comes out. She lifts her hands to her neck and collapses to her knees, unable to draw the breath she urgently needs. I find her assailant a few feet away and send out the strongest surge of power I can, wobbling unsteadily when the attack drains a large portion of my magic. The Elemental loses her balance and falls, head slamming against a rock on her way down. Blood gleams on the gray stones, and she doesn't get back up. Threat neutralized, I turn back to Raya. She's collapsed into the dirt.

"No, no, no," I murmur and kneel beside her.

I search for a pulse, but I can't find one. She's dead. Jaw set, I sink back onto my haunches and send out a silent prayer. It takes effort to stand, but I manage it, oddly numb to the tragedy I've witnessed, and I hope I'll stay that way as I rush through the shadows, more desperate to find Crowe or Clio or anyone who can help me make sense of things.

Another yelp sounds nearby, this one chilling my blood with recognition.

Helena. My oldest and dearest friend.

I dash in the direction of the scream, fear becoming the fire that fuels me as I cross the boundary into the Grove. Helena lies in the thick foliage at the edge of the clearing, hands clutched over a deep gash on her thigh. Blood flows around her fingers.

"Helena!" I gasp, dropping beside her. All the emotion that's been locked up finds its way free. I've already lost so much. I can't lose her too.

"Lilith!" she says, voice a strained whisper.

I pull a handkerchief from my pocket and tie it around her leg in an attempt to slow the bleeding.

Helena looks at the blood on my wrist. "Are you okay?" she asks, and a tear runs down my cheek. My friend is in danger, yet she's still worried about me.

"It's not mine," I say tonelessly and think of the Elemental I'd brained. "We have to get you to Ambrossi." I don't mention that I have no idea where he is. By some miracle maybe I'll find him if I wish hard enough.

I loop Helena's arm over my shoulders and push myself up, wincing as her weight pulls hard against my injured side. Every step feels like a battle, the strain in my leg screaming beneath me. I summon the last flickers of magic I can muster, threads of energy weaving through my muscles to keep us upright. We move forward, slow and unsteady. Each step drains what little strength I have left, but I force myself to keep going. I stumble, heart pounding, but catch myself before I fall.

Ahead, the field stretches on endless and exposed. Open land that offers no shelter. Dangerous. As if to prove my point, a sharp sting cuts through the skin of my left arm. A thin line sags open, revealing the meat underneath.

Horrified, I spot a male on the other side of the clearing. The culprit. Another blast of energy comes as soon as I notice him. As sharp as a knife, it sweeps across my side, slicing my pants to expose the skin underneath. Another line opens along my ribs. The impact unbalances me, and I lose hold of Helena.

A final blast of magic rips through my flesh below the first cut. I close my eyes, ready to hit the ground, but it never comes. When I open my eyes, Clio cradles me close, eyes shining in the darkness as he holds me up. I look past him in time to see a surge of energy pierce Helena's body. For a time, she remains oddly still. Then she falls sideways to the ground.

"No!" I shriek, fighting against Clio's hold. "We have to

help her! We have to help Helena!"

"We have to get out of here." Clio pulls me close against his chest, the steady beat of his heart grounding me as he carries me away from the danger on the other side of the field.

I stare at Helena's body over his shoulder. A flare from a nearby fire lights the area enough for me to see the absence of life in her eyes. Clio drops down into a crevice in a group of rocks, and she disappears. Sobbing, he collapses to his knees but doesn't let go of me. He hugs me tighter, exhaustion clear when he pulls back to study the wound along my ribs.

"I'm gonna get you help," he promises, and I slide from his warm embrace to the cold ground, made colder compared to the warmth of his body.

"D-don't go. Please, don't go," I plead.

"I'll come back." Clio puts his fingers under my chin, lifting my face to kiss me softly. I close my eyes, hoping to keep him with me, but when I open my eyes, he's gone.

"Clio?" I cry out.

Hyperventilating, I struggle to stand, and that's when I finally feel the pain. The cut across my ribs is pouring blood. I fall on my hands and knees, shuffling the dirt around me. A single tear sinks into the soil beside my hand. I've failed. As the Sage's successor, I'm theoretically supposed to be the second strongest witch in the Land of Five, but I couldn't save any of the witches who matter the most to me.

Nearby foliage rustles, and I look up. "C-Clio?"

Three figures in red robes emerge. They aren't Clio or Crowe, or anyone I know. I try to force my body to stand, further depleting what little magic I have left.

"Help!" I try to call, but no sound comes from my tightened throat.

"Don't fight," one of the figures says and takes two steps closer.

I clamp my eyes shut to prepare for the inevitable: my death. I'd known this was a possibility when the Sage sent Crowe and I on our mission, but thinking of the possibility and staring death in the face are two very different things.

The figures close in. I open my eyes and lock gazes with the silvery eyes of the figure who'd spoken. An odd tingling starts in my fingers then passes slowly up my arms. The skin it travels through numbs in its wake. It slips through my chest. Spots dance in my vision.

I can no longer hold myself up.

I collapse. Arms snake under my body, grabbing me before I hit the dirt. As my mind cuts to black, I'm left with a final, haunting thought—death is more peaceful than I would have ever imagined.

# Chapter Two
## Prisoner

SILENCE WAKES ME, jolting my senses like a burst of electricity. After the chaos of the battlefield, it's unsettling how loud *nothing* can be. Have I gone deaf? Have I died? There's no way to tell. My mind is a hazy web of confusion. I try to wiggle my fingers, but it's hard. Considering I was completely paralyzed the last time I was conscious, this is remarkable progress. I strain harder, trying to sit up and open my eyes, when sharp agony sears across my ribs. Memories flood my mind, and I cry out.

Can I call it luck that I'm still alive, or is it more of a curse at this point?

My face hurts from lying on a hard surface. My neck is stiff when I try to move, but as my memories return, it's low on my list of priorities. The Elementals *got* me. I'm a prisoner of war.

Where are my captors?

Eyes the color of a violent thunderstorm fill my mind. I can picture the boy who brought me here, but that memory doesn't help.

I force my eyes open, fearing the idea of not being alone in this place. Wherever I am, it's dark. In all directions, the darkness remains unchanged. That's probably for the best. If my situation is as dire as I imagine, I most likely don't want to see what's waiting for me. I strain to pick up any sounds, but all I hear is the blood pounding in my ears and the steady thumping of my heart in my chest.

Only slightly relieved, I try to move again, but my wrists are firmly bound in front of me. I struggle against the bonds, sending fresh discomfort through my body when my elbow accidentally grazes my side. To keep from crying out, I clamp my jaws together until my teeth clank. I may be alone for the time being, but I have no idea where my captors are or when they'll be back.

They could be watching me through magical surveillance for all I know. I need to get out of here. Tapping my telekinesis, I reel my mind in long enough to untie the ropes on my wrists with the telekinesis I've carefully manipulated the past few weeks. The bonds thump to the floor, and I rub the tender skin, wincing at a particularly raw patch at the base of my palm.

My weak leg offers no support when I try to stand, and I collapse to the floor, mind racing for any two-bit plan. As my hand grazes my side, I feel the cuts, every single one. Strangely, it's not the physical pain that overwhelms me, but the emotional. The wounds will heal, given time. Most of them, anyway. Only one truly matters, a scar I don't expect will ever heal—Helena's death.

*Why am I not dead, too?* I let out a slow wail of agony that sounds more animalistic than human.

I know why. I mean something to the Council. I'm *valuable* in a way. My death was never really part of the Elementals' plan. They need me for something, though what that something is, I haven't the foggiest. I'm the most useless of all the Council witches. I'm confident in that. I can hardly control my powers. Hell, I can barely *walk*. Now I'm here to stay, even without their restraints. My leg makes sure of that.

As I sit in the dark, I contemplate my options. Do I call for help or try to make a break for it? I sit up, leaning against the bedframe for support. The scabs across my ribs crack, serving as an instant answer to my dilemma. Between my leg and the injuries sustained in battle, I'm in no shape to go anywhere.

*You have to fight for her,* I tell myself. The image of Helena dropping to the ground is the horrible accompanying image. I struggle to stand again. Prior to their deaths, I thought my parents' betrayal was the worst agony I would face. How wrong I'd been. I collapse back to the floor with an audible *thump*, fight completely gone. If everyone I love is dead, where can I go if I do happen to escape?

Nowhere.

I stop struggling. What's the point of fighting? That horrible existence is the one I'm trying to go back to, isn't it? The one without my best friend, without my parents, without *anyone.* I bite my bottom lip to stop it from quivering. Crying has never helped me, and it certainly won't do the trick now.

But how can I do anything else? Everyone's dead besides Clio. And he abandoned me in the middle of the war, to try to guess what happened to him.

I slump to the floor, lost in despair. Time has no meaning in this dark pit. When the door finally opens, it could be two hours later or two days. I have no idea. I groan at the light trickling in. It's *watery*, as if I'm seeing through a filter.

I can't run, I can't fight, and now, to make matters worse, I can't even *see.* The door creaks to its full extent, and I lift a hand to block some of the light. It doesn't help. A shadowy outline appears. Someone is standing there, watching me.

"Finally come to torture me?" I sneer, hoping my captor has no idea I'm temporarily blind.

Whoever it is remains silent. I wish I could see them. What are they doing? Brandishing a knife or some other primitive weapon, searching for new ways the Council hasn't thought of to strip me of my dignity?

"At least you're not in shock anymore," a deep voice finally says. "That's good."

My jaw sets. My kidnapper. The one with the silver eyes who snatched me from the battle that most likely destroyed my entire Coven.

"You," I snarl, trying to move away from the light. A grimace has me stop. If he's watching me, there's no way he doesn't notice it.

"Tensions are high, I understand that, but you must listen to me when I tell you we won't hurt you."

That's the opposite of what I expect. I scoff, softly at first, but the sound changes into a chaotic stream of laughter. I shuffle, trying to see him better and kick the abandoned rope aside. "You won't?" I lift my arm to reveal the myriad of bleeding wounds down my ribs. I can't see them, but *he* can. I hope they look as bad as I imagine they do. "You killed my best friend… my parents… everything's gone because of you."

"We're in the middle of a war," he states as if that answer justifies every tragedy his people have inflicted.

"How can you be so cold?" I whisper. "How can you not care?"

"Everything we do is for a reason. A purpose."

If that's the truth, I already know why I'm here. I'm the Council's pride and joy. "Kill me, then. I have no information for you."

"I knew you were stubborn, but I didn't think you would downright *ignore* people. I told you we aren't going to hurt you, and I'm not here for information, either." His voice is louder now. He's closer.

"Then go away."

"I can't do that, Lilith. I have orders."

That can't be good. *Orders* sounds so official. "Leave me alone," I growl, striking out, though I have no idea if he's close enough to hit.

"Relax. You're hurt. I need to take you to our Healer."

Words fail me. After everything my loved ones have suffered, why in the world do their executioners care about *my* wounds?

*That's what the whole thing has been about, remember?* a voice in my head says. It's not my own. *Chastity warned you this would happen.*

I've heard this other voice only once before, at Chastity's execution. I have no idea to whom it belongs. Swallowing heavily, I push away my unease. The voice likely belongs to another Elemental, but who? And why contact me now? Are they in the room, too?

Someone grabs my elbow. In the blip of confusion, I forgot about my kidnapper. "Let go!" I bark, but he doesn't.

He pulls me up with ease, and as soon as my feet hit the floor, I forget about my fear. Pain jolts through my body. "I'm sorry, Lilith. I know this hurts," he says, but I pay him no mind as he pulls me across the room in what he probably imagines is as gentle a manner as possible.

The floor tilts. Or maybe it's the ceiling. My vision tunnels, shrinking into a narrow pinprick of light. I try to say something, but the words dissolve before they leave my lips. A low hum builds in my ears, and my knees buckle.

Then everything goes dark.

# Chapter Three
## Old Friends, New Enemies

WHEN I COME to, I'm lying on a cold metal table. The chill seeps into my shoulders. My vision is still blurry, forcing me to rely on my other senses to piece together where I am and what danger I might be in. A faint breeze brushes my skin. I try to sit up and immediately become aware of how exposed I am beneath the thin blanket someone has draped over me.

My movement is met with instant protest. "Don't move too much, Lilith."

*Ambrossi.*

It's a new sensation, being so confused that I'm at a loss for words. He's my friend, my Healer… the smartest person I know in all of Ignis. He's watched over me like a goofy older brother for as long as I can remember. I've literally put my life in his hands on more than one occasion. I can't comprehend the fact that it's *him*. Here in the pit of my tragedy, *sharing* this moment with me. I'd suspected him of having ties to the Elemental Coven but never put much stock in the theory.

I guess I should have.

Stunned, I don't notice the blanket slipping away from my most vulnerable places. It feels like I'm floating above my body, watching this scene unfold from far away like a dream, or maybe this is the strange way my mind is processing a coma.

If I'm awake, where is this? Am I still trapped in the depths of the Elementals' prison? Did the Council somehow rescue me while I was unconscious? Or am I back in Ignis, with whatever remains of my Coven?

Am I dead?

A harsh light floods my vision, clearer than before. I blink, forcing my eyes to adjust. The room around me is stark white and bare. Ambrossi is beside me. Behind him, a man with silver eyes smiles. My kidnapper is here, and Ambrossi seems less than concerned.

The hair on the back of my neck stands on end, and I grab the edge of the table. "What's going on?" I demand, voice raw and brittle, scraping up my dry throat.

I've been unconscious far longer than I realized.

Ambrossi ignores my protests and gently guides me back onto the cold metal table, carefully adjusting the cloth as he does. At his touch, the weight of the situation settles over me. I'm painfully fragile in this dangerous place. Glancing down, I notice a few drops of red bleeding through the white fabric. A shiver runs through me as the cloth shifts just enough to reveal the full extent of the damage beneath.

Ambrossi catches my expression. "You were hurt in the battle," he says, "but you're going to be okay."

"Y-yeah… I know."

My wounds are the least of my problems. I might've trusted Ambrossi at one point, but everything's upside-down now. The last thing I want is for these people to know I'm anything less than confident. "Then I was kidnapped, don't forget that," I say with a pointed look at Silver-Eyes, "but that doesn't explain why *you're* here."

"Come on, Lilith, you're a smart girl."

Ambrossi isn't one to beat around the bush. He's open, *honest…* so much so that I'm prepared for him to say three words in response—*I'm an Elemental.* But he doesn't. He won't, and that makes me sick in a completely different way. I don't know him, not really. He's been living a double life of darkness and secrets, as much of a stranger to me as Silver-Eyes.

"You're one of them?" I say at last.

"It's my understanding that you're one, too," he replies calmly as if the statement doesn't carry all the weight in the world. "Hold on. This will sting." A pinch of his magic jabs through the deepest gash in my side as he weaves the wound closed.

I grit my teeth, determined not to show how much it hurts. "You knew Iris and Chastity, didn't you?"

Ambrossi sets his fingers to the freshly sealed laceration. He's going out of his way to avoid eye contact, and I'm not sure whether I'm angry at him for it or relieved. I don't think I could handle the unfamiliar personality coming from a person I thought I loved.

"You helped Iris attack the ceremony," I mutter, piecing it all together.

"I had help," he says, mouth set in a grim line as he finally brings himself to meet my eyes. "Stop moving." Another sting sears my flesh, and I grasp the metal bar of the bed for support.

"Who? Are they still in Ignis, waiting to hurt more innocent witches?" He pretends not to hear me, eyes on the next cut on my side. I tack on, "When were you planning to tell me the truth?" The ache makes my voice much rougher than it should be.

Part of me hopes he'll *hear* it, that he'll *know* it's not me, and that'll be enough to bring back the Ambrossi I *do* know.

Instead, in a cold voice, he says, "I wasn't." I stare down at the floor. "There were plans, and I had orders. Everyone has their roles to play. You'll learn soon enough."

"Is that right? Do I have a *role*, too?" I hiss.

Ambrossi drums his finger on the newly formed scab on my side to test its strength.

My nostrils flare, and I have to resist the urge to sit up again. "How are you so *calm?* Did you not hear the part where I said I was *kidnapped?*"

"In time, it'll come to feel like home," he replies, focusing on the last two wounds.

Instead of responding, I go limp, and Ambrossi offers a small smile, probably with the assumption that I'm cooperating, when really I don't know what else I can do.

This isn't Ambrossi.

I wave a hand in front of my face, testing how well my body responds, and hope for some kind of delay, anything to support my dream theory. It doesn't hold up. I'm awake. But if that's true, how can this overwhelming sensation of living outside my body be explained?

Everything I've held in since my Arcane Ceremony rears its ugly head. My goal has always been to save my loved ones, but I never considered the idea that all the people I want to protect may not be on the same side of this fight.

*I can't save everyone.* That thought is accompanied with the image of Helena collapsing in the battle, the light dancing in her lifeless eyes as Clio dragged me away. One sob passes my lips, and after that, there's no stopping it.

Ambrossi prods the tender flesh on my side, but I don't look at him, unable to bear the thought of risking eye contact when I'm like this. I'm too vulnerable, and this situation is still too uncertain. When the tears finally dry, I'm inevitably embarrassed at putting my fears on display.

Ambrossi senses my silence and doesn't press me to talk. Instead, he continues his work, healing me with as much tenderness as he can muster. He could have finished much faster, but he's deliberately slowing down, giving me the time I need to process everything.

As much as I hate him right now, I appreciate his thoughtfulness.

My gaze stays fixed on my hands, both embarrassed and surprised by the sudden surge of emotion. The outburst is long overdue, and there will be many more to come, but I hate that it had to happen here, in front of my kidnapper.

From time to time, my attention strays to Silver-Eyes, but he doesn't say anything. He's watching the scene with a lack of emotion. I'm sure I glare every time I look at him, but he doesn't speak, and neither do I. It's like the tension between us has bonded us to an oath of silence I don't remember taking. When Ambrossi's magic recedes from my skin, he sits back in his chair, thoughts impossible to read.

"How do you feel?" Silver-Eyes asks.

"What do you care?" I snarl, glad he's the one to break the silence.

He gives an indifferent shrug. "I don't, really, but I thought I'd attempt to be nice. I need to make sure you're okay before you meet Willow."

Out of everything that's happened over the course of the last twenty-four hours, those words strike me the hardest. Willow, the woman everyone refuses to speak of. The woman who had been *executed* for her abilities.

The girl who was like me.

"But she's—"

"Dead?" Silver-Eyes guesses. "Well, things change." He grabs a cloth from the table beside him. "Get dressed."

He tosses the dress to me, and a flush rises to my cheeks at the reminder that I'm essentially naked. I quickly pull it on, the slim-fitting black fabric clinging to my body in unfamiliar ways. As it brushes against the fresh scabs on my side, I pick at the material and catch Ambrossi's gaze.

"You'll come back if you have any issues, right?" he asks.

I never was one to complain. It's always taken a lot for me to seek help. After everything that's happened, I can't see myself confiding in him again. Looking him full in the face, I say, "No."

A hint of concern tightens his features, but he doesn't push it. That's also unlike him. Normally, he would stubbornly pester me until I agree.

Shoving away my irritation, I dip my head and jump off the table, gathering what few manners I have left. "Thank you."

It's been a while since I stood on my own, and I've forgotten how bad my weak leg hurts. I stumble, lurching forward, but I don't hit the floor.

Silver-Eyes catches me just as I'm falling, pulling me close so my chest presses against his while my injured leg drags behind. Gathering my strength, I push him away. All I can think of is Clio and how he'd knock him out if he were here.

*But he's not,* I remind myself. I'm alone.

How can these witches even pretend to care about me after everything they've put me through? Healing my injuries is the *least* they can do. I should demand more. A wiggle of power moves inside me, then bursts without further warning into a wave of energy, slamming Silver-Eyes into the wall.

I face Ambrossi, trying my best to seem intimidating, but I'm far off the mark. Naturally, I'm small and in the aftermath of the battle, I can't do much damage. This is a real stuck-between-a-rock-and-a-hard-place situation. I don't want to hurt Ambrossi, I've *never* wanted to hurt him, but I'm not sure I have a choice. He admitted to being one of the Elementals, one of the people who've worked to systematically tear my life apart.

"Lilith, I'm sorry," he says.

His eyes flicker to my leg, and that familiar, burning anger flares up inside me again. What exactly is he apologizing for? Has he known the truth about my accident all along? Was he involved in what my parents did? I try to unleash the same force I used against Silver-Eyes, but my powers falter, slipping away and retreating deep into my core.

Silver-Eyes climbs to his feet, gray eyes illuminated by the force of his powers.

A tingling spreads through my fingertips, and panic wells in my chest. If he knocks me out again, how can I be sure he won't kill me this time? The thought of Willow being alive, of her being one of *them*, gives me the courage to fight through the despair that was so ready to consume me ten minutes ago.

"Lilith! Relax!" Silver-Eyes demands.

I don't acknowledge him. With the tingle spreading through my limbs, I *can't*.

"I'm not going to paralyze you again, okay? But I need to lock up your powers for now. You can't go to Willow like this. Hell, you can't leave this *building* like this."

"You're too unstable," Ambrossi adds in a much nicer tone. As if that'll make a difference.

I try again to push my powers out, but they won't budge. The attempt proves too much for my already limited energy supply. This time, I *do* collapse, and neither of them try to save me. I hit the floor with a *thud* and see stars. The metallic gleam in my kidnapper's eyes disappears. With his magic receding, I see myself through his eyes.

Small. Weak. *Pathetic.*

"Lilith, I really think we've gotten off on the wrong foot."

I lift my head, glare at him, spit a mouthful of blood on the floor from the fresh wounds in my tongue, and wait for him to continue.

"I never even told you my name," he says. "I'm Maverick."

I'm unsure what to do with the new information. In no way, shape, or form is it useful.

Then he says, "Are you ready to meet Willow?"

## Chapter Four
### The Land of New Life

WILLOW, THE WOMAN of a thousand mysteries. Can meeting her really be this easy, after everyone avoided the topic like the plague for so long? My head swims with many unanswered questions. If Willow died when the Council executed her as the Land of Five believes, how did she come back, and why does her Coven seem unfazed by such a miracle? Did the Council lie about executing her?

Maybe the most pressing of all my questions: What could she possibly have to tell me?

As I step outside the building, reality crashes back in. This place is unlike anything I've ever seen. Towering, amethyst-hued plants stretch high into the sky, their thick, leafy tendrils weaving together to form walls of living green. The air beyond the strange, enchanted forest is a deep, almost suffocating purple, teetering on the edge of blackness. I have no idea where we are, but I can already tell it's nowhere near The Land of Five. Whatever I imagined waiting beyond my prison… this hadn't been it.

Maverick swats aside a handful of plants as he leads the way. Being a good foot shorter than him, I don't have to worry about it. I trail behind, my steps light, eyes wide with wonder like he's about to show me something magical. I should be scared. I have no idea what waits for me at the end of this journey, but oddly, I'm not. I could lose myself in this lush, vibrant forest for days, letting the beauty of it all wash over me. I'm starting to think whatever magic pulses through this place might be influencing my mood too.

For the briefest moment, everything fades away. I'm a kid again, seeing the world with fresh eyes. No pain or anger or bone-deep exhaustion. This place is nothing like my old home in the desert-Coven, Ignis. It feels more like a fairytale land.

My mind stops on the word *fairy*. It reminds me of my friend Fern. Like Clio, I have no idea whether she's alive or dead. I didn't see her in the battle, but since it's *her* oasis that's been drained, I can imagine she's grieving right now if whoever sabotaged her land didn't hurt her.

The thought grounds me, and with it, my anger rises again. I lower my head, no longer distracted by the beautiful foliage. The ground beneath my feet shifts to smooth, gray pavement, easing the strain on my bad side. As we push forward, the maze of plants eventually clears, and the land begins to rise. At the top of the hill, a Victorian-style mansion looms, its silhouette sharp against the sky. It reminds me of Crowe's mansion in Aquais.

"That's Willow's home," Maverick says.

And I thought the Council was immoral for their lavish lifestyle. "Why is it so big for one witch?"

"Willow's... *special*. You'll see."

I've already been told she's dangerous. Do they have to keep her tucked away from the rest of the Coven because she's a risk to them?

"Why can't you tell me?" I ask anyway.

"It's hard to explain."

I'd anticipated that response, so I don't press him any

further. If the truth doesn't lie within the mansion's walls, then it simply doesn't exist. I follow Maverick into the foyer, a vast space adorned with elegant bronze statues in each corner, framed by rich red tapestries that drape along the walls.

I clasp my hands together, wary of touching anything. A smell washes over me, steady and acrid. It's a scent I've encountered before, but still I slip my hand over my nose.

Eyes streaming water, I ask Maverick, "What is that smell?"

"Death," he says, tone unchanging. He doesn't cover his nose, either.

I stop. How can I willingly venture into a place reeking so strongly of corpses? Either Maverick is madder than I guessed, or there's more to this story than anyone's told me. For all I know, this could be the Elementals' dumping ground, and I've done them a favor by waltzing in here myself rather than forcing them to carry my dead body. The whole Willow thing could've been a ruse to lure me here.

And look at that. It works.

Maverick walks on. Other than glaring at the back of his head, there's not much else I can do. My magic is still locked in my core, and my scars are far too fresh for a physical confrontation. I push away the chills running down my spine and follow him. The smell of rotting flesh grows stronger, and breathing through my mouth doesn't help.

The last thing I want to do is *taste* it.

We round a corner, and a low growl cuts through the air. Maverick halts, raising a hand to block my path. I stop instinctively, more out of surprise than anything else, and scan the shadows but see nothing that could have made that sound.

"Careful," he warns.

"What is it?" I ask in a whisper, scared that if I speak any louder it'll draw the creature's attention directly to me.

Whatever it is dodges past us, letting out another growl that echoes down the empty corridor. I can't place the source. Heart pounding, I look to Maverick for answers, but he only offers a smirk. Then the beast materializes from the shadows. Four paws, whiskers, tail lashing. A tiger stalks toward us, ears flat against its head and teeth exposed, looking as real as Maverick and myself, though it appeared out of *thin air*. There's something *wrong* with this creature. Stitches cross its face and run down its sleek side to a patch of missing fur, revealing bloody flesh on its shoulder.

It *reeks* of death.

"It's a work of art, isn't it?" Maverick asks.

The cat pauses to sniff the air, and its ears flick up. The growl fades, and it lowers its head to lick its paw. It seems to have decided we're no threat, and I'm grateful for that. I don't think I could bring myself to kill something that looks as bad as I feel. The massive cat gives us one last, lingering look before melting back into the shadows.

"What's wrong with it?" I ask Maverick. I don't know how much longer I can tolerate the smell. I already feel as if it's burning the inside of my nose all the way up to my brain.

"It's dead," he says simply, as if it's the most obvious thing in the world, and continues walking, passing the spot in the shadows where the tiger disappeared.

"Oh," is all I can manage. I eye the spot warily and follow

Maverick deeper into the mansion.

There's another concept I need to wrap my head around. If Ignis is the Land of Fire, this place must be the Land of New Life. First Willow, and now animals, too? Her powers makes death temporary.

I glance nervously into every shadowy corner. If there's one tiger, who knows how many more there are. And who's to say it's limited to tigers? There could be grizzly bears or lions—anything waiting to rip me limb from limb the second I step out of line.

Maverick walks onward, unshaken.

"How does an undead tiger not chill you to your bones?" I finally ask.

"Just doesn't."

He's seen it before. If he's as close to Willow as I imagine, he's seen it a hundred times at least.

"Are there others?"

"You ask a lot of questions."

I push my lips into a straight line. "Yeah, that happens when I'm *kidnapped*."

"Oh, get off it, will ya?" Maverick rolls his eyes and walks faster.

I don't bother trying to match his pace, falling back a few steps instead. I distract myself by studying the featureless walls. The farther we go, the less impressive the mansion feels. The rooms here are barren—empty walls and cold, uninviting floors. The stillness, the lack of anything personal, speaks volumes about Willow. There's such a lack of personal touch I could believe this place to be a stage or theater.

But not a home.

Crowe's mansion had boasted paintings, photographs, and tapestries on every possible inch of the walls, things that show some shred of the owner's taste, or even *existence*.

This mansion, filled only with shadows and silence, is a tribute to Willow's mysterious legacy.

# Chapter Five
## Willow

WE'VE BEEN WALKING for what feels like an eternity, though I'm pretty sure it's only been ten minutes, at most. The mansion's interior is a maze, and the endless blank walls don't help. My head throbs as I try to piece together my bearings, staying close to Maverick, unable to risk losing him. If I do, I'll be left here, wandering the empty halls with nothing but the tigers for company.

He's talking to me, but I can't focus on his words. At the end of the hall sits a gothic archway barred by a set of red imperial doors. Willow is somewhere behind them. Maverick doesn't give me much chance to prepare before pushing the doors open and leading the way inside.

On a bookshelf to our left sits a cat with three legs, stitched together in the same manner the tiger had been. It's hard to look at, but it doesn't seem offended by my cringe. It blinks its one remaining eye and pointedly turns its nose away. This one doesn't blend into the shadows, and I give Maverick a questioning look. Does only the tiger have that ability, or does this cat happen not to?

"I think it depends on how long they've been dead," he says in way of an explanation.

"Oh." Not only have they come back from the dead, but some of them have *powers* too.

"Miss? Are you here?" Maverick calls into the seemingly empty room.

It's silent. *Too* silent. Paranoia creeps back. This could be some kind of trap. No one can live in conditions like these, right? Around the corner, red-carpeted steps lead up to a matching throne. Perched there is a woman sitting sideways in the lavish chair so her legs drape over the armrest.

She's at least a decade older than me, but she looks young, nothing like the way I pictured her. Her long, curly hair flows down her back, a few strands falling into her face to obscure her sharp cheekbones and black eyes. She's striking, but not in a beautiful way. Her appeal is more otherworldly. The effect is punctuated by the array of undead tigers and lions lurking in the giant pit in the floor a few inches in front of her throne. There are a dozen of them at least, all wearing varying scars and marks from their demise. The pit is deep enough to drop them out of view from a certain angle, but there's a slope angled enough to allow them to come and go as they please.

Some of them eye us suspiciously, but for the most part, they mind their own business. I have a feeling if we move any closer, they won't be as calm. These cats aren't here to be cute, cuddly pets. They're protectors, warriors, and they're already dead, so they have nothing to lose in a fight.

"Hello, Maverick. Is this her?" the woman asks, sliding her legs to the floor to prop herself on the edge of her seat.

Maverick dips his head, fingers laced in front of him. "Yes, ma'am."

My face scrunches. He sounds nervous although he's nearly twice Willow's size. *That's* power.

"There was a brief confrontation in Ambrossi's chambers," he adds, "but I was able to subdue her. She hasn't said much since. I would think a witch in her position would be more vocal." Maverick raises an eyebrow and looks my way. "She loves your pets, though."

I know the comment is meant to get a rise out of me, but I don't want to play his game. I *don't* mind her pets much. As long as they keep their distance, of course.

"See? She's the queen of this game."

I force down a smirk. He knows exactly what I'm doing. Playing the silent game, waiting them out. "The queen, huh? Can that be my official title?" I ask, lifting my chin. This is the first thing I've said in Willow's presence, the first time she's heard my voice. I want her to sense my strength, if not from my physical appearance, then through my confidence.

Willow swipes her long dark hair over her shoulder. "No. The only *queen* around here is *me*. And I hope you didn't spook my pets with all your stomping around. They're a little excitable."

"*Me* spook *them*?" I ask, jaw hanging open. "Look at them! They're *monsters*. *Maybe* try hanging some kind of warning sign outside the door."

Willow smiles coyly at Maverick. "She's talking now."

My shoulders sag. I fell for her game. Maverick raises his eyebrows but doesn't say anything else.

"You've done well, Maverick. I'll let you know when I need you." Willow gives him a dismissive wave, and all signs of playfulness are gone. Things are about to get real.

He leaves, slamming the door behind him. The dead felines seem the same for his absence, but I eye where he'd stood in envy. I'd rush away from the smell of this place too, if I could.

Willow puts her odd black eyes on me, and I shiver when our gazes meet. "You must be wondering why you're here," she says at last.

I scan the undead felines around her then meet her gaze again. "Among other things." The more I look at her, the easier it becomes. How does her magic work? And to what extent does it affect the witches she encounters? *What all can she do?*

"You'll get your answers in time," she promises.

I want to believe her, but I don't. I *can't.* The words sound too empty. I scoff. "Yeah, that's what the Sage tried to tell me, too."

"I bet you were told many lies over there," Willow says, cupping her chin in her hand.

"As I'm sure will be the case here." I'm a captive of *war,* after all. I can't imagine she'd want to tell me battle secrets.

"The lies end here, Lilith. I mean it when I say we want to help you."

I narrow my eyes. Can she read minds, or was that a fortunate guess on her part? "You do? Really? And why should I believe that? After everything your people have done, you want me to believe you care about me?"

Willow breathes deeply through her nose, keeping an absence of emotion on her face as she processes my words. It's a face I'm sure I make a lot. "I understand your hesitation. If I were in your position, I'd feel the same. You've been through many trials in the past few weeks, but I want you to understand that we're not the bad guys."

Maybe I'm not as good at composing myself as I think I

am. Her voice is so calm, like everything hasn't changed in the past twenty-four hours. That's because *her* world hasn't. She doesn't care about Helena or my parents. She didn't know them. Their deaths are nothing but another casualty.

"How dare you?" I spit, clenching my hands into fists. "How dare you face me with your good-for-nothing promise like it'll fix everything you've destroyed?"

Willow stays silent.

"You killed my best friend. My parents. You tore my Coven to shreds. You don't care about me or my people. This was never about us. It's all about you. You've been gunning for me ever since I stopped your attack on the Arcane Ceremony. Am I right?"

Her gaze flickers for a moment, then she speaks, voice calm, almost regretful. "I'm sorry you feel that way, but you're wrong. I never wanted to hurt you. Honestly, I loved hearing the story of how you rushed in like a lioness to protect your friend." She taps her finger thoughtfully against her lip. "This whole situation? It's a lot more complicated than you think."

My chest tightens with rage. "But *you* destroyed my Coven. Not them. *You!*"

Willow's expression doesn't waver. "On the contrary. We *saved* it."

My rage threatens to take me over. "Saved it? You wiped them out! The survivors, if there are any, are dying. They have no Healer. No herbs to treat their wounds because you burned them all. No water, no way to survive. What the hell are you talking about?"

Her eyes lock on mine. "*We* didn't burn it."

"Then who *did?*"

"The Council."

"Bullshit. I was with Crowe and Tarj when it happened," I tell her, not wanting her to be right. Flashes come through my brain of running through the battlefield, searching for some sign of them and not being able to find either until the damage was already done.

"Mm-hmm," she says, not looking as if she believes me. "And where were Tricia and Hyacinth?"

"The Sage sent them to Aens for… for a special mission."

Her eyebrows shoot up. "Are you sure?"

No. No, I'm not. I'd taken the Council's word at face value. When they blamed the Elementals for all the death and destruction, I believed them. Even worse, I'd *helped* them. I'm a pawn, too. A *stupid* one. "Why would they do that?"

"What better way to not only draw out the Elementals, but unite the witches capable of rebellion by giving them a reason to fight?"

I feel like the floor is about to disappear from beneath me. I've had my suspicions about the Council, haven't I? Especially after the Sage's admission. Could it be that this entire time, I've been fighting on the wrong side of the war?

"You're wrong," I say, unwilling to admit defeat.

Willow puffs out her cheeks and looks up at the ceiling for so long that I look, too, to see if she's got another pet that I need to worry about. There's nothing there, but finally, she says, "This conversation would best be saved for another time, one in which you're more comfortable and willing to listen. If it means earning your trust, how about a peace offering?"

*A peace offering?*

I fold my arms tightly across my chest, trying to hide the hurt in my body and heart. My leg threatens to buckle. Ambrossi's magic hasn't dulled the pain in my side. It pulses with a vicious throb as if hot metal is buried beneath my skin. The tiger closest to me sniffs the air, then licks its muzzle, its gaze fixed on me. It smells the weakness, the injury. Likely, it knows more about me from my scent than I do. If it can sense my vulnerability, then surely Willow can, too. So why, then, does she care about making peace with me?

"Consider this a token of goodwill," she says and claps once.

A set of doors, similar to those I entered through, open in the wall behind her. They move in slow motion, revealing a girl with bright red hair. She walks through the archway, her eyes a mix of black and green.

Helena.

# Chapter Six
## Helena

I'VE FAINTED MANY times in my life, but nothing compares to how my brain shuts down now. My legs buckle, and my mind disconnects from the rest of my body. Everything moves in slow motion. I'm grateful I pass out before I hit the ground because I'm sure the impact is rough.

When I come to, I blink to clear my eyes, grateful to still be able to see. Silky fur brushes my arm, and I jolt away from it in reflex. An undead tiger passes me, not acknowledging my presence as it stalks away. My fingers clench, feeling the stones beneath my body. It takes time to remember where I am, then all at once, everything comes back.

I'm in the tiger pit. I must've fallen right in. A deep breath brushes against my ear, and I freeze. The tiger is right next to me, its massive form looming over my head. It must have crept back while I wasn't looking. Our eyes meet, and that same chill races down my spine, the one I felt when I stared into Willow's eyes. If eyes are the windows to the soul, maybe these creatures are so unsettling because they've lost theirs. The tiger blinks, its black-and-amber gaze locked on me, as if I'm the most fascinating thing it's ever seen. I groan and try to push myself up. The cat jerks its head back, looking like it's been struck, and pauses mid-sniff, watching me with an intense, unnerving focus.

I raise my hand to my head, searching for injuries. Willow

kneels beside me with her hand on my knee—the reason for the cats' watchful eyes. "Lilith, are you okay?" she asks evenly, black eyes boring into mine. Can she see into my soul? I feel like she can. "You hit your head pretty good."

I dig my fingers into my hair until I find a lump. "I-I'm really not sure anymore," I say, dropping my hand. I want to verify that what I had seen wasn't a dream, but things feel surreal.

Helena hasn't moved from her place beside Willow's throne. An ethereal white glow surrounds her. I don't know how I manage to pick myself up off the ground without magic, or how I do it so *fast*, but the next thing I know, I'm holding my dead best friend in my arms. I never want to let her go, despite the potent smell of decay wafting from her body. I ignore it, burying my face in her orange curls and knotting my hands together in the small of her back.

Nothing can tear us apart right now.

"Helena, when he killed you…" I stare at the wall behind her. I have absolutely no idea how to finish that statement. I can't make eye contact; the emotions in me are too raw, too *unstable,* as they were in Ambrossi's chambers. Letting anyone, even Helena, know how much I'm aching is a risk I can't take when I have no idea what Willow and the Elementals want from me.

Helena pulls back, and I don't stop to wonder if I squeezed her too tight, or if that even matters anymore. She's so pale, I can see all the bluish veins in her face, but there's *life* in her eyes. In the back of my mind flashes the all-too-vivid image of what they'd looked like dead. No words pass her lips, but they don't need to. I know by the gesture alone that she understands what I want to say. What I *feel.*

"Now that that's out of the way, do you accept my gift?" Willow says from behind me.

She sounds closer as if she's also climbed out of the pit, but I don't check. I nod slowly without taking my eyes off Helena. I've never been more grateful for anything in my life. Willow sets her hand on my shoulder, and very hesitantly, I pull my hands off Helena.

"Your friend will be here later," she assures me.

"Mm-hmm," I mumble, ignoring her way of trying to politely get down to business.

"We have much to discuss, Lilith. Helena, you're dismissed."

Unease creeps down my spine. Bringing Helena back to life had most likely *not* been an easy task on Willow's part. If I were her, I'd expect something in return, but I have no idea what that is. More importantly, I'm not sure I can afford it.

Helena dips her head and leaves the room. I watch her go, full of questions. I need to focus on Willow, but it's hard now that my mind is split. Maybe that was the point of this. What better way to win than by lowering your enemy's guard?

When the stately doors swing shut behind Helena, I have a suspicion that something is wrong. She hadn't spoken. How badly has she been damaged by the battle that ultimately killed her? And more importantly, how much of that had Willow fixed when she brought her back?

"It takes time to adjust," Willow offers as if answering my unspoken questions.

"Huh?" I ask, tearing my eyes away from the door.

"You're worried about your friend, but you don't need to

be. She'll be okay." Willow reaches out an eerily white hand to pet the head of the massive feline beside her. The beast purrs and licks her palm.

I want to believe Willow, but that skeptical voice in the back of my mind is loud. What if this is all a trick to get me to agree to her terms… whatever they may be? Elemental powers are unconventional. I wouldn't be surprised if Willow has a witch somewhere who can make people see things that aren't really there.

"I was the same way when I first came back," Willow adds.

My concern shifts to wonder. I've been through a lot, but I haven't *died*. Not yet, anyway. Willow knows what it's like on the other side. She's seen it firsthand. Now Helena has, too.

No wonder her gaze is so chilling.

Furrowing my brow, I consider my words. "The Council… *killed* you, right?"

"They did." Willow's thin lips curve into a faint smile. "I have the power of resurgence, Lilith. I can bring anything back to life."

"Even yourself," I murmur with a new sense of awe.

"The comfort I find in death, other creatures could never understand," she says and pets the tiger again. "Eventually, we all die. That's our ultimate destination, but it doesn't have to be terrifying. Every aspect of life is beautiful. It's not a matter of *if* we die, but rather *when*."

She's right, in a way. We're all promised death, or at least we're *supposed* to be. The tiger stares back at me, an anomaly, a challenge to everything I believe to be true.

"At least, that's what I used to think," she admits, dipping her chin to cast a shadow over her eyes. "Now? I'm not so sure."

Neither am I. Before my time in the Elemental Coven, there's only one thing I've ever been certain of, death, and now that's not even a guarantee.

"Still. Whatever *this* is—" she says, gesturing to her body and the massive cat beside her, "—it's easier than living. Without having to eat or go to the bathroom, it's a very low-maintenance existence."

She looks so normal, so *sweet*. If the story Crowe told me is true, she led a rebellion against the Council once. That's *why* she died or at least the reason the Council had chosen to give for their decision. Not that they have a record for truth-telling. "Why did they do it?"

"Kill me?" She smirks. "I'm sure you've heard theories."

"Yeah, well, the third side of every story is the one that actually happened. That's the one I'm after."

"That's a tale for another time."

The tiger she's been so intent on petting shifts its gaze to me, its dead face curling into what could almost be a sneer, though its rotting lips barely move.

Willow had promised my time with her would be different than what I went through with the Council, but so far, it's the same. I'm being given bits and pieces. Not enough to complete the story, but enough to change the way I see it.

Petulantly, I try, unsuccessfully, to pry into her thoughts. The barrier around her mind is the thickest I've ever encountered. No wonder she's the leader. You don't get to the top by letting just anyone wander through your head.

"So, what happens now? Are you forcing me to stay?" I

ask.

"Do you not want to?"

Her voice is soft, lilting, as if my answer to that question won't change *everything*. Of course I don't *want* to be here, but how can I leave, knowing Helena and Ambrossi are here, too? That Willow is *alive?* That the Elemental Coven is thriving outside of the Land of Five? That I've found a place where I can live forever if I choose it.

"Will the Council look for me?" I counter her question. "Do… do they want me back, or have they already labeled me a traitor?"

"Does it matter? Either way, they'll find a replacement. They have to," Willow says, moving toward her throne at the top of the tiger pit.

For any other witch, that's a given, but I'm not so easy to replace.

I'm the Sage's apprentice, next in line to take the most powerful position in the Land of Five. My results in the Arcane Ceremony haven't been matched by anyone else. I have the potential to develop five powers at least, and that's not something *anyone* can do.

Instead of mentioning any of that, I say, "I don't think you've told me what it is I'm doing here."

Willow plops down in the throne, making it a point to meet my gaze as she says, "Isn't it obvious? You're my sister."

# Chapter Seven
## Blood, Bonds, and Breaks

A TINNY SOUND pierces my eardrums, low at first but gradually rising to a crescendo that blocks everything out. Spots dance in my vision. I brace myself, convinced I'm on the verge of fainting again, but I don't. Closing my eyes, I try ridding myself of the swirling motion. The sensation passes, but Willow's haunting words remain. My *sister*. How can she be my sister? How can I be related to *her*, this ghost of a woman?

Willow rushes toward me and puts her arm over my shoulders as if she thinks I might collapse. I focus on her eerie black irises and pull out of her grip.

It can't be true. "Did I hear you right?" I force myself to ask.

"Yes," she says, gathering her white gown to sit on the edge of the tiger pit. She swings her feet in a way that makes her look young, fragile even. I have a hard time telling if she's angry or hurt. Either way, it leads me to believe she's telling the truth.

That somehow makes me feel worse. So, instead of doing something, I do nothing. I sit on the floor, staring at my hands. The undead cats leave a wide circle around me as if they sense something in me is off kilter. I don't know how much time Willow gives me time to absorb the news, but I'm grateful, though not as grateful as I'd be if I never knew the truth at all.

My real parents are most likely dead, and my adopted

parents are too. But now a sister I didn't know I had is alive, in a manner of speaking, and she's less than five feet away.

"Where have you been all this time? Why…" I find myself as tongue-tied as I'd been when face-to-face with Helena. There are so many holes in the story of my past that I don't know where to start trying to make sense of the few pieces I have.

The one thing about my childhood I *do* know is that my adopted parents, Raya and Haze, had gotten me from my real parents somehow. They'd been Mentis witches. Fearing that the Council would make a connection, they crippled me in an attempt at hiding my real powers.

I run my tongue along my teeth, casting another glance at Willow from the corner of my eye. Can it be possible that other members of my family are out there somewhere, hiding until the war blows over?

"I understand this must be distressing," she says as she catches me eyeing her.

A flash of indignation crosses through my confusion. "You *think?*" Distress isn't a strong enough word to describe the chaos in my mind. She's had *years* to deal with this, knowing who she is the entire time. She had never been left to wonder, never abandoned in the web of lies and darkness like I have.

"Take a breath," Willow says.

I obey, but it doesn't stop the world from spinning.

After Raya told me the truth, I thought I had my life figured out: no more secrets, no more surprises, but I've barely scratched the surface. How deep does the rabbit hole go? Who *are* my real parents? And how did I get torn away from them?

I finally ask, "What happened to them? Our parents?"

Willow's face remains expressionless, but I can see a thousand memories in her eyes. I'm not the only one this conversation hurts. "They didn't abandon you if that's what you think. They're dead. Both of them."

"I figured that. They were Elementals, weren't they?" *Your parents—your real parents—were Elementals,* Raya's words echo in my head.

She glances down at her hands, pressing her palms together as if deep in thought. "Powerful ones."

"And you've kept up the family legacy," I say, unable to hide the venom in my voice. I don't know what's a lower blow: learning that I'll never meet my real parents or learning that they're the reason I'm in this mess in the first place.

"Lilith, you must understand, it's not as if they *planned* this. Any of this."

I raise an eyebrow. For her to still be so trusting after everything she's gone through really says something about her character. How does she do it? "But they did," I reply, my voice tight. "Even if it wasn't intentional. They knew what joining this war would mean for them, for their family. They *sacrificed* us. Don't you see that?"

She shakes her head, eyes distant. "No. What I saw were two people who gave it their all for the sake of the greater good." Willow pauses. "You're too young to remember, but they loved us *so* much. They only wanted the best for us."

"Then what happened?" My words are sharp, harder than I mean them to be. "Both of us have had terrible lives, and we have them to thank for it." I force myself to stand, my legs shaky.

"Life is nothing but a series of events, Lilith. They fought for what they believed in, and they did what they could to make the world a better place for *us,* even though they knew it could and probably *would* cost them their lives."

I snort, but the longer her words hang in the air, the more my resolve fades, morphing into something else. "They died with you, didn't they?"

Willow shakes her head, a tear caressing her cheek. I didn't know she was capable of it. Apparently, her existence isn't as low-maintenance as she believes. "They died in battle. Dad died saving me, and Mom died for you."

Now it's my turn to cry. I'm tired of people *dying* for me. "If we were born into this, as enemies of the Council, why aren't we dead, too?"

Willow simpers and rises to her feet, taking two steps along the edge of the tiger pit. "You forget, I *did* die."

"When?"

"I was executed not too long after the battle that claimed our parents. In all honesty, I don't know how I brought myself back, but here I am. I will never let them do that to me again."

Iris and Chastity had been burned to ash, impossible to distinguish from a handful of dirt. It's hard to imagine Willow taking a similar pile of nothingness and building herself back cell by cell.

"I don't remember any of this," I say, staring blankly at the floor.

"You wouldn't. You were so young."

I pause to let the information sink in. "If I was a baby when you were executed, that was less than twenty years ago," I say. When Fern told me about her, the stories had made it seem as if Willow's death had happened *centuries* ago, so far in the past that the information had no hope of existing now in the Land of Five.

How had people forgotten about her so quickly?

"I know." Willow reads the question on my face. "The Council has a witch who can make others think certain thoughts, or forget them. Her name is Tabitha. She's the Council's lifeline, for obvious reasons. If people think things are the way the Council wants them to think they are, then there's no reason to rebel."

"So... she wipes memories?"

Willow quirks her lips to the side. "Essentially."

I knit my eyebrows together. "How come I've never met her?"

"No one has, but the Sage."

I've been through so much that I'm willing to suspend my level of belief to a degree, but  this conversation is putting a strain on it. The Sage is the only one who knows she exists? That's impossible. "Then how do you know she's real?"

"We've seen her inside the Sage's memories."

I consider this. "What you're saying is that Tabitha's erased your story from every mind in the Land of Five, but not *ours*? And she couldn't keep it from the people who told me about you. Why?"

"There's something to be said for dying. Mentis magic seems to have a weaker effect on us." Her words come out light and airy, but there's a dark undertone to them.

The weight of her statement sinks in as a cold silence stretches between us, heavy and thick. "What's it like... to *die*?" I ask, skimming my fingers down the nearest tiger's back. The skin beneath the fur is cold and stiff, but a low purr rumbles up its throat as if it's very much alive.

"I don't remember much. I doubt Helena does, either. When the brain stops, it also stops making memories," she says and tilts her head. "One moment I was burning alive. The next, I was lying in the mud, gasping for air. There's a big, black gap of nothingness in between."

I try not to do it, but her emotions create an opening in the barrier around her thoughts. Through the hole, I see her demise and her rebirth. I don't know which one is more haunting. "You brought Helena back, but who else? Are my adopted parents here?"

I didn't have the best relationship with Raya and Haze toward the end, but they did raise me, and for that, I owe them *something*.

"No. No, they're not."

"Why bring back some people and not everyone?"

Willow doesn't answer right away as if she's carefully choosing her words. "Think of what a horrible place this world would be if I brought back *everyone*, Lilith. In order for there to be life, there must also be death."

"I wasn't asking you to bring back *everyone*. Just my parents."

Willow swipes her hair out of her face. "This is difficult for me to say, but if you must know, I could've brought *one* of them back."

My eyes drift to each of the undead felines around us. There are at least ten here. Far too many for me to show any aggressive tendencies toward their master and hope to walk away unscathed. Still, it's hard to keep the suspicion out of my voice. "Only one?"

"I… it exhausts me… using this gift. Have you ever used your magic until your reserves ran out?"

I have. It's a terrible, empty feeling I wouldn't wish on anyone.

"Bringing back *one* life, whether animal or human, does that to me," she says. "And it takes time to recharge."

"But your pets—"

"Are all in varying stages of decomposition," she points out.

When I study the cats, I see she's right. Her power isn't as straightforward as I'd thought. With any miracle comes a catch, and Willow's ability is no exception.

"I had so many of my warriors to help in the aftermath, and I thought you'd be over the moon with Helena. You have to believe me when I say I wish I could've done more, but I couldn't. We went back for them, but the Council had already taken possession of the bodies."

I'm careful to keep my face angled toward the floor so she can't see my emotions.

"And… wouldn't it have hurt you more for me to bring back one, knowing I *chose* which one got to live? At least this way, they're together."

I swallow once, rough and jagged, as her words settle. I can understand where she's coming from. I would have preferred my mother, and if she'd chosen my cold-as-ice father, I might've grown to resent her for it. Who knows?

"Why was I spared, then?" I ask, trying to change the

subject and the trainwreck of my thoughts with it.

Willow draws her eyebrows together. "I told my fighters not to hurt you."

"No, not in *that* battle. The one that killed our parents."

"The grace of the Gods, I'd imagine."

I snort. If the Gods have any role in this, I'd hate to think what they have planned for me in the future. "They wouldn't talk about you, you know. *Anyone* I mentioned you to, clammed up. You're taboo in the Land of Five."

The room falls silent as the three-legged cat on the bookshelf jumps to the floor. Tail held high, it makes its way to Willow, and she scoops it up.

"Why did no one tell me the truth?" I ask as she scratches it behind the ears.

"*They* probably didn't even know. Honey, if there's one thing the Council is good at, it's lying."

A chuckle rumbles up my throat, and I start to laugh so forcefully the scabs on my side crack open and start to bleed.

Willow eyes the fresh blossoms of red in concern. "Are you okay?" When a drop of my blood hits the floor beside me, she says, "I think you need to lie down for a bit."

"What I *need* is to figure out how to get back at these people."

Willow beams wide enough to show the gap between her two front teeth. "That's what sisters are for."

# Chapter Eight
## Settling In

I GENUINELY LIKE Willow.

Once my initial shock fades, that's the thought I'm left with. When I first heard the hushed whispers of Willow's existence back in Ignis, I had already built up my own image of what she must have been like. That image doesn't come close to the truth. She's strong. Like a phoenix, she rose from her ashes and took charge of her life. She rallied others to follow her and get back at the people who ruined her.

The rest of the day passes in a kind of quiet anticipation. Willow speaks little about the details of what's to come, but she doesn't need to say much. There's a gleam in her eyes that tells me everything I need to know. In time, the pieces will fall into place. And when they do, I'll be part of it.

In a way, Willow reminds me of how Helena used to be before life stole away her hope. I frown at the thought of my best friend. What do her next steps look like? Does she want to be with the Elementals? At one point in time, I would've been able to answer that. Now, I'm uncertain. After our Dedication Ceremony, Helena had withdrawn from everyone she loved when it became clear she would never develop powers. Could be possible that she was in talks with the Elementals before the battle that stole her life? Did she choose for all of this to happen?

*Or is she a prisoner too?*

I consider the word. Am I a prisoner if I don't want to leave?

While I might not care for Maverick, he hasn't harmed me, even when he could have in Ambrossi's chambers. Willow said I'm safe from her warriors but wandering around the manor full of undead pets gives me the distinct feeling that I'll be met with opposition if I try to leave.

"Are you hungry?" Willow asks.

I've been so wrapped up in my thoughts that biological necessities like food and sleep are easy to forget. While she needs neither, she still keeps track better than I do.

"Yes, I am," I reply as we step into the grand hall.

The room feels richer than anything in the Council's quarters. In the center, a long dining table stretches out, its surface draped with a crisp, white tablecloth embroidered with intricate patterns that catch the light. Surrounding the table are tall, blue chairs, their gothic curves and sharp angles giving them an elegant air. Above, a glass chandelier hangs like a crown, its crystals glinting in the light. The walls, in stark contrast to the opulence, remain bare.

"I'll get you something," Willow murmurs. "Wait here."

I plop down gratefully onto the nearest chair. When she returns, she's carrying a plate of the most amazing food I've ever eaten. Midway through the meal, one of her tigers wanders up to me, sniffing for a bite. I pause, eyes darting between the chicken and the tiger then to Willow. She nods, and I slip the rest of the bone to the cat, who happily accepts with a *crunch* of its jaws.

"You can pet him if you want. I know they look rough, but they're sweethearts," Willow says.

I've already touched a handful of them, but the fact that this one holds my gaze makes it intense. My hand shakes as I move toward the cat's face, but it accepts the gesture with a bow of its head.

"I didn't think they needed to eat anymore," I say, stroking the soft fur along its jaw.

"Some of us do, some of us don't. Depends on how long we've been dead," she says.

I translate that to mean it depends on whether their internal organs have rotted away or not. The tiger licks its muzzle and plods away, tail swishing happily with each step. It doesn't have a care in the world. Watching Willow's pets only adds questions to the pile I already have. Do they keep rotting until they're nothing, or does Willow's magic actually make them immortal? Can these creatures die again?

"Will they... will you... *die* someday?" I ask.

Willow shrinks in on herself and says in the quietest voice, "I don't know."

"You've never seen one of your pets die?"

She shakes her head. "They've disappeared. Runaways, I've always believed."

"Maybe," I reply, but part of me isn't convinced. Maybe they *did* die, and she wasn't aware. But that doesn't explain their missing bodies. In an attempt to lighten the mood, I ask, "So why tigers and lions?"

She shrugs, seeming grateful for a change of subject. "They're my favorite. What's your favorite animal, Lilith?"

My first thought is a cat as I remember the silver ball of fur that used to belong to Helena. "Something I can depend on,"

I tell her. "A dog."

Willow watches me take another bite of chicken. "Good choice."

WILLOW TRIES A handful of times to send me to bed after I finish my meal. The more I fight it, the more my resolve crumbles. I don't want to sleep, but I can't deny how tired I am. The wounds on my ribs are still in bad shape, worse now since I've given them no chance to heal. They'll never improve if I continue to push myself.

Willow has me stay in a room alone. It looks like it was a bedroom once, but now it contains a handful of bookshelves, a desk, and a chair. It's oddly quiet inside, and though I don't hear her lock the doors on her way out, I'm paranoid she did. She didn't tell me where she had to go, and I'm unsure how long it'll be until I see her again.

When she comes back, she's alone. "Sorry about that. Had some business to take care of," she says and pauses as if she sees the question on my face. "You're not being put back there," she informs me matter-of-factly. "There's no need for it."

"So, I'm *not* a prisoner anymore," I state as I search the room behind her, expecting another witch to enter.

"Do you feel like you are?"

"No."

"Good. You'll come to like it here, I promise."

It's too soon for me to guess either way.

"Let me show you to your room."

*There's* a phrase that gets my attention. In my time spent

with the Council, I was promised a room but had never been given one. Instead, I was forced to bunk with other councilmembers.

I follow her down the empty hall. This wing seems to be the farthest from the main portion of the manor. Is there a specific reason she chose it? When Willow finally selects a door to push open, a dog sits in the middle of the room. White fur covers it, making the ugly, lengthwise scar down its side more visible. I shiver, guessing it had been completely cut in half at one point. It hops up on its hind legs, letting out a happy little yap.

"How do you like him?" Willow asks from behind me.

I try to regain myself the same way I had after my first encounter with the undead cats. "How long has this dog been dead?" I ask, staring at its shimmering outline. I expect it to jump into the shadows like Willow's tiger, but it doesn't. Its stumpy tail thumps on the floor as it anticipates my next move.

"Not long enough to have any powers."

"So he's just a regular zombie dog, then? Fantastic." My comment doesn't dampen his energy. He walks toward me and licks my hand. He's big, his back coming up to the middle of my thigh, but I don't feel uneasy with him like I do with the tigers. There's something endearing about his personality. Sweet, even.

"What's his name?"

"I was hoping you'd tell me."

"You want *me* to name him?" I ask, letting my fingers sink into the soft white fur on the top of the dog's head.

"Well, yeah. He's *your* dog now, after all."

The dog looks up at me, and the ice melts in my heart a bit. How can I possibly say no? "How about Kado?"

"That's a strong name," Willow says, holding her finger to

her chin. "I like it."

Kado yips again, and I pretend he's adding his approval.

"I'll leave you two to get acquainted," she says and departs with a dip of her head.

Then I'm left alone with Kado. He gives another happy yap, and I pet him again as I pass him to wiggle into the clothes Willow left on my dresser. I lie in bed, and Kado's quick to join me, lying in the curve of my legs.

Time seems to stretch endlessly, but sleep remains elusive. In the stillness, the undead tigers creep through the shadows, their slow, deliberate steps a reminder of how surrounded I am. Yet, as I lie there in the dark, a quiet sense of peace settles over me. It's strange, unsettling even, how I find comfort in the beasts. For the first time in weeks, I feel... safe.

*Maybe Willow's right. There is peace in death.*

Kado noses a bit closer to me, and I hug him tight, like a stuffed animal. He doesn't smell like death or maybe I'm already more used to the scent than I thought. I've seen so much lately. Raya and Haze are still dead, and possibly Clio and Fern too. Tears steak down my face when I remember Clio saving me from Helena's fate, his promise to get help echoing in my mind.

Where is he now? I don't want to accept the possibility of his demise. *Surely Willow would bring him back, too.* I try to reassure myself, but the hope fades quickly. She hadn't been able to bring back my parents. Of course, there's a chance she doesn't know who Clio is or how *important* he is to me. Even worse, she might've thought he'd sided with the Council as the Ignis Adept and left him for dead.

*I can't keep doing this to myself.* Enough things are fighting me without my mind joining the fray. I force my eyes to remain closed. Maybe when I wake in the morning, things will make sense again. *For now, focus on the positives.*

Helena is alive. That gives me more reason to live than I had this morning.

When I feel as if I'm on the verge of sleep, light knocking sounds at the door. Kado's head pops up, a tiny *err* coming from deep in his chest. I groan and consider ignoring the visitor.

The knocking grows louder.

"Come in," I call sleepily, face pushed into the pillow.

The door *pops* open, and Ambrossi steps in. I sit up, surprised to see him. "Ambrossi?"

Uncertainty crests his face. "Is this a bad time, Lilith?"

I glance at Kado as if he'll answer for me. "No, I guess not. What do you want?"

"We got off on the wrong foot today," he says. "And I wanted to apologize."

My lip quirks up, though I'm not sure if it's the beginning of a grin or a sneer. "You could say that again."

"If it's any comfort, I'm glad you're here."

"*Are* you? That wasn't the impression I got."

"Yeah, I am."

"Then why the evasiveness? Why the—"

"I never lied to you, Lilith."

"You haven't told the truth either, though, have you?"

He tries to smile, but it comes out more of a grimace. "It's complicated."

"What isn't?" I stifle a yawn and look longingly at my pillow. The initial curiosity at Ambrossi's appearance has faded with the answer, and I can't wait to go back to sleep. "What happened?"

Ambrossi tugs at the black band around his throat and turns his back to me.

Did I say something wrong? "Ambrossi?"

"I'm sorry. I can't look at you when I say this."

I open my mouth to ask when I realize he's *ashamed* of whatever it is he's about to say.

"The week before your Arcane Ceremony, the same week you started developing powers, I received a message from Alchemy that my mother was sick. *Really* sick," he begins. "My father wanted me to come home to see if I could help her. And I *wanted* to, but…"

"The treaty," I say. It isn't unheard of for Healers to travel across boundaries, but those who are assigned to a Coven aren't given the same amount of flexibility.

He bobs his head. "I sent in a request for travel, but it was denied. I was heartbroken. I didn't know what to do. Then your fairy friend—"

"Fern?" I perk up, surprised at the mention.

"*Fern* came to me. She said… she said she could help me. I was so desperate, Li, I was ready to try *anything*, so I listened to her. She introduced me to a witch who helped me sneak into Alchemy, and I *saved* her," he says, finally meeting my gaze with that last sentence. "I saved my mother. She'd be dead without Willow and the Elementals."

I silently digest his words, flipflopping from one extreme to another. When I'd woken in the holding cell to see Ambrossi here, I'd immediately assumed it was for some selfish reason but of course it's not. He's not that type of witch. I stand up and wobble unsteadily, pulling Ambrossi into an awkward embrace.

It's good to know that not *everyone* loses the battle against their personal demons.

# Chapter Nine
## Hopes and Expectations

IN THE MORNING, I expect to see Willow as soon as I open my eyes, but I'm alone. The room is silent. Kado is still tucked into the curve of my legs, and I groan at the stiffness in my joints. I haven't moved all night. The dog's fuzzy head pops up as I nudge him gently with my heel and sit up, gritting my teeth against the discomfort in my side. The skin feels tight and tender. It's freshly infected. I can only imagine what kind of bacteria has gotten into it during the multiple times I've broken it open.

I poke at the wounds once, grimace, and listen to the thump of my hand on the mattress as I send another useless glare around my room. There's no note saying where Willow's gone, or any hint of what I'm supposed to do with myself. I run through my memories of last night, but she hadn't told me then, either. I should've asked.

*Too little, too late.*

I flip over, staring at the wall. Kado, oblivious to my melancholy, lets out his happy little yelp and watches me, paw set on my knee.

"Are you hungry?" I ask, running my hand across the scar on his side.

He jumps off the bed, and I can't tell whether he's excited by the prospect of breakfast or upset that I paid so much attention to his wounds. Either way, he stands beside my bed, watching me.

I'm not as enthusiastic as he is about my next move. No one had said I *have* to get up. I can simply lie back down until someone comes to get me for whatever it is they have planned, but that choice reeks of pathetic. Not the vibe I want to give. I'm still not convinced I can trust these witches, and part of me imagines Willow feels the same way. Why else would she stick me in the room farthest from everyone else?

That leaves me with one option: leave the room and risk the labyrinthine halls in the hopes of finding my sister. Kado jumps back on the bed, his massive paws barely avoiding the scars on my side. He bares his teeth, and I lift my arm on reflex to protect my face. I'm ready to fling him away, but his eyes aren't on me. His attention is on something *behind* me. A snake as thick as my arm is coiled around the bedpost. I scramble to the other end of the bed as Kado growls, ready to dive into combat. The snake watches us with an expression dangerously close to amusement on its scaly face. An ethereal glow shines from its dark emerald back.

It's another one of Willow's pets.

Does she have an entire *zoo?*

Swiping my bangs out of my eyes, I glare at the snake and pat Kado on his side. He's not happy with my new roommate, but I'm not about to move it. I don't think it's a threat, or it would've made its move while we were asleep. Kado is nowhere near relaxed but stops barking. He growls once more at the snake then jumps down.

I prepare myself to step onto my bad leg. Like my side, it's tightened up during the night, making progress to the door considerably more difficult. Pausing a few times, Kado offers his support, helping me across the room. I pet him appreciatively, already glad for his companionship. When I open the door, he pads away to growl at the snake again, and I'm left to stare at Maverick on the other side.

"You're not Willow," I say, folding my arms across my chest as petulantly as possible.

"Your observation skills are remarkable."

"Oh, yeah? How are yours?" I ask, stepping aside to reveal the snake and Kado. "See anything wrong with this picture?"

Maverick glances over my shoulder and grins. "Gave you a fright?"

I barely manage to bite back my rage as I say, "You guys could've warned me about the snake."

"But then it would've taken the joy out of the meet and greet!"

"I could've killed it. Willow would be upset," I say, then glance at Kado. "*He* still might."

Maverick rolls his eyes. "They'll be fine. Trust me."

Now there's sound advice.

"Go get dressed," he says, eyes on the spot of my dress clumped with dried blood. "We don't have all day." He points to the bathroom. "Willow left you a fresh outfit."

"Wonderful," I retort, not mentioning the fact that I *do* have all day to waste. Instead, I make quick work of dressing. "Good enough?" I spit when I approach Maverick. A stubborn lock of hair curls into my eye.

He raises an eyebrow. "Can't brush your own hair?"

"My hair is none of your concern, thank you. Where's Willow?"

"If you want to walk around looking like you've got a mop on your head, be my guest," he says and shrugs. "Willow's busy. She sent me."

"For what?"

Kado stops barking and joins us, his posture stiff. He's feeding off my emotions toward Maverick, unsure whether to perceive him as a threat or not.

I'm liking this dog more and more.

"To keep you busy. Or, if you want the honest answer, to keep you out of *trouble*." His eyes shift toward the snake again.

"That is *not* on me."

"I suppose not."

"Where's my sister?" I try one more time. I think of shoving him aside, but I'm not cocky enough to assume myself physically capable of it.

"She's *busy*. Remember, she runs this *entire* place. That isn't done with magic. It takes hard work. A lot of people depend on her, and being her *sister* doesn't make you any more important than the rest of her Coven."

"So I've learned," I state, thinking of the trip my old mentor, Crowe, had taken me on through the Land of Five. So many people had been missing from their Covens, and if our guess is correct, they're all here.

Willow really has her work cut out for her. I'll have my own share, too, I'm sure. Helena's recovery alone will make sure of that, and if Clio comes back the same way… I cut that thought off. It's too much.

"Fine. Can I see Helena then?"

"Later," he says, walking into the hallway.

I ball my hands into fists at my sides and follow him. He doesn't have to like me, but a bit of civility would be nice. "So, mind telling me where we *are* going?"

"Willow wants me to take you back to Ambrossi, first of all," he says, eyeing the bloody spot on my side. "Then I need to introduce you to a few people."

"Afterward, can I see Helena?"

"*Afterward* is not my problem."

My lip twitches in a mixture of amusement and annoyance. Maverick is brief. Stoic. I can relate to him in that way. It's nice meeting someone else who doesn't take any bullshit.

We walk through the building in silence, Maverick leading the way to Ambrossi's room. Inside, Ambrossi looks up from his cluttered workstation with an unreadable expression that morphs to a heavy frown. "You didn't give them a chance to heal, did you?" he asks as he glowers at the array of ugly scars down my ribs.

I don't look at them or Ambrossi as I plop down on his table. "You think I had the opportunity?"

"You used to be such a sweet little girl, Lilith. I never would've guessed you'd grow up to have such… *bite*," he says with a sign and goes to work slathering the wounds with green paste.

I narrow my eyes at Ambrossi, knowing that wasn't what he really wanted to say. I might've been sweet at one point. Hell, I might've been innocent, too, but she's not me. Not anymore. The world's broken me.

"That's not me anymore," I tell him.

Ambrossi scrunches his face, and I recognize that look, that need to argue. The expression passes as he finishes his work.

Setting his tools down he looks me in the eye and says, "From now on, take it easy, please. I'll be sure to pass the message to Willow, too, so no more excuses."

I give in. It doesn't seem worth it to push the topic further. "Sure." I peer at Maverick over Ambrossi's shoulder. "Are we good to go now?"

Ambrossi and Maverick exchange a look as the healer steps away from the table. I jump to my feet, well, *try* to jump to my feet. It comes off as a scramble as I make my way to Maverick's side.

"Alright, that's done. Who are these people I need to meet?" I ask.

"Your sister's right hands," Maverick explains as he leads the way out of Ambrossi's chambers.

"Take it easy, Lilith!" Ambrossi calls after us.

I don't respond. Taking it easy has never been my style.

Outside, we cross through the eerie plants and purple sky. The path leads back to the building where they'd held me prisoner. It's large, Romanesque. The doors and windows look cozy, homey even, but I know better. This place is all business. Is this the heart of the Elementals' land or just the edge?

I freeze, digging my heels into the dirt in case Maverick decides to drag me. "I thought I *wasn't* a prisoner anymore."

Maverick laughs. "My, my, aren't we a little self-centered? You do realize, this building has more functions than what you've seen? This is the Community Villa. It's got the cafeteria, meeting room, hospital wing—"

"And prisons? That's friendly."

"All part of the community."

He holds the door open, gesturing for me to go inside. Hesitantly, I obey. He takes the lead, guiding me through kitchens, living rooms, and even a laboratory. This building doesn't seem to hold out on any luxury. It's much homier than I would've imagined a prison could be. When Maverick finally picks a room to enter, it's empty. No furniture, no witches. Just a window on the other side overlooking the strange amethyst plants. Maverick places a hand in my path to stop me.

"What?"

"You don't want to be rude, do you?" he asks, smiling at me as if he's told the funniest joke.

I must be the punchline, because I don't get it, and my confusion has to show.

"Lilith, I'd like you to meet Grief," he says, gesturing to the vacant room.

I blink once, twice, three times, trying to process the situation. Is he crazy? Or does he really want to piss me off? I can't decide. "Is this a trick?"

*In a way,* a voice replies.

I startle at the familiarity and draw my eyebrows together, glancing around. I've heard it before. It's not Maverick's. It's the disembodied voice in my brain, that I hadn't been able to connect to anyone.

A few feet away, the air shimmers. The abnormality takes shape, and a second later, there's another boy in the room. He shakes out his long black sleeves and avoids eye contact. After a minute of complete silence, he doesn't make a move to introduce himself.

I glance at Maverick, but that annoying smirk is back on

his face. "This is Grief," he says.

"Hi," he murmurs.

"Grief, I'd like you to meet Lilith."

Grief makes no further effort to communicate. He disappears back into the air as suddenly as he'd appeared.

"What the *hell?*" I ask.

"Grief's shy. Spends most of his time hiding. He's the champion of hide-and-seek."

"Why doesn't Willow make him show himself?"

"Hard to make a witch do things when he can literally disappear at will."

What a way to rebel. "Is that right?"

"He'll come around eventually."

I doubt that. All I can think of is that I've heard his voice before, but I can't tell Maverick. A witch with the power of *invisibility.* It seems surreal, but then again, so does Willow's power.

"Where did he go?" I ask.

"He cares for Willow's pets mostly. They take to him better than any other witch." Maverick glances around the room. "And it's impossible to know where he is if he doesn't want you to."

I think back to my time in the holding cell. The feeling of being watched. Had Grief been with me then? Or was it all in my head? "So where to now?"

"Breakfast," Maverick says simply.

The response catches me off guard. I manage a surprised, "Oh."

I want to keep exploring, to see what else this new land has to offer, but a meal sounds good too. Maverick leads me to a beautiful room with elegant dining furniture. It's not as lavish as the kitchen in Willow's mansion, but it's far fancier than the kitchen in my Ignis home. Willow, Ambrossi, and Helena are already there, empty plates in front of them.

"What's this?" I ask warily. I've learned to not like crowds. They usually mean trouble. Of course, this gathering isn't big enough to be considered a "crowd," but there's enough people to unnerve me the same way.

"We want to welcome you into the Coven properly," Willow says.

Maverick eases me into a chair and takes the one beside me. A witch moves gracefully around the table, her robes whispering against the floor as she fills our cups with a sweet, tropical juice that smells like mango and something floral. Willow strikes up a conversation, light and easy, and soon Maverick and Ambrossi join in, their voices weaving together.

Across the table, Helena catches my eye. She smiles, and just like that, the tension unravels. Jokes pass back and forth with Ambrossi and Willow, and for a moment it feels like the war never touched us. Like I'm back home in Ignis, before everything cracked open.

The shadows of Clio's absence, and the horrors I've witnessed, fade into the background. There's no room for them here. Not now. For the first time since the world started falling apart, I'm fully present instead of in the past.

# Chapter Ten
## The Truth Hurts

THE HAPPINESS DOESN'T last long. New, unfamiliar witches flutter in and out of the room. Footsteps announce someone's arrival, but unlike the others, they don't come in. They stand in the doorway, watching us. My skin crawls, and I look up. With his wavy blond hair and chocolate-brown eyes, the man could pass for innocent. If I didn't know better, I might believe that.

"You!" I snarl, stalking toward the witch who killed Helena.

He might have a pleasant expression now, but all I see is the image of him covered in blood. I grab his shirt, curling my fingers into the fabric as tightly as possible. "How *dare* you show your face to me after what you did to her?"

"Lilith! No!" Maverick yells. He grabs my shoulders, trying to separate us, but I'm a pawn to my anger now. The harder he tries to separate us, the tighter I grip.

"I'm sorry about your friend," the man says, voice dripping with contempt. "I am, but the UnEquipped have no place in battle. It was as much her fault as it was mine."

I see red, and I hit him so hard in the face that it's red as well with the blood oozing from his nose. I raise my hand, ready to strike him again, when the anger drains away. It's a familiar sensation. The work of another Elemental.

By the time her magic fades, and I regain control of myself, Maverick has dragged me far from Helena's killer and into the purple plants outside the Community Villa. He storms through them, hands on my upper arm to stop me from rushing back into the fight, and I let him pull me along, feeling my sanity slowly settling back into place. Grudgingly, I find myself glad Maverick stepped in before things could get worse.

"You can't do that again," he tells me when he eventually releases me.

"Why not?"

"Because Sabre's one of our best fighters. He deserves respect," Maverick spits, voice thundering with anger.

"No, he doesn't. He killed Helena. I won't *forgive* him for that."

Maverick raises his hands in surrender. "You don't have to be his best friend, but you *do* have to be civil. Willow expects it of you." I roll my eyes, and Maverick sighs. "Look, I have work to do, and if you're intent on knives and fire, this isn't going to be easy for either of us. I can't risk you going off on anyone else like you did with Sabre… like you did with *me*."

"So what are you saying?" I ask, raising my eyebrow.

Maverick stares at me for a long time as if I've completely exhausted him already so early in the day. With a wave of his hand, says, "You're free to go for now. Just stay away from the Villa."

"Great, thanks," I say and watch him depart through the plants. That probably wasn't the smartest choice he could've made, but it works for me.

*Don't take it personally,* a voice says in my head. *Grief's* voice.

I whisk around, but he could be standing beside me, and

I wouldn't know. He's *been* following. Not just today, but for some time. That only leads to more questions. Why did he decide to reach out at Chastity's execution? How long had he been following me before that? Has he always been there, a shadow following my every move?

With my mind focused on Grief, my feet take me through the entrance of the building in spite of Maverick's warning. I'll take the punishment for this later, but for now, I need to find Grief. If Maverick had never pointed him out, I would've never known he existed, and the handful of times I've heard his voice would be nothing more than another mystery.

Now that I know what Grief sounds like, he's so much easier to find. I filter out the streams of thoughts from other witches and round the corner into the room he occupies, I can't see him, but I know he hasn't spotted me, because his train of thought hasn't changed. He's thinking through a to-do list of tasks. One of Willow's tigers sits in front of him, grooming itself. I keep my pace slow, using my telekinesis to muffle the sounds of my awkward footsteps. When I'm close enough to feel the heat of Grief's skin, I lunge and grab the back of his shoulders.

In his surprise, he drops his focus on remaining invisible and turns to me with wide brown eyes. "Lilith! You almost… gave me… a heart attack." He clutches his chest, and I almost feel bad.

*Almost.*

"You have a lot of explaining to do," I snap.

"I can't do that if you kill me first," he retorts and tries to pull out of my grip.

I don't let go. "You were at Chastity's execution."

His silence is answer enough.

"Why?"

"It's… complicated."

"Try me."

"Well, it all depended on you, I guess," he says. "If Chastity had successfully captured you, I was supposed to help bring you back."

"And if she failed?" I demand, staring at him with so much contempt that he wiggles under my gaze.

The air shimmers, and I recognize his effort to disappear again. I squeeze hard enough to make him yelp, and the undead cat growls in protest. It lifts a threatening paw, and I drop Grief's arm.

"What were your plans if she failed?" I ask again, calmer this time to appease the beast.

He rubs his arm. "To help you," he says, looking up from the ring of red fingerprint bruises I've left in his skin.

"Help… *me?*"

Grief trains his gaze on the floor.

Then it clicks. "*You* lit the fire… Chastity. I—"

He looks up, eyes haunted. "Yeah."

That one word is enough to overwhelm us both in emotion and memories. I couldn't light the fire to end her life, but it had been done anyway. "But… if you were there, have *always* been there, why wouldn't *you* grab me? I would have never seen it coming."

Grief shakes his head. "Willow didn't want you to know about me. We had… an advantage."

"All this time, I thought *I* killed her." I nearly choke on the words.

He gives one last, haunted look and disappears. I let him go this time. I can't look at him anymore. Not with the weight of all I've learned. His thoughts tell me when he leaves the room, but I don't follow this time. The undead cat who growled at me earlier paces to my side, butting its head against my hip for attention. Its big amber eyes look concerned, and my fingers unconsciously stroke the fur between its ears.

Maverick's voice slices through the tension behind me. "What trouble are you getting yourself into now?"

Throat tight, I manage to say, "Nothing."

His gaze sharpens, a knowing look passing through his eyes, but he doesn't press me any further.

"What do you want?" I ask, embarrassed that he's caught me not only where I'm not supposed to be, but crying while I do it.

"To see if you were okay," he says.

I blink, momentarily thrown off guard. His response is so unexpected that I can only muster a terse, "Oh."

"And that you were staying out of trouble," he adds, his gaze lingering on me a beat longer than necessary, like he's trying to figure something out. "Took me a minute to find you. You know, for having a limp, you move fast."

I manage a smirk, but it's hollow, drained of any real humor. The sharp edge of his words doesn't cut as much as it should. Maybe because I'm too tired to care. Instead, my mind drifts, caught in a bitter tide of longing. I envy Grief. More than anything, I want to slip away from this conversation, from my entire *life,* and never have to worry about being found ever again.

# Chapter Eleven
## Witch Warriors and Fairy Friends

SOMEHOW, I MANAGE to convince Maverick to take me to see Helena. Maybe it's because he caught me with Grief, or maybe it's something in my eyes. I'm not sure. He groans, just like I expect, but eventually gives in, probably worried about what I'll do if I'm left alone again. He feels responsible for me, like most people feel about their pets. If I end up mauling someone, it's on him.

I don't want him to see it, but after the incident with Grief, I'm on edge and filled with so much self-doubt, I'm convinced everyone can see it radiating off of me. It's becoming harder and harder to believe that this is real, that this is what my life has become. I need to see Helena to prove that I'm not as crazy as I think I am.

Maverick leads me deeper into the labyrinth of violet plants, the dense thicket closing in around us. Twisted tendrils brush against us, as if they're alive, intent on either guiding or trapping us. The air shifts too, sweet and heavy, and for a moment, I wonder if my mind is playing tricks on me. Is it so starved for something untainted by death's foul stench that it's weaving the scent of meadow flowers out of desperation?

We finally emerge into a small clearing where Helena's home stands. It's smaller than the other structures I've seen, but there's something oddly charming about it. A little cottage with red siding and a white roof, almost whimsical in appearance, but there's something about the design I don't recognize from any of the Covens. Is that significant?

When Maverick opens the door, I realize the outside is nothing more than a well-crafted illusion. Inside is something far different. The walls, the floor, and the low ceiling are all shades of cold gray. The room is furnished, yes, but the space feels more like the holding cell I'd been locked in yesterday rather than a home. The only splashes of color come from the red sheets on the bed and the matching rug on the floor.

Helena stands by an open window, the only window in the building, staring into the strange wilderness beyond. The corners of her lips curve up, and I recognize that wonder in her eyes. This version of her is more like the Helena I grew up with than the depressed one who'd taken her over after our Arcane Ceremony.

"As requested," Maverick says sarcastically, jolting me back to reality.

"Yeah, thanks," I retort.

Maverick takes his leave, and I let my shoulders sag with relief. When Helena's eyes meet mine, I rush across the room to pull her into my arms.

The smell of death on her is fainter today. Is that because she's recovering or has my nose has already become so used to the smell that I hardly notice it? When we break apart, she opens her mouth to speak, looking flustered when no sound comes out.

I pat her on the shoulder. "It's okay. You'll get there eventually."

Helena tucks a strand of wild orange hair behind her ear. Her green eyes bore into mine, but I don't understand the excitement I see there. If I were her, newly resurrected from the dead, I don't think I'd be able to feel anything close to joy for a long time.

Helena points at my side. "I'm okay," I say, interpreting her hand gestures. "Ambrossi says I'll be fine if I take it easy."

She nods, relieved.

"How are *you*?" I ask.

"She's recovering well," a voice says from the doorway. I jump as Willow walks into the room, her long hair swinging with each step. She looks smaller somehow, more like a ghost than human. "You are, too."

I nod, my gaze still lingering on Helena, who's barely moved since we entered.

"She's eating again," Willow adds, gesturing to the empty bowl on Helena's gray nightstand. Somehow, I overlooked it on my initial survey of the room.

"That's good. Really good." There's a strange swell of pride in my chest, unexpected but undeniable. Helena's been through so much, and hearing that she's eating, actually taking care of herself, feels like a victory, a sign of hope when everything else has been so bleak.

Willow's lips curve into the smallest of smiles, pleased with my reaction. "I thought you'd be happy to hear it." Before I can respond, her tone shifts, and she adds, "Can you come with me for a little bit, Lilith? Helena has some exercises she needs to work on."

I draw my eyebrows together, standing my ground protectively between Helena and Willow. "I can help her do them."

"I know you care about your friend," she begins carefully, "but if she's going to get better, she needs to work alone."

Stubbornness settles deep into my bones. "But I *just* got here."

Her expression softens, but she doesn't back down. "I understand that," she murmurs, fingers absentmindedly twining a lock of her long brown hair around her finger. "But I can't have you blowing off Coven duties."

"Coven duties?" I echo. "I didn't know I had any. According to Ambrossi, I'm supposed to do nothing until I'm healed."

"This isn't strenuous, and my word supersedes his." She winks, and I suppress a deep-seated urge to argue.

*Willow's your sister*, a voice whispers. *She worries about you.*

The voice sounds like Helena's, but she hasn't moved her lips. When I make eye contact, no thoughts come to the front of her mind. I glance at Willow, but her face remains stoically expressionless, giving no hint that she's heard anything.

"Come on," Willow says, her petite frame nearly dancing through the doorway.

"I'll be back," I promise Helena, though I'm not sure Willow will let me make good on it. Once the door closes behind us, I ask her, "Where are we going?"

"I want to introduce you to a friend of mine," she says, leading us through the odd, purple plants.

Interesting. Who does she trust enough to call a "friend"? I haven't found many witches who fit that role, and I'm average compared to her. "Maverick said you were too busy for me today."

"I was, but I moved some things around, and my day opened up. I'm going to take you on the tour you *should* have had."

I don't care for Maverick, but her slightly bitter tone suggests someone will be punished over this. Oddly enough, I feel bad thinking that someone may be him. "It's not his fault, you know. Maverick's. He kept me from doing something I'd regret. I... I saw him... *Sabre*. And I lost it."

Willow holds up a hand. "You don't have to explain yourself. Maverick informed me of the situation, and I understand why you did what you did."

I dip my head in appreciation.

"But..." she continues.

I squeeze my eyes shut. *Here it comes.*

"That doesn't excuse anything. You might be my sister, but I can't condone that type of behavior. We all have our demons, and trust me, throttling Sabre will not make them go away."

"You don't know unless you try, right?" I ask with a chuckle.

Willow glares at me, and I flinch. She's right, but part of me still wants to make Sabre pay for what he's done. I wait for her to spell out my punishment, but she doesn't. It's like we're at an impasse, neither of us wanting to further the conversation that's clearly not over. Our walk continues, utterly silent, as we surrender to our thoughts. Willow's light steps and my irregular ones stomping through the foliage keep it from being too quiet.

"You really make people live all the way out here?" I ask, smacking a broad leaf out of my face. I thought it was insane to keep me from everyone else in the same *building,* but apparently, I could have it worse.

"I don't make anyone do anything they don't want to do," she says pointedly. "He *chooses* to be out here."

The questions double when she stops at a pile of boulders. I glance around in confusion. There's no house, no tent, nothing to suggest anyone *lives* here.

"Malcolm, I'd like you to meet my sister Lilith," Willow says. I cringe and look over my shoulder. Are there *more* invisible witches than Grief?

A fairy emerges from the rocks. Red wings encase the tiny body, and when they open, I'm shocked to see the fairy is *male*. A gothic fairy had taken me by surprise, but that's *nothing* compared to this feeling. I hadn't thought male fairies existed. Fairies, after all, are believed to be immortal, but this singlehandedly shatters that idea; a male implies reproduction.

Malcolm is all warmth and hospitality, oblivious to the chaos his existence has created in my mind. "She… she looks like you," he says to Willow, and in some strange way, I've blown his mind too.

"Yes. She's my sister, and she'll be staying here for a while. So, if I'm not around, I'll need you to look out for her, okay?"

Malcolm nods like an obedient child, eyes alight with wonder as he watches her. The dynamic between them is a far cry from what I had with Fern. *Fern.* Just the thought of her name sends a ripple of chaos through my mind, especially when I remember Ambrossi's story. Fern had been the one to draw him into the Elementals.

*What happened to her?* If she's on their side, they have no reason to harm her. But the Council… that's a different story.

By the time my mind comes back to the present, Willow is saying her goodbyes to Malcolm. He slips back into the rocks, and I stare at the spot, wondering how he fit through with such ease.

"Let's head back," Willow says.

As we trek through the plants, my arsenal of questions begins to fire. "No offense, but Maverick said you'd be introducing me to your *higher-ups*. Malcolm doesn't seem to fit the title."

Willow shrugs, unconcerned. "So maybe this isn't the *exact* tour I instructed him to give you."

I struggle to come up with a reasonable response. Over the course of a day and a half, my world has been flipped upside-down, and in the silence, I hear the destruction. Willow's smiling as if this is normal. I have to remind myself that to her, it is. Her world might've gone through the same turmoil at some point in the past, but she righted it a long time ago.

"How long have you known Malcolm? You seem... *close*..." I say, for lack of a better word.

She slows a bit to match my pace. "I found him when he was a baby."

At the word *baby* everything fails me. First *male* fairies, and now *baby* ones, too? I'm sure there are fairies in all five Covens, ranging in age and gender, but I've never met them. I can only imagine how different each one is from those I've already encountered. Maybe somewhere in the Land of Five are more male fairies like Malcolm... and his father. Whoever that might be.

"Where's his mother?"

I watch the strange way she crawls in her skin as she says, "Bonding with a fairy is hard to describe. I guess it *is* like being a parent, you know? Especially when they're young like Malcolm."

"I was bonded to one back in Ignis," I offer, hoping it will make her say whatever it is that's clearly on her mind.

"Fern?" she guesses.

*"Fern came to me. She said… she said she could help me,"* Ambrossi had said.

My stomach does a little flop. This is my opportunity to ask, but I'm not sure I'm ready for the answer. "Yeah. How do you know her?"

Willow's lips curl into a small smile, like she's amused by my confusion. "Isn't it obvious?" she asks with a little chuckle. "She's Malcolm's mother."

"What?" My knee buckles, and I stagger slightly, but I catch myself, and thankfully don't fall face-first into the muck.

Willow's expression doesn't change. "She's his mother," she repeats.

I stop dead in my tracks, unable to move. "Then why isn't she here with him?"

Willow pauses, taking a breath as if she's preparing herself. "Because I asked her not to be."

I grab her arm to stop her mid-step. "I'm sorry, but what? Why would you make her leave?"

For the first time, Willow's usual composure falters. Her shoulders droop, the weight of whatever's coming next settling heavily in the air between us. She exhales slowly, then glances away, staring off into the distance as if the memory is too painful to face head-on. "I think I need to tell you a story."

I wait for her to continue, but she doesn't look at me. Instead, she seems to drift back in time, her eyes focused on something I can't see.

"After our parents died," Willow begins, her voice dropping lower, "Fern helped me escape from the Council."

I blink, struggling to make sense of her words. "I was told the Council *recruited* you as one of them. Not *captured*."

"They have a way of twisting the truth like that," she says, bittersweet smile on her lips. "I was never *one* of them. The Sage forced me to live in the Grove to keep people from searching when I disappeared from my Coven. To keep them from asking questions. That's the same reason no one fought the decision to have me executed. The Council made it all so easy to digest. They said I betrayed them, and everyone knows no one lives through treason." The similarities of her story and my life are too close for me to be comfortable with. Were they grooming me for the same fate Willow faced?

"Before any of that," she continues, "I found this place. I was safe… everyone was, and I made a mistake by leaving. Exactly what Fern told me *not* to do. After I died, I came back here to recover, and by that time, Fern had already given birth."

"And she *chose* to leave her child?"

Willow looks away as if the conversation is finally making her uncomfortable. "Fairies are complicated."

That's not limited to fairies. "It was for me, wasn't it? The reason you left?"

Willow opens her mouth, then closes it, resolved. "Yeah. I thought I could help you, and I couldn't. Fern knows how much you mean to me so she volunteered to find you, watch over you, and bring you back when the time was right."

"I guess that time never came," I say dryly, glaring at the base of the nearest purple plant. And now there's a possibility she might be dead because of me.

"Things got far more complicated than any of us could've anticipated," Willow says, her voice heavy with regret.

"Where is she now? Is her disappearance part of your plan?"

"I wish I could say it was, but I don't know where she is, or if she's safe," Willow admits. "I'm not giving up though. I've got people who'll find out the truth, one way or another."

A flutter of hope warms my chest, but I'm too afraid to acknowledge it. Hope is a dangerous thing. "You have people who can do that?"

Willow stares into my eyes until a chill runs down my spine. "My people are capable of many things."

My body floods with adrenaline. Now is as good of a time as any to ask. "Can… you find someone for me? In Ignis?"

A sparkle lights Willow's black eyes. "Of course. Anything for my dear sister. Who is it?"

A blush creeps into my cheeks as I think of the right way to pass the information to her. "His name is Clio. He's my…" I don't know how to finish that sentence. He's not my best friend, that title belongs to Helena, and he's certainly not an ordinary acquaintance. He's my rival, my friend… my *lifeline*.

"He's special to you?" Willow guesses.

At least she can make sense out of me swallowing my tongue. I nod once.

"I'll do my best to have him found."

# Chapter Twelve
## Meet and Greet

WILLOW'S WORDS CARRY me through the night. I have *faith* in her that, come Hell or high water, she'll find Clio. The night brings dreams about him, and when I wake in the morning, I'm clutching Kado like a giant teddy bear. He catches my gaze and rolls over to rasp his tongue across my cheek.

Bright and early, Maverick comes to take me on the rest of the abandoned tour. The day follows almost the same routine as yesterday. The only difference is Kado walks by our side, confident. I watch him from the corner of my eye, not entirely sure what his reaction will be should we happen to cross paths with any of Willow's undead cats.

I'm learning quickly how important regularity is around here. Witches hustle from room to room, chatter echoing up and down the halls that seemed so lifeless before. Everyone has tasks, and somehow, Willow keeps up with them all. I'm impressed by my sister's attention to detail. The Elemental Coven might be an unconventional group, but they're the best-run Coven I've ever seen.

"So how do you like it here so far?" Maverick asks in an attempt at small talk as we round the first bend in the corridor.

"It's okay." I don't bother pointing out that I haven't been here long enough to form a real opinion.

Maverick chuckles, his tone dry. "I was hoping for a bit more enthusiasm than that."

I smirk, meeting his gaze. "Were you jumping for joy when they recruited you?"

"Actually, yeah." He shrugs, a small smile tugging at his lips. "I was excited to join the Elementals."

"I thought everyone was here because of some tragedy."

"For a lot of witches, maybe."

Slightly intrigued, I ask, "But not you?"

"No. I learned early on that I was Equipped even though I came from UnEquipped parents."

That's a situation I understand too well. "How'd you learn you weren't like them?"

"We had a cat when I was real young. It was a pretty thing, with stripes and all. I loved her, but every time, she tried to jump in my lap, she immediately fell asleep. Like clockwork."

I roll my eyes, not taken by the story. "And? That's what cats do."

"She didn't do it for anyone else."

"How'd you figure out that was an *ability*?"

Maverick shifts uncomfortably, scratching the back of his neck. "Our neighbors had a dog. I could make him go out the same way."

"Ah," I say, piecing it together. "So, you figured it out with animals first."

Maverick sighs, a deep sound coming all the way from his gut.

I get the feeling this isn't the first time he's had to explain himself. "I bet your parents were shocked."

"I never told them. Too scared to. My parents had never been fans of the Equipped. Never knew anyone who was. So I kept it to myself."

"And no one noticed you could do this?"

He shakes his head.

When my powers started to develop, they were sporadic and wild. It hadn't mattered how much I wanted to keep them hidden, because they couldn't be contained. "You had help," I say.

"Yeah. Sabre and I both did." He pauses, a small, almost nostalgic smile forming. "That's actually how we met."

"Who helped you?"

"A girl from Aquais. She had this power to calm the worst of my temper."

I know that witch. I saw her yesterday, in the Community Villa. *She's* an Elemental, too, which means she's here, somewhere.

Maverick continues, taking no notice that I'm no longer listening. "She sensed how upset I was the day I realized I was Equipped, and she came to soothe me."

"But she had to cross the border to do that," I point out. "That goes against the treaty."

"I didn't think about it at the time. I never got any bad vibes from her. She was always nice so when she told me there was a Coven that takes in witches like me, I didn't question it."

"And you believed her?"

"I had no reason not to."

"So you pretended to be UnEquipped?"

"Yeah, and it worked. As far as my parents were concerned anyway."

"How did you trick the Arcane Ceremony?" I ask,

genuinely curious. My most heartfelt prayers hadn't been enough to change *my* results.

"I didn't. I skipped it. Disappeared the night before. I didn't have any other choice."

A rock settles in my stomach when I remember how much of Aens had been missing. Maverick looks to be about my age, which means we should've been at the same ceremony. "That sounds about right, actually," I finally say.

Maverick stops walking and faces me so suddenly that Kado lets out an anxious whine. He folds his hands together, his eyes meeting mine. "I won't lie to you. Today will be stressful."

"More so than usual?" I ask as I pet Kado, wordlessly soothing the anxious dog. I can't remember the last day that's passed without stress.

"Willow is introducing you to the entire Coven today."

Kado's black eyes search my face as I try to hide exactly how uneasy that statement leaves me. "That's good, right?"

Maverick starts walking again, and I have a feeling he does it to avoid eye contact. "All depends on how they receive you."

"That's comforting." Although my snarky comment sounds like it's founded on confidence, it's not. What happens if they *don't* receive me well? Will Willow have to send me back to the Land of Five?

"You'll do fine," Maverick assures me.

Not surprisingly, I don't find much comfort in it.

As we near the end of the hall, Willow's voice echoes from a room I've yet to enter. Maverick gives me a long look then pushes open the double doors and gestures for me to step inside. I obey, heart pounding.

Willow stands on a platform in the middle of the room, looking much fiercer than I thought her capable of. Rows and rows of benches fill the space, each packed with Elementals. A hundred witches, maybe more. I don't recognize most of them. Then I spot the empty chair on the platform beside Willow.

Before Maverick says the word, I know that chair is meant for me. The blood leaves my face as I imagine hobbling over to it in plain view of everyone. That will be their first impression of me. The girl they risked life and limb to obtain.

"Go," Maverick whispers.

I repress the urge to glare at him, choosing instead to thrust my energy into my telekinesis. It's strong for the first few steps but falters and dies as the nervousness takes over.

"I can help," Maverick whispers again, a little gentler this time.

I smack his hand away, drawing murmurs from the nearest handful of Elementals. Doesn't he understand he's only making things worse? Kado lifts a paw as if he's trying to help me too. I narrow my eyes at him, and he sits down, tail wagging uncertainly.

I move forward. The sound of my uneven footsteps draws more Elementals' eyes, all of them burning my skin like hot needles. My gaze stays on the chair. If I make eye contact with anyone along the way, it'll be the end of me. They'll see *through* me and decide that I don't belong here. In a way, I feel like I'm taking my first steps all over again, except falling down here won't be met with encouragement to keep going.

What feels like an eternity later, I reach the chair and plop into it as if my bones are made of clay. Willow beams at me, and I try to copy the gesture, but my face feels heavy, too.

"Right on cue. This is my sister Lilith," she announces.

The room goes silent.

The tension doesn't lessen as the witches scrutinize me. They whisper to each other with quick glances in my direction as if they haven't gotten their fill from the initial stare. The image in their minds, the one built up from Willow's stories and words, is the complete opposite of what I really am. I can feel them piecing it together. They're learning how badly they've been tricked.

If Willow notices the tension in the air, she doesn't comment on it. Instead, she launches into a discussion of other Coven goings-on, leaving me to wallow. I should feel bad for glaring at them, for stooping to their level, but I don't. I want them to know I'm not afraid of them.

Not anymore.

Maverick is perhaps the only one who doesn't look disgruntled, and I tell myself I have no right to be angry. Just as these people have left their mark on me, I've also sculpted them. Chastity was captured and executed for *my* attempted abduction. I hadn't lit the fire, but I was still responsible for her death. At her execution, no one cried because that had been done *here*, in her true home.

"Maverick will be helping her settle in," Willow says when I finally come back to the present. "Any more questions?"

No one speaks, and I'm mad at myself. What did I miss when I was in La-La Land?

"All right, then!" Willow claps her hands together. "Remember, vigil is at eight o'clock sharp tonight. Meeting dismissed."

I stand quickly, desperate to prove my strength, my

worthiness. All around me, the Elemental Coven grunts and groans as they file out of the room. A few of them aren't shy about sharing their displeasure at having me here, whispering curses and insults so Willow won't hear. One even bumps me with his shoulder. Reading his thoughts lets me know he'd intended to knock me down.

When the room is nearly empty, Willow moves to Maverick. I grasp her sleeve, holding her back. Curious, she asks, "Is something wrong?"

I'm dumbfounded by her honest confusion. Had the hostility been in my head? "They *hated* me," I say, my voice more brittle than intended.

Willow tilts her head, her brows knitting together. "That's a pretty strong word."

"Maybe. But it's how they feel." I glance over at Maverick, hoping to gauge his reaction.

He offers a small, unreadable shrug.

"They'll warm up to you," Willow says, her tone reassuring. "Right now, you're a stranger. It'll pass."

Those words change nothing. I can't suppress the unease creeping up my spine. "How do I know they won't try to kill me in my sleep?"

Willow laughs softly, but there's no humor in it. "You're overthinking it."

"What if I'm not?"

Willow runs her hand through her long brown hair, frustrated. "I guess my word isn't enough?"

I shake my head.

"I suppose that's fair. This is a big Coven, and while I'd

like to trust everyone with my life, I can't speak for all of them. That's why I gave you Kado." She nods as the dog pads up to my side, his tongue lolling from the corner of his mouth. "He'll keep you safe. We can *both* trust him."

I glance at the undead dog. In spite of my initial fears, he's becoming my best ally here—perhaps the *only* one besides Willow herself. "Thank you, Willow."

"You're welcome," she replies as chipper as ever. Then her voice drops to a whisper. "If you ever feel your life is in danger, come to me *immediately*."

"Of course," I say, surprised by how quickly the good cheer left her.

"Good," she says briskly, then resumes smiling at Kado and tugs on his collar once, to lead him away for breakfast.

"You handled it well," Maverick says. "Didn't cut any throats."

"Yeah, well, I'm sure they wanted to cut mine."

He shrugs, and I take that as a yes. "That's why we need to get you back in shape for training."

"Ambrossi told me not to do that yet," I remind him, gesturing to my injured side.

"Well, it's a good thing he's not our only Healer then, isn't it?"

I perk up. "You have others?"

"Mm-hmm. We're going to see her now."

That statement both excites and worries me. Yesterday, Maverick was on Ambrossi's side about me resting, and now he's encouraging my training? He must know something I don't or maybe his Coven's hostility is as apparent to him as it is to me.

## Chapter Thirteen
### The Lost Aquais

MAVERICK WALKS WITH confidence, but his mind is torn, split between disobeying Willow's direct orders and making sure I get the training I need. I listen to the internal struggle, trying to find the perfect moment to jump in, but it doesn't come. The pros outweigh the cons in this situation so I let him work through it on his own.

We round the corner, and Maverick halts. I mirror his movement, my gaze following his to a woman standing in the center of the hall. Her curly blue hair is swept into a loose bun atop her head, and her lips press into a tight line. She watches us intently, her tawny eyes sharp with focus.

I'm struck by her familiarity. I've never spoken to this witch, but I know her name.

"Katrina," spews from my mouth on reflex.

She narrows her eyes at me, but it doesn't hide her confusion. "Do I know you?"

She doesn't. We've never been properly introduced. The only time I've seen her is through Crowe's memories, and it's hard to shake the image of that night when his eyes were filled with heartbreak. Finding out that Katrina had left Aquais to become an Elemental shattered him so much, it compromised his entire belief system.

"Hello?" Katrina snaps her fingers in my face.

"No, you don't," I say finally, "but I'm a friend, I promise."

She wrinkles her nose and looks at Maverick for confirmation.

"As well as any," he offers and shrugs.

Katrina quirks her lip and folds her arms across her chest, indecision obviously still unresolved. "Okay, *friend*. Where are you off to?"

"We're on our way to see Laura. Lilith's due for a checkup," Maverick says. I barely hear him, still impossibly distracted by Katrina's presence.

Katrina meets my gaze. There's an odd look in her eyes as if she wants to ask me something, but whatever it is, she doesn't want to say it in front of Maverick. "Have fun," she quips and we continue our journey down the hall. I'm stuck on the look in her eyes. Whatever is bothering her, she'll tell me when the time is right.

When we get to the door at the end of the hall, Maverick cracks it open. "Knock, knock," he calls inside. "Can we come in?"

"Of course!" a soft voice replies.

Maverick pushes it the rest of the way, revealing an eerily white room smelling briefly of healing herbs. They're different from those in Ambrossi's room. Sweeter somehow. The girl who'd spoken, a petite thing with a pointed face and tangled, light-brown hair, beams at me.

"Laura," Maverick greets her.

I look past her. Two hospital beds fill the room, one against the wall on each side of the room. One is empty, but

Helena sits on the bed to Laura's left.

I rush to her side. "I-is she okay?" I ask, glancing between Laura and Helena.

"Yes, of course," Laura replies, wringing her hands together. "My job is to assess how well she's recovering."

I clutch the side of the bed for balance. Right now, Helena is my lifeline. I don't think I can bear to hear anything bad happening to her.

Maverick's voice breaks through the silence. "I need you to check Lilith, too, please."

"She's a Healer?" I ask him.

Laura shifts her weight, her head tilting as she considers the question. "Of sorts," she says, her tone measured.

I frown, still not understanding. "What does that mean?"

"She cleanses auras," Maverick explains.

The woman grins, showing all her teeth. "While traditional Healers can manipulate the illnesses of a human body using herbs, I've learned to do it with magic."

I'm both skeptical and fascinated by her statement. Healers are different from other witches in that their ability *isn't* based on magic. It's learned and passed down generation to generation. There isn't as big a distinction between the Equipped and UnEquipped in Alchemy because they can all be *taught* their gift. I've never heard of magic-healing beyond Lynx's isolated incident.

"Take a seat," Laura says, oblivious to my temporary distraction.

I know she means for me to sit in the empty bed, but I'm stubborn, and insist Maverick help me sit beside Helena. On instinct, I reach into my pocket for Ambrossi's amulet, only to remember I no longer have it. "How does this work?"

"You relax and leave the work to me," Laura says.

Maverick takes a step back, as if he's about to view something extraordinary, leaving my skin to prickle with anxiety. I don't know what an *aura* is or how it can heal someone. Not knowing what to expect leaves me anxious.

"Will it hurt?"

"No," Laura says and chuckles. "Auras are basically a chart of your energy. They can tell me quite a bit about someone."

Helena looks more prepared than I am for what's about to happen. She's *excited*. She can *see* her aura in Laura's mind. Mine, too.

*Helena… can you hear me?* I think.

*Yes,* comes the soft reply.

I stare into the window of Laura's mind, unsure whether I'm more amazed by the auras or by Helena's sudden ability. Helena's aura has Willow's signature white ring, rising into a flare of blinding light. Unlike Willow's other projects that display a clean glow, Helena has flecks of black crackling through it like fire.

Judging by the tension in Laura's mind, it's a bad sign, though not entirely unexpected. What it reveals about my aura remains unclear since it's completely black. Her frustration only amplifies the one that's been with me my entire life. Even if she can't unravel the mystery of my confusing aura, I can. It's the same reason for my limp—my childhood "accident."

"Helena, you're improving," Laura says.

Helena reaches over to squeeze my hand. She's too

preoccupied with her brief mind-reading stunt to hear what else Laura has to say. When Laura combs through my aura, she doesn't look so hopeful.

"Is everything okay?" I ask after a long tense minute of silence.

"I... don't know," she admits, shoulders sagging in defeat.

Maverick's brow furrows first at her, then at me. "That bad, huh?"

"It's impossible to tell." Laura admits and frowns as she looks me up and down. It doesn't suit her. "How do you feel?"

"I feel fine."

"Really?" She clicks her tongue, looking torn. Her eyes stray to Maverick. "Then I would say light training should be fine. Just don't exert yourself, okay?"

Maverick and I nod at the same time. Those are terms in which we can both agree. Laura dismisses us, and regardless of Maverick's complaints about time, he agrees to tag along while I take Helena back home.

"So... mind reading, huh?" I ask her.

She bites her lip, a flicker of excitement shining in her eyes.

"Funny how we both ended up with Mentis powers," I say, smiling.

She doesn't respond, her gaze trained on the ground.

Slowly, my smile drops. Confused, I glance at Maverick, but he offers no explanation.

I bite my lip to keep from repeating the question, hoping she'll offer something on her own. As we step into her yard, Kado pads out of the forest, yipping happily with his stump of a tail flopping. He's alone.

Helena stares at the dog, shoulders tense as if she's suddenly upset.

"Are you okay?" I ask, confused.

She pets Kado and ignores me.

"Come on," Maverick says, gently grasping my elbow. "Let's give her some time alone."

I follow him but glance over my shoulder to see if Kado is following. The dog glances at me, but then his eyes land on Helena. He senses her sadness too. If I can't make her feel better, I'm glad that at least Kado can.

"What was that about?" I ask Maverick when Helena is out of range.

"What your friend went through is a lot. It's going to take time for her to come to terms with it all, and she's gonna have moments like that."

"I know," I admit. I can't imagine what it's like to grapple with your mortality the way she must be, but it doesn't make it easier to watch her struggle.

Maverick leads the way to the training fields, a sparse lot of green grass that stands out from the purple plants. It doesn't look like it belongs here.

Maverick stares at me expectantly from the other side of the clearing.

I search for some sign of what I should do. When I don't find anything, I ask, "What do I do?"

"Show me your magic," he encourages.

Suddenly, I'm not in the Land of New Life with Maverick, but in the Grove with Crowe, trying to force powers that won't come. The look in Katrina's eyes comes to me again, and I understand what she wanted to ask. Most likely, she wants to know about Crowe. If he's okay. If he's talked about her.

The last time I saw him, he was going to Tarj's home for dinner. Then everything had fallen apart. What became of him in the Battle of Ignis? Is he still alive? Is he injured? One thing is for sure, he hasn't given up his place on the Council. If another member disappeared besides me, Willow surely would've heard about it, but why he would stay with the Council?

I don't know whether he's my friend or my enemy.

"Earth to Lilith!" Maverick calls, and I snap out of the memory. Dwelling on it won't help. I'll ask Willow about him later.

For the next ten minutes, I push myself, demonstrating every way I can wield my telekinesis. Normally, it's a rush, but today, the exhilaration fades quickly, replaced by a creeping dizziness and a hollow weakness in my limbs. Maverick notices almost immediately. He calls it quits and guides me back to my room, the walk dragging longer than the last time I made it.

When we reach the door, he doesn't deliver his usual cold dismissal. Instead, he studies me until my skin crawls.

"What?" I snap. Every moment I'm forced to stand is agony, and all I want to do is lay down. To rest.

"That's how I know you belong here," he says.

I scrunch my eyebrows. "What?"

"Today must've been hard on you, but you don't show it. Instead, you tuck it all inside, keeping your head. Strength like that must be genetic. You and Willow, you both have it."

I breathe out slowly, unsure how to respond to the

compliment.

"She has a lot of faith in you. We all do."

The hair on the back of my neck rises. The last person who depended on me was Helena… and she *died* for it.

I BARELY SIT down on my bed when someone knocks on the door. Kado, who returned shortly after me, jumps to his feet, alert for any sign of danger. I expect Willow, so I'm taken aback by a flash of blue hair. As soon as the door cracks open, Katrina bursts inside my room like her pants are on fire, causing Kado to let out an uneasy *yap* as she barely avoids stepping on his paws.

"Um… hi," I greet her, scrunching my forehead. For the life of me, I can't imagine why she would want to visit *me* at this time of night.

"I'm sorry. It's late, I know," she says, closing the door behind her.

"It's okay," I reply, folding my arms across my chest. She's making me uncomfortable at this point, but I probably did the same to her earlier, so it's only fair.

She plops down on my bed, eyes glued to the wall. "You know me. How?"

I give her the answer she's after. "Crowe told me about you."

She squirms on the edge of the bed, her face lighting up. "He did?"

"Well, not in so many words, but… he looked for you in Aquais."

Katrina bites her lip. "And?"

"It *devastated* him that he couldn't find you," I admit, remembering how hard it had been for him to not look at her house.

"I didn't want to leave like that, but I *had* to. I wanted to tell him goodbye, but I never got the chance." She drops her gaze. "I hoped he would understand."

She's wounded by the same heartache overwhelming Crowe; the type of agony that comes from being separated from the people you love.

"Then why not leave something to let him know? Why make him worry like that?"

"Couldn't risk it. The Council was cracking down on Elementals after Fleur was nearly caught. Not to mention Iris' fiasco. It'd be a matter of time until they found me."

It's hard not to mention the fact that an innocent fairy nearly died from Fleur's pointless attack. I almost point that out, but somehow manage to bite it back by reminding myself that I'm one of these people now.

"I miss him, Lilith," Katrina says, twining her thumbs. "Perhaps my biggest regret in joining the Elementals is that he couldn't come with me."

"You should be worried about what happens if you have to face him in battle. I mean, if you run, you'll be labeled a traitor, and I don't think I have to mention what happens if you pick the other option."

"My plan is to capture him," she replies without missing a beat. There's such confidence in her words that it's obvious she's put a lot of thought into it. "This way, he'll be here, and he'll be *safe*. Even if he doesn't want to be."

"That's… that's a plan," I manage to say. Should I tell her how messed up it is?

Her wide tawny eyes look glassy with uncertainty. "Promise me you'll do the same if it comes down to it."

When I first met Crowe, all I wanted to do was strangle him, but he's grown on me. He was there for me at my lowest. I don't want him to get hurt. I don't want *anyone* to get hurt. "Katrina, believe me, I have no intention of hurting him."

"I need to talk to him." She scrunches her eyebrows, then releases the tension. "If we could somehow get a message to him, maybe we could convince him to join us."

She sounds so optimistic, I can't help but agree, though we both know that attempting to contact Crowe is not only a suicide mission, but it would put all of us in direct danger.

# Chapter Fourteen
## The Vigil

AFTER RUNNING OUT of ideas on how she's going to make contacting Crowe a possibility, Katrina eventually leaves, and I'm left alone with Kado to settle in for the night. Sleep, however, is hard to come by after everything that's happened today. When a knock sounds on my door, I'm tempted to ignore it, thinking Katrina has returned to tell me she's finally got a plan. Kado grips the edge of my sleeve in his teeth, pulling gently to get my attention. I roll toward him, and he lets out a soft yip, which I recognize as his impatient whine.

"Fine. You win, traitor," I say and get up. After a luxurious stretch, I grumble, "This better be good."

Kado's eyelids flutter indifferently, tail wagging at having gotten his way.

"What's going on?" I ask as soon as I open the door. The reason for Kado's impatience is that it's not just *any* visitor at my door. It's Willow.

"Vigil," Willow replies simply.

She's cloaked in a flowing black dress that looks almost like a poncho in a regal sort of way, if that's possible. Heavy red marks scour her porcelain face. She's been grieving while I've done my best to try and forget about it all.

"You're coming with me."

I narrow my eyes, unsure if I've heard her right. Ignis was

my home, but the Elementals have made it clear I'm not wanted here. "I don't think that's the best idea," I tell her.

She quirks an eyebrow.

"I might make things worse for them. I hurt some of those witches." I pause, not wanting the words to leave my lips though I'm sure she already knows. "*Killed* one."

Willow simpers with all the fragility of ice. "I know, but you can't be so quick to forget that my warriors hurt you, too. They know all the things you've gone through on their account."

I can't think of a solid way to refute her. I've never been a coward, but I absolutely do *not* want to attend the vigil. Kado climbs back onto the bed to settle down to sleep, and I wish I could switch places with him.

Willow catches the hesitation. "Look, I know this is hard, but I can't think of a better way to bond with your new Coven than by being there for them in their time of need. Yes, you might be to blame for some of their pain, but you're also here to pick up the pieces, and that says something. You need to show your place here. More importantly, you need to show that you're not afraid."

"I'm *not* afraid." I made a show of it earlier, or at least, I thought I had. Witches on both sides of this are hostile toward me. That's nothing new. If I'm afraid of anything at this point, it's failure. My failures have cost me so much already.

"Then you have no reason *not* to go," Willow counters.

"If you say so," I murmur, sentence punctuated by Willow thrusting a dress into my arms.

"Put this on."

Too drained to argue, I shuffle to the bathroom. Willow settles onto the bed beside Kado, waiting patiently. I change quickly, then splash cold water on my face, hoping to bring a little life back to my complexion. I've always been pale, but now my skin nearly matches Willow's. I avoid the mirror. There's no need to see my lifeless eyes staring back, reminding me just how grim tonight feels.

When I step back into my room, Willow is petting Kado, and for a fraction of a second, I catch real emotion contorting her expression before she wipes it away.

"Ready?" she asks, jumping to her feet with a fake smile plastered on her face more.

A thousand words race through my mind, but I choose silence instead. Tonight will be hard on her, too. Despite the weight of sorrow pressing down on her, she carries herself with quiet dignity, holding her head high all the way to the meeting hall.

Maverick's words echo in my head again. *"That strength. You and Willow both have it."*

I'm starting to see what he means.

The meeting room is dark, aside from a few candles, and as packed as it was earlier, but the atmosphere is different, homier, like a real Coven. No benches divide witches from one another, and there are barely any chairs. They huddle together in groups, forming an enormous mass in the middle of the room.

The far wall is covered in photos. When I get closer, I understand these are the deceased. I don't recognize a lot of them and take it to mean these are the deceased Elementals. Then I startle when I see Raya and Haze. A few other UnEquipped Ignis witches as well. Did Willow hang them here for my benefit or someone else's?

Willow leaves my side to begin her rounds of consolation,

and I keep staring at the pictures, guilt heavy in my stomach. They believe me to be a monster. And maybe I am. If enough people believe something, doesn't that make it true? If I were brave enough to meet anyone's eyes, I'd probably see confirmation on *someone's* face.

Willow offers an encouraging bob of her head when I glance her way. That means I stay. Pushing my anxieties to the back of my mind, I shuffle through the crowd, trying not to draw attention to myself. I plop down in an empty chair at the back of the room.

Maverick makes his way toward me. Whether by choice or by order of Willow, I'm not sure. When he catches the distant look in my eyes, he says, "You're thinking."

"Yeah."

"Mind cluing me in?"

"It's just… Willow's strong. I don't know how she does it."

"Duh. And you don't know the half of it."

I cut my eyes at him.

"See that ring?" He gestures to a heavy silver band around Willow's middle finger.

From this distance, it's hard to make out details. I squint until I spot the glint of silver. "What about it?"

"That ring connects her to this Coven in ways you can't dream of. Especially the Reanimates."

"Wait. *Other* Reanimates? Besides Willow and Helena?"

"There are always a few Willow resuscitates after every battle. See the group over there?" He gestures to a group of witches in the corner, slightly separated from the others, as if they're unsure of their place too. I hadn't pegged them as anything different during my initial inspection. "They stay in Willow's mansion."

"*All* of them? Really?" I ask. I hadn't seen any of them until now, but Willow's mansion is huge, and I'm in the farthest wing from everyone else.

I try to make sense of the Coven structure. The Reanimates live with Willow. Living members of the Elementals have their own houses, but Helena is an exception. Do the other Reanimates care? Do they want their own homes or are they content where they are?

"They're all bonded," Maverick says by way of explanation. "To her and to each other. That ring lets her know where her Reanimates are at all times, and it gives her the ability to control them if need be."

"No way!" I gasp, eyes focused on the band again. Just when I thought she couldn't get any more fantastic, she proves me wrong.

Then my thoughts take a detour. Helena had been in such a strange mood earlier. Had she picked up on something going on with Willow?

"How do you know?"

"She told me once. It gets hard holding the weight of what she can do."

A sharp pang of guilt twists inside me. I've been too wrapped in my own emotions to consider what she must be going through.

My eyes shift from Willow's finger to her face. She's silently crying. Dewy tears glitter in the corners of her eyes, and her teeth gnaw her bottom lip until its red. Maverick must see it, too, because he says a quick goodbye and goes to her, caressing her elbow and murmuring comforting words into her ear. She simpers, but it doesn't look real. At least not to me. Maverick doesn't notice.

Shifting my attention from them back to the pictures, I skim each of the faces. What other details have I missed? The witch who killed my adopted parents isn't here, and she's not on the wall either. Had Willow chosen not to bring her back? Or is she in recovery?

Willow's life must be a constant battle. It can't be easy to *choose* which of her covenmates to bring back. They're marked by their glowing white rings, reminders that they survived what others did not.

What an awful twisted survivor's guilt the Reanimates must feel. I want to say something comforting to them. That none of it is their fault. Standing on shaky legs, I make a move to approach the witches, but when I lock eyes with one of them, my words die. Nothing I say can fix their torment.

"Stop looking at us." One of the younger ones, a girl with a blue dress and brown pigtails hisses. Surprised, I gape, trying to backpedal a response when she gnashes her teeth and springs to her feet, bolting from the room. Willow comes to my side.

Face frozen with shock, I say, "I wasn't trying to offend anybody."

"I know," she assures me. "We all handle it differently." She's calm as if this isn't the first time something like this has happened. "Amelia just needs time."

No one calls after Amelia. They barely acknowledge her

absence which is a strange thing to witness after everyone had seemed so joined together at the Coven meeting. Perhaps it's their mutual hatred for me that had made it seem that way. When I really think about it, I can't remember if there were any Reanimates at the meeting or not. An uncomfortable flutter blooms in my chest. If Reanimated witches are outcasts in their own Coven, what kind of life does that offer Helena?

I'm not sure what spurs the decision but I go after Amelia. Maybe it's the thought of Helena, but it could also be guilt. Either way, I hear her sobbing when I take two steps into the hall. She's sitting against the wall, head buried in her knees.

"Hey," I call to her.

Amelia's head pops up, hair matted to her blotchy red cheeks. "What do you want?"

I raise my hands, unsure what to say. Usually, I'm the one losing control so it feels strange to be on the other side for once. "If I offended you, I'm sorry. I didn't mean to."

She sniffles and wipes her nose with the back of her hand. "But you were staring at me… like… like I'm some kind of freak."

"No, you're not. I'm sorry if I made you think that. It's just… you looked so sad, I wanted to reach out to you. You remind me of my friend Helena."

"R-really?" she asks, looking torn.

"Really," I say. When she stays quiet, I add, "I like your dress."

While fashion is the last thing I care about, her blue and purple dress *is* pretty, and Amelia seems proud of it. With a twitch, I remember how similar it looks to the one Raya made me for my Arcane Ceremony.

It all seems like eons ago.

Amelia wipes her face with the back of her hand. "Thank you."

Cautious of setting off another outburst, I say, "Come back in. You shouldn't miss the vigil…"

She wipes her face again and grasps the end of her pigtail. "You're right." She stands and makes her way back into the room with me trailing behind.

Amelia makes a beeline for the Reanimates, and Willow approaches me. Rather than speaking, she sets a hand on my shoulder, proud.

Chasing down Amelia? That's something she'd do. Not me. But maybe this place is changing me. *Willow* is changing me. As the vigil goes on, any trace of hostility starts to fade. Everywhere I look, witches are crying. No longer strangers, we're one family, united in our grief, mourning the brothers and sisters we've lost to this senselessness.

I lose Willow again in the crowd, and I'm about to track her down when a pair of arms wraps around my shoulders from behind, a strand of curly orange hair drifting into my vision. Helena.

The vigil isn't only for the fallen Elementals, but for Ignis as well. The only home I've ever known is destroyed. My Coven is gone. My knees threaten to give out, and Helena manages to steady me. *This* is why Willow insisted I come. Not to appease the Elementals, or to prove some point about Coven rank, but to *mourn* for my parents' deaths and for the covenmates I'll never see again.

With that, I dissolve into tears, another witch in mourning.

# Chapter Fifteen
## The Battle of Mentis

SOMETHING SHIFTS IN me that night. Up until the vigil, part of me had stayed hopeful that I would somehow wake up back home in Ignis and everything I had experienced would end up just being a dream. Seeing the grief in Helena's eyes solidified the fact that there *is* no going back. This is my life now. My Coven. My family. My friends.

My future.

A week goes by, and I fall into a new routine. Life almost takes on a sense of normalcy. Maverick keeps up my training, taking me to the field day after day to help me get a handle on my magic. Prior to Laura's "clearance," I'd felt as if my wounds were healing well enough. But it's much better now. I can manage basic movements without pain. Even my bad leg hurts less. Heavy training still goes against Willow's wishes though so I practice my telekinesis in short bursts on simple tasks like opening windows and lifting my blanket. My magic is nowhere near what it used to be, but it'll take time to work myself back to full health.

I wish the process was faster.

One morning, I'm woken by shouts and footsteps pounding down the hall. Bolting up in bed, I stare at the door with wide eyes. I do my best to get out of bed and hurry outside of my room in time to catch Willow running by.

"What's happened?" I ask.

"The Council blacked out Mentis," she says, swiping her frantic brown hair from her face.

In any other Coven, that wouldn't be a cause for concern. Most witches hate electricity and function just fine without it. Mentis is the only Coven who *depend* on it for survival.

"Why would they do that?" First Ignis, and now Mentis? Why is the Council bringing innocent civilians into the crosshairs?

"They… they got Larc," she says. A tear trails down her face. "They scoped his mind."

Her panic sets alarms off in my head, but I don't quite understand the context of what she tells me. The only witch I've ever met named Larc was an odd middle-aged UnEquipped man, the scum of his Coven according to the Mentis Adept, Dawn. What does it matter if they read his mind?

"So?"

Her features contort into an expression of betrayed disappointment. "He knows me. He knows you. He knows the *truth*," she says, and I can hear how much effort the words take. "He knows *everything.*"

Then it clicks. He was an Elemental too, hiding in plain sight. By making himself an embarrassment, people looked the other way, giving him clearance to get away with whatever he needed to do. "I…you…" I struggle for words.

"We'll talk later," she says and tries to pull away again.

"It's a trap, Willow."

"Maybe," she says. "But I have to try to help him."

"Why would they go after him now?"

Willow wipes her eyes with the back of her hand, and I close my mouth, already knowing the answer. The day he approached me in Mentis, there must have been witnesses.

It's my fault.

"I have to go," Willow says, her voice strained as she tries to pull free again.

"Then I'm coming, too," I growl, tightening my hold, refusing to let go.

"No." She snaps the word sharply, fists clenched so tight her knuckles whiten. "You're to stay here and heal. That's an order."

My fingers dig in deeper, unyielding. "I want to help."

Her eyes blaze with frustration. "Then find Maverick and stay put."

I shake my head, voice low but fierce. "He's not here, obviously, and you knew that. Willow, with all due respect, if there's a battle, I should be on the front lines with you. This war is mine as much as it is yours."

The mix of fear, desperation, and guilt behind her eyes breaks my heart when she glances at my side, as if she can see the damage through my clothes. "Yes, but you're in no shape to fight, Lilith. If something happens to you, I couldn't bear it. Here, you're safe. I can make sure you're protected.

My nostrils flare. My entire life, I've been "protected," hidden away from everything, and I'm sick of it. Sick of people dying for me. "You can't honestly expect me to sit back and do nothing while you put your life on the line. I don't *want* to be protected anymore. That's been my entire life. While you've had to live yours fighting, I've done the opposite. It's my turn to do something *useful*. Our lives were shaped by this war. What's the point of hiding me from it?"

Willow eyes me for such a long time, that the corners of her bloodshot eyes well with tears. "There's no stopping you, then, is there?"

"The only way to stop me would've been to never tell me in the first place."

There's no more arguing. Next thing I know, we're on the move, nightclothes and all. We dash through the labyrinthine halls, where more and more witches join us, dressed in their own mixed variety of pajamas and battle gear. The group is not quite as large as the one that had gathered for the vigil, but it's impressive nonetheless. Maverick walks on one side of me, and Katrina on the other.

I somehow end up in the middle of the throng, and I assume Willow has something to do with it, even though she hasn't spoken since we left the room. We emerge from the mansion and into the purple plants. At night, they have a luminescent glow, outling paths so thin we have to walk side by side to traverse them. It feels as if they go on forever. Eventually, I start to lag behind, my leg throbbing, but I don't want Willow to see and demand I stay here. With a huff, I gnash my teeth and tap my telekinesis to push onward.

Then the group stops. Confused by the sudden halt, I shoulder my way to the front and find a witch I've yet to meet. Willow stands beside him, a massive bulk of dark skin and muscles easily three times my size. He has the same ethereal beauty as Willow: a white aura and black eyes. Then I notice the thick, ugly scar across his neck.

He's a Reanimate.

"Zane," Willow greets him.

The hulking man salutes her. He doesn't ask what she needs, and she doesn't say. He reaches out a large hand to pat her head, tousling her brunette hair. She speaks one word that I assume to be a code between them, and he pulls a tiny, curved tool from his pocket. It's as black as his eyes and shaped like a miniscule scythe. It glitters in the soft moonlight as he lifts it up, then slings it downward, a deafening, tearing sound filling the air before it parts, revealing a fuzzy layer of colors on the other side.

Unconsciously, I grasp Willow's wrist. "What is this?"

"Teleportation," she says. "It's safe."

She twists her wrist to grab my hand and lunges through the portal. The strange ripple of air swallows us. I expect it to hurt, but it doesn't. When we emerge on the other side, I recognize the sandy borders on the outer edge of Mentis. The land of sweet scents and purple plants lies behind the shimmering veil, and my heart pounds with anticipation as the others join us. I don't know how Willow keeps her fear at bay, then I realize it's because she has no other choice. Too many people depend on her for this to go any other way.

Maverick dips his head to catch my gaze. "You okay?" he whispers as the portal seals behind us.

I nod. It's the best answer I can manage.

"You're ready for this?" he asks, voice sharper this time.

I glare at him.

"Don't give me that. I need to make sure because things are about to get real." As soon as the words leave his mouth, an explosion fills the air.

I cower, hands covering my ears against the sound, and that's all the time it takes for my covenmates to scatter. Dazed, I try to scope out the scene around me, standing alone where an army had been seconds prior. Screams echo through the air, and the world spins as I try to process what's happening. This place looks nothing like what I remember of Mentis.

What was once a tropical paradise has been reduced to a warzone. The air is thick with the smell of blood and ash, blurring the line between the chaos around me and the memories flashing through my mind from the battle that destroyed Ignis. Half of Mentis lies in ruins. Only a few buildings remain standing around the empty oasis.

Somewhere between panic and indecision, I start moving. Injured witches from both sides of the war are scattered across the sand, blood staining it in dark, cracked patches. I try to walk past them, tuning out their desperate pleas for help. One reaches out to me, trembling, and for a moment, I consider stopping, but I force myself to keep going. I can't help them. My Healer skills are weak, barely enough to patch a wound. These witches need someone better.

Laura or Ambrossi will see to them.

Willow and Larc. That's *my* mission.

As if to hammer the point home, another explosion rips through the air, slamming into the heart of the empty oasis. The shockwave throws me off my feet, the world spinning as my ears ring. Sand and blood fill my mouth, bitter on my tongue. Dazed, I force myself up, every movement heavy with the sting of pain. A quick glance reveals a thin trickle of blood running down the back of my arm, but otherwise, I'm okay.

I catch a flash of color beneath a nearby pile of rubble. Someone is trapped beneath it.

I rush to it, throwing stones aside to get to the witch. "Lavina," I gasp.

Mentis' Healer. I only met her once, the day Crowe and I traveled to Mentis. With shaking fingers, I roll her over. A trickle of blood runs from the corner of her mouth, and her wide brown eyes stare at nothing. I can't see the wound that killed her, but she's already gone. There's no mistaking the emptiness in her eyes.

"Lilith!" shouts a familiar voice.

I recoil and whip around, ready to fight as I search for the voice's owner. On his knees, leaning his shoulder against what I assume are the remains of his house, is Quinn, brother to Councilmember Tricia. Like Lavina, I only met him once, but he's a friendly face.

*He had to be nice,* I remind myself. He owes me no such loyalty now.

I wait for an attack that doesn't come. He's nestled into a crook of rubble. Blood splattered into the sand around him. He's bad shape. Pushing past the haze of adrenaline, I reach his side and quickly check his injuries.

Blood trickles steadily from a deep cut on his knee, soaking into the sand beneath him. His arm rests at an awkward angle across his chest, and he holds it gently but firmly. Each shallow breath causes him to wince, his skin damp with sweat and dust. A slight tremor in his hand shows he's doing his best to stay alert.

"Quinn. How bad are you hurt? Can you walk?" I ask, silently begging for him to tell me yes. Slowly, I ask again, "Can you walk?"

If he can't, I won't be able to move him, but I'm not sure

I have it in me to leave him behind. He gives the smallest bob of his head.

"Come on," I urge, trying to pull him to his feet.

He tries to obey, but shrieks and stops. A thick plank of wood protrudes from his thigh. I stare at the situation unfolding, brain flailing to create the best plan of action. The most sensible option would be to remove the wood, but without the proper Healer skills, I'll cause more harm than good.

I look from the bloody mass of flesh to his eyes. "I know this hurts, but we have to move," I say, my voice wavering. If there's one person who understands leg pain, it's me. "It's not safe here."

Something sharpens in him, and he says, "It won't be safe where you take me, either. You're one of *them*. You did this."

Reeling from the sudden venom, my mind fractures between choices. The primary tells me to leave him. Finding Larc and Willow is urgent, my priority, but leaving Quinn behind feels wrong. If he sees me as the enemy, what else can I do?

"Who took Larc?" I ask, fearing I may have run into a dead end. "Do you know where they went?"

"What? Why?" Quinn asks, thrown by the question.

I have neither the time nor the patience to explain. "Who was he last seen with?"

"Tricia but—"

That's all I need to hear. "The explosions? It was all a trap. They took Larc to draw us here. *They* bombed Mentis to get rid of us and didn't bother to pull you out of the way first."

"Tricia would never," he growls.

"Keep telling yourself that," I say and stand. I don't want

to leave him, but if he's made up his mind to stand by the Council, there's nothing else I can do.

"No," he says, softer this time as if his resolve is wearing down. The fire in his eyes goes out, and he reaches his good hand toward me. "Lilith… please don't leave. I need your help."

"I know," I say, wrapping my hand under the forearm that's not mangled. "I have no intention of leaving you behind." Inside, I'm cursing for the time this argument has cost us, but I give it my all to get him out from beneath the rubble.

Helping Quinn to his feet is the last real memory I have. The next is complete blackness.

# Chapter Sixteen

## Regrets

I'M HOME IN Ignis. The heat of the desert sun presses against my skin, familiar and comforting. Clio and Helena are beside me, their laughter echoing across the sunbaked sand. They talk like nothing's changed, like it's just another carefree day in the desert Coven. The kind of day we used to live over and over, without a care in the world. The kind I thought we'd always have.

I stretch out my hand to join them, to pull myself back into the moment, but my fingers slip through the air like smoke, vanishing before I can touch them. The warmth of the sun still kisses my skin, but everything else—everything real—feels distant, like a fading dream.

"Hey!" I call, but they don't hear me.

Something's wrong.

I step directly into their line of sight, heart pounding, but their eyes don't land on me. Don't even flicker. The scene crumbles to nothing.

Silence.

Darkness.

I don't know where I am or what this void is, but inside, I'm hollow with my memories of times I can never experience again.

"Is she okay? Please tell me she's okay." A voice breaks

through the blackness. It's familiar, but the waver in it is hard to place. Fear? Sadness? Concern?

"She lost some blood. Nothing too serious. I've given her a poultice. She should come around soon."

The second voice is much easier to recognize. Ambrossi. I groan at the thought that he's here to see me at my lowest once again.

When my eyes crack open, light filters into my vision. I'm back in the hospital room. People are gathered around my bed, but only one stands out. Helena.

"What happened?" I groan, touching the side of my head. I have a slight headache, and my skull radiates pain to the touch, but other than that, I feel fine. "Why am I here?"

"You were hurt," Ambrossi says.

Remembering the battle, I check myself over, finding nothing more serious than a skinned elbow. It certainly doesn't seem like a hospital-worthy wound. Lavina's body flits through my mind. It can always, *always*, be worse. "Quinn!" I gasp and sit up so sharply, a zap runs through my head, making me squint. "Is he…"

"He's okay. He's healing as we speak," Helena offers.

Am I still dreaming? "You're talking," I state stupidly.

Ambrossi smiles, a flicker of pride in his eyes. "She's recovering well," he says, clearly relieved.

"What… what about Lavina?" I ask, the image of her bleeding body still at the front of my mind. I catch a glimpse of Ambrossi's reaction and almost regret asking.

Helena doesn't share her partner's expression. "Who?"

"Mentis' Healer. Sh-she was dead… and… Willow can

bring her back. Right?" I ask, glancing desperately between Helena and Ambrossi.

Ambrossi's regretful frown doesn't change. "No, Lilith. I'm sorry. Her body is still in Mentis. Quite a few are, actually."

"Why?"

"Recovery efforts take witches, and we can't risk sending anyone else out there."

I don't know what hurts more—knowing it's my fault Lavina's been left behind or that I hadn't been able to save her in the first place. The door creaks open. Willow steps into the room, jaw set and eyes clouded over with rage when she focuses on me. Something happened, and based on that look, I'm somehow at fault.

"Give us a minute," she says to Helena and Ambrossi, though her eyes never leave mine. "I'd like to speak to my sister alone."

Helena gives me a parting glance as Ambrossi drags her from the room.

The door clicks shut behind them, and Willow spins on me, eyes bloodshot and burning. "I told you to stay here, Lilith," she says, shaking with fury. "I *knew* you weren't ready for combat. I said it again and again. So why lie to me? Why pretend you were fine?"

Her words hit like a slap. I blink, struggling to clear the fog clouding my thoughts. I hadn't expected anger, at least not from her, and it throws me. I rewind the battle in my mind, searching for the moment I went wrong, but nothing stands out.

"Larc's dead," she says, her voice breaking as she wipes her cheek with the back of her hand. "Dead because I had to choose between saving *him* or saving *you*."

The world lurches beneath me. I open my mouth, floundering for something to say. "What's the big deal? Can't you bring him back?"

Her black eyes blaze fire. "No, I *can't* bring him back. They have his body. He was a war criminal, Lilith. That gives them the right to do whatever they want with it." Her voice hardens. "That usually means cremation."

"I—I'm sorry," I whisper, my throat suddenly dry.

"You should've stayed here," she spits, and now the fury makes sense. She blames me. Not just for disobeying her, but for *losing* him.

"What happened wasn't my fault," I say quietly, though even I can hear the doubt behind it.

"It was because I had to save you."

"You could've left me there," I shoot back.

Willow's lip pulls up into a snarl. "I couldn't leave my sister for dead."

"You could've saved him, *then* come back for me."

Her jaw tightens. "Then they would've taken you instead."

I want to sympathize with her, but she's making it increasingly difficult. "You're better off without Larc anyway."

A dry chuckle leaves her lips. "You think you know everything, but you don't know a damn thing." She pauses. "Larc wasn't some *pervert* as you keep calling him. He was the one who saved you from the battle that killed our parents. Didn't you know?"

No, I didn't. "I don't believe you." My words stick in my throat.

Willow's eyes are wild with grief, and fury crosses her face in a way I've never seen. "Then you're dumber than I thought. He saved your life, housed you, fed you, and did everything he could to keep you safe until the Council found out and took you away."

Her voice cracks, and I understand the mistake I've made. Larc *means* something to her beside being a member of her Coven. Apparently, he should also mean something to me. If he was my guardian at one point, he's risked his life for me, and there was nothing for him to gain out of it. He'd done it for Willow because he loves her and above everything, she loves me. Willow cares about him, possibly as much as I care for Clio, and on top of having to choose me over him, I've thrown her decision in her face.

"Because he valued your life more than his own," she says, "he was captured, stripped of his powers, and crippled for life. I'd think *you* of all people could appreciate that type of agony."

My face twists. "He lost his powers because of *me*?"

Willow's eyes are two pieces of flint as she stares at me.

I sit in the silence, taking it all in. I can't go back in time to save Larc or even tell him I appreciate his silent sacrifice, and all the apologizing in the world won't take back what I said. I stare at Willow, but instead of my sister's face, all I can see is when I met Larc. The odd things he said at the time.

Pulling myself from the memory, I ask, "Who's Ivy?"

Willow stiffens. Her eyes narrow, and for a moment, it's like I've hit her. The fire in her expression doesn't vanish, but something dims behind it. "She was our mother," she says, voice tight. "Why?"

"It… was something Larc said. That I look like her."

A tortured smile bites her face. "You do," she murmurs and abruptly storms out. The door slams shut behind her, and a muffled sob trails into the hall.

I stare after her, too stunned to move. The silence that follows feels too big for the room.

Helena creeps in, her steps cautious, with Ambrossi close behind. She glances toward the closed door, then back at me.

"That didn't go well, did it?" she asks gently.

I bite my lip, struggling to meet her gaze. "How much did you hear?"

"All of it," she admits, shoulders sagging with guilt. "I didn't mean to, I just—"

I turn away before she finishes. I have no right to be mad at anyone. "She's right."

A thick, awkward silence settles over us. I can feel Ambrossi's presence behind me, his thoughts pressing at the edges of mine. He's searching for the right thing to say, but he must not find it because he stays silent.

*You can't fix this one, buddy.*

"Do you want to see Quinn?" Helena asks as if she senses how desperate I am for a change of subject.

"Of course."

I'm up on my feet without their help. My memory of the battle is nothing but a black hole. I don't know who bothered to save Quinn, or me, in Mentis, but maybe he has the answers I don't.

Helena guides me through a maze of sterile white rooms, each indistinguishable from the last, until we step into a larger space. The air feels colder, the lighting harsher. Rows of makeshift cubicles line the walls, sectioned off by thin gray curtains.

"Careful, Lilith," she says, eyeing me as she pulls the first curtain aside to reveal Quinn.

He lies on the narrow bed, fast asleep. Bandages trail down one arm and wrap across his forehead, stark against his pale skin.

My shoulders sag with relief. "Does he know where he is?"

She shakes her head. "He's been out since he got here so I don't think so."

"Who brought him?"

"I don't know, but Willow brought him to Ambrossi at the same time you were brought in."

I can imagine how they must've found us curled together in the sand, bleeding and barely clinging to life. "I want to be here when he wakes up, if that's okay," I say. When he realizes where he is, he'll fight it like I did. I don't want him to do that. He doesn't know it yet, but this place is his best chance of survival. His Coven, much like Ignis, is gone. If he leaves here, he'll be Covenless. If Tricia didn't care about hurting him this time, who's to say she won't target him again? Maybe on purpose next time.

"I'll make sure you are," Helena replies, giving my hand a comforting squeeze.

A set of footsteps in the hall announce Maverick's presence before he pops into the room. "Willow's called a meeting."

No further explanation is required for my anxiety to kick into high gear. A meeting… *now?* Is it possible she wants to evict from the Coven for my role in what happened in Mentis?

Maverick shoots me a sideways glance as if he's had the same thought

"I'll catch up. I have a bit more work to do first," Helena says as she checks Quinn's vitals.

I hesitate but finally nod. Maverick waits silently by the door, and I step away, following him through the labyrinthine halls.

He doesn't speak, and the silence between us grows heavy, making the walk feel colder and more foreboding than it truly is. At the meeting room, the scene is much the same as it had been the first time I was here. Willow sits where she always does, her expression unreadable. But the chair next to her is gone, an empty space that leads me to believe that at least this won't be about me.

Maverick moves steadily down the narrow aisle between the benches, and I cling to him, closer than usual, seeking some small refuge from the scorching gazes burning into my skin.

Has Willow already told them what I've done?

Across the room, her eyes are red-rimmed and swollen from crying, but beneath the pain, a fire burns. When she calls the meeting to order, her voice is sharp, laced with a fury that slices through the heavy silence.

"That was a disaster," she says, hardened voice echoing through the room. "We lost people today. Good people." Her gaze finally lands on me. "And that can't happen again."

Filled with shame, I lower my head, wishing I could curl up so tightly on myself that I disappear completely.

"We need to refocus our training efforts. After what happened, that *defeat*, the Council sees us as weak. Breakable. We can't have that."

Murmurs of agreement ring through the room.

"Grief, Laura, Katrina, get on it," Willow says.

All three state, "Yes, ma'am," and gather various Elementals for their missions.

I wonder who'll pick me when Maverick sets his hand on my shoulder. "Come on."

I arch an eyebrow.

"*Someone* needs to teach you," he adds.

I appreciate the gesture and translate it appropriately. None of the others will pick me. Not with Willow as angry as she is.

Somehow, I keep my head held high as I follow Maverick out of the room. Willow may have lost her faith in me, but it's good to know not *everyone* has.

# Chapter Seventeen
## In the Face of Danger

WITH GROUPS SORTED, dinner is served and we're sent to bed with strict instructions to rise early in the morning. When I wake, I make my way to the Community Villa to meet up with Maverick. He doesn't say much while we eat. Likely his way of staying neutral between me and Willow. I try, unsuccessfully, to forget her angry words, but they buzz around the front of my brain like angry hornets. Every time, I feel worse for insisting I go, for thinking I could make a difference. The Council had built my confidence in a very subtle way by telling me what great things I could be capable of. I didn't consider the harm I could also do.

As soon as breakfast is finished, witches find their designated group. Willow appears just before we head off for the training grounds to make sure no one is missing from their duties. She doesn't look at me as she does a head count, and I'm fine with that.

Leaving the building feels almost like stepping out on a field trip, the air fresh and full of promise. I lose Willow in the crowd, but I know she's somewhere up ahead, guiding us. I think about asking Maverick where she went, but the impulse fades. I keep my mouth shut, avoiding the risk of saying something stupid.

Maverick and I fall toward the back, naturally, as part of the smallest group. The quiet feels almost comforting, a space I can sink into. But then, the excitement of knowing I'll soon be training again sends a flutter of energy down my spine. I quicken my pace, moving faster than Maverick, passing him, and stepping onto the familiar stretch of grass that marks the training grounds.

I pause for a moment to take in the scene. The witches around me are an imposing sight. Some wear expressions of quiet determination, others seem lost in thought, but all are marked by the same resilience. Outcasts of the Land of Five. Maybe none of us made a decision to be here but we were welcomed with open arms anyway.

I glance to my left and familiar green eyes give me pause. "Why is Helena here?" I ask Maverick.

He shrugs. "Maybe she's volunteered to practice healing."

That *could* be it, except Laura hadn't been gathering Healers in the meeting hall. She had picked soldiers, people who can hold their own in a fight. Shouldn't Ambrossi be here to make sure she's using the right techniques? Or maybe the goal is to see if she can develop more powers than mind reading.

*She won't get hurt here,* I tell myself. Coven training is safe… safer than combat at least. Then I notice how few Reanimates have been chosen for this training session.

*Why?*

Undead soldiers seem like the perfect weapon to me. Harder to kill than regular witches.

Katrina lays her hand on Helena's shoulder and whispers something in her ear. I don't invade either of their minds, but the scene comforts me. Though we haven't talked since the day she came to my room, we've bonded in a way that's hard to explain.

Secrets can do that.

Grief, Laura, and Katrina lead their groups to different parts of the field. Maverick takes me on a looping walk around the field to search for a place that hasn't been claimed. Spells fill the air as the Coven engages in their collective practice. I'm amazed by how smoothly it all goes. Witches of all different backgrounds and powers work side by side, dodging and moving in sync, as if they share one mind.

"They're strong," I say.

"That's what happens when a Coven is bonded." The leaves rustle softly around us, muffling the distant sounds of training that drift through gaps in the foliage. Through those breaks, I catch glimpses of figures moving with purpose on the other field, spells sparking faintly in the morning light.

He stops just inside a smaller clearing, shielded from prying eyes. With a half-smile, he asks, "Ready to give it a go?"

"As ready as I'll ever be," I say, and we get into position.

A one-on-one duel reminds me of all the times I dueled Clio when our lives weren't on the line.

Things are so different now.

I have no idea how to go toe-to-toe against someone like Maverick, but this isn't the first time I've faced an opponent with unconventional powers. Paralysis is impossible to counter even if I was in pristine shape. I need to use wits.

Tingling starts in the tips of my fingers and toes, slowly bleeding upward. I can tell he's taking it easy, and I try to use that to my advantage. When I connect to my telekinetic powers, I force what energy I have into my next move. The power that comes out is disappointing. Maverick doesn't move an inch. Paralysis takes hold of more vital parts of my body, and I collapse to my knees.

"Concentrate, Lilith!" Maverick calls, watching my struggle with a mix of concern and hope.

Instead of an attack, I put my effort into defense, but the result is the same—failure. Maverick retracts his magic. The skin tingles as I start to feel again, and I stare at the ground, disappointed in my lack of fight, and the amount of sweat I produced to do it. My leg demands I sit down, but I don't want to be the first to call it quits. I force myself back to my feet and catch a glimpse of Sabre through the gap in the foliage. As if he feels my eyes on him, he meets my gaze.

Then he makes an error in judgement.

He decides to *approach* me. I tense as he squeezes through the gaps in the plants, no longer hearing the list of commands Maverick rattles off. He doesn't exist as Sabre comes closer and closer. "Get him away from me," I state, never taking my eyes off him.

"Lilith, calm down," Maverick says, holding his hands out as if he's unsure whether to grab me or not.

But I can't calm down. Not with the all-consuming rage that accompanies Sabre's presence.

"Lilith," Sabre greets as he steps into the clearing.

"Get him away!" I screech, rage exploding out of me.

A blast of wind soars across the field and into the next, knocking down everyone in its path. All eyes fall on me, both from those still standing and those who were affected by the attack. No one speaks. Looking at the aftermath douses my rage. That was me... *I* did this.

"Lilith, you have *that* power, too?" Maverick asks, neck craned to see me from his place on the ground.

"I-I…" I stutter but come to no coherent conclusion.

The Sage once told me there was a possibility I'd develop one power from every Coven, maybe more, but I didn't believe her. After being lied to so much, it had been easy to dismiss everything she said.

This isn't one of those things.

An *Aens* power. That's three out of five Covens. Who knows how much further my powers will go?

* * *

AFTER THE INCIDENT on the field, I don't know what I expect to happen, but it certainly isn't being sent to my room like a kid being punished. I obey, but it does nothing to assuage my worries. Pacing across the room helps my anxiety slightly, but not much. A thousand scenarios of what can happen next runs through my mind, none of them good.

Kado's eyes follow me from his place on the bed, tracking me from one end of the room to the other, but he doesn't intercept me. He whines softly and sets his chin on his paws. I pet him a few times every few laps, but I can't take my eyes off the door. No one told me to expect company, but I can't shake the feeling that someone will show up. When the knock finally comes, Kado and I spring to answer it at the same time Maverick pokes his head inside.

"Willow wants to see you," he says, emotions under wraps.

"I figured she would," I reply, wiping my sweaty palms on my dress. If nothing else, at least this will be the ice breaker I need to get her to talk to me again. "Wish me luck," I say to Kado.

He whines again as if he senses something big is about to go down.

Maverick leads me through the labyrinth of halls to a part of the building I haven't seen yet. Willow greets him as soon as we enter the nearest room. There's a 4-poster bed in one corner and a vanity dresser on the other side. The middle of the room is filled with a dining table and matching chairs with red cushions. Willow is seated in one of them, a cup of tea clenched in her hand.

This must be her bedroom.

She sticks her nose up at me, and if I didn't know any better, we could be strangers. "Your powers are developing well," she says in that same icy tone though she doesn't look at me as she says it.

"I'm sorry about what happened. Really, I am." I blurt out and take a small step toward her. "I want to protect this place. I want to protect *you*."

Her jaw clenches. "The way you do that is by *following orders*, which, so far, you haven't been willing to do." She punctuates her statement by slamming her mug on the table. "If you're so willing to prove yourself, then we should work on developing every power you possess. Since you've just gotten in touch with your Aens powers, it follows that those are currently your weakest."

I bob my head.

The door creaks open, and a pointy face peeks in. A *very* familiar face. "Ma'am, you sent for me?"

"Lilith, I believe you've met Fleur," Willow says as the girl takes her place at Willow's side.

My breath catches, a sudden jolt of disbelief tightening my chest. Fleur? Because of *her*, Callista almost died. Close to the Council or not, she's a gentle soul who hadn't deserved what happened. And this woman didn't deserve the likely praise she got for making it happen.

*But she helped Maverick,* a tiny voice wars in my head. *She's not all bad.*

Grief.

*Stay out of this,* I shoot to him.

I stare, struggling to mask the shock that threatens to unravel me. "*Her?* You expect me to get along with *her?*" The words come out sharper than intended, trembling on the edge of anger and disbelief.

"You can't have a problem with *everyone* and expect to stay in my Coven," Willow says, tapping her foot.

I pull my lips tight into a bitter smirk, running my tongue along the inside of my bottom lip. She would never toss me out of her Coven, but she can't show favoritism so this is my *punishment.* "I don't have a problem with *everyone*, just the ones who have problems with *me*. The ones who have no problem hurting innocent witches or fairies."

Willow taps her fingers on the chair's armrest. "Tensions are high. We've had to do some unforgiveable things. I get it, but *this is war.* If you're really one of us, you need to be here body, mind, and soul. Your petty bickering isn't helping anything or anyone."

Stunned, I stare at the floor. I hadn't expected her to be happy, but I hadn't thought she'd be this angry, either. What if she stays like this toward me forever?

The door creaks open again as Willow continues, "She's here to help, but you won't be training under her."

"Then who?" I ask.

She smiles stiffly, watching the witch who just entered. "There's your teacher now."

I lock eyes with Sabre. He smiles at me. I don't smile back. A dry chuckle falls from my lips.. "You're joking, right?"

"No, Lilith. This isn't a game, and I don't appreciate you acting like it is," Willow says, matter-of-factly. "You're my sister, and I love you, but I'm beginning to think you're using that against me. I'm taking charge now, like I should have done sooner. I get that you don't like Sabre, but he's the one who brought these powers out of you, so you'll learn what he has to teach whether you like it or not."

My hands clench into fists, and I'm ready to shout obscenities at Willow, Sabre, and even Maverick. Then the anger leaks out of me like water from a broken pail. Fleur's magic at work. She pulled the same thing the last time I encountered her. I hadn't bothered to prepare for it, and now it's too late to counter.

Willow tucks her hand beneath her chin to prop it up. "Sabre is one of my best Aens warriors, and he's more than qualified to teach you proper air-manipulation techniques."

I scowl at him, but with Fleur's magic tightening its grip, that's as close as I can get to showing what I really feel. His face remains unreadable and that blankness makes my blood boil. How can he be so detached, so indifferent?

A sudden surge of raw emotion pulses through me, bypassing Fleur's control and fueling my telekinesis. Seizing the moment, I lash out. Fleur crashes to the ground with a thud. Freed from her restraint, I blast Sabre, sending him stumbling to his knees.

"I know all too well what you can do," I howl. "Look… look, you bastard!" I hike up my dress to show the scars dappled across my side from the wounds he inflicted during the Battle of Ignis. It doesn't occur to me that I'm flashing my underclothes until a blush blooms across Sabre's face.

"I've seen *plenty* now, thank you," he says as he climbs back to his feet.

Willow jumps up and stomps toward me. She grabs my elbow, fingers digging into the skin as she drags me to the corner of the room.

"You're hurting me," I say with a grimace.

"What the hell is wrong with you?" she hisses, as if she either doesn't notice how tightly she's holding me or doesn't care.

I give an innocent shrug.

"Honestly, do I need to put you back in the holding cell until you learn your place? Or are you capable of self-control?" she asks, finally letting go. Her eyes are smoldering pits. Fleur, Maverick, and Sabre stare at me, and I realize what I must look like to them. Wild. *Crazy* even.

I flare my nostrils but take in a deep breath. Given Willow's current mood, she'll have no problem tossing me into a dark hole and throwing away the key.

"No, I'll stop," I say, resigned.

"See that you do," she says, then to Sabre, "Begin her training tomorrow." She starts to walk to the door but stops long enough to tell Maverick, "Oversee it."

# Chapter Eighteen
## The Wind Warrior

WHEN NIGHT COMES, I struggle to fall asleep. The events of the day replay in fragments. My new Aens powers take all my thoughts. Developing these skills means having to learn from a man who tried to kill me. Who succeeded in killing Helena.

What's become of my life? Friends are now enemies and enemies are friends. My transition into the Council had been easier than this. As mad as I am at Willow for assigning me to Sabre, I understand her reason for it. She'd needed my help, and I became a liability instead. She can't extend me anymore pleasantries for fear she'll regret it later on.

*Never again,* I vow.

*Then you need to listen to Willow,* Grief's soft voice lilts through my mind.

*Easier said than done.*

I fall asleep, and when I wake, Maverick's ready to take me straight to Willow. The thought of seeing her so early in the morning makes my stomach churn since I can't guarantee how the interaction will go, but I don't want her to know that.

I push it down, trying to keep a neutral expression on my face. Inside her room, Sabre, Helena, and Laura are already present, lounging about as if they've been awake for a while. Willow sits in the biggest chair, an empty chair beside her. I glance at her, waiting to see if she'll greet me. She makes a point of avoiding eye contact even while kicking the chair toward me. I wonder why she didn't offer it to Maverick.

Another glance around the room alerts me to Fleur's absence. Then my gaze lands on Sabre and how close he stands to Helena. They're talking and smiling; he even has the audacity to put his hand on her shoulder, as if he hadn't murdered her in cold blood a few weeks ago.

A low chuckle escapes my lips, but no one notices. "He should apologize to her."

The conversation in the room fades as everyone's attention shifts to me. Willow voices their question. "What?"

"Sabre should apologize to Helena," I say, gesturing to the two, who step apart under the attention. "He *killed* her, after all."

Helena's eyes go wide. "No, he…" She stops and clears her throat before trying again. "It's fine, Lilith," Helena chimes in, voice sharp as if she's embarrassed by this, embarrassed by *me*.

I stare at her, thinking I misheard her. "Huh?"

"I said it's *fine*, Lilith. No harm done."

"No ha—" I struggle for words. "How can you *say* that? What of your scars? You'll have them for the rest of your life!"

"I like my scars. They show I fight back," Helena replies, head held high.

Pausing, I'm torn between her optimism and the quiet wisdom in her words. I wish I could share her sense of hope, but there's no simple way to explain what it felt like to watch her die. I project the memory to her.

She stiffens, but her voice flows out sweet and lilting. "I know," she starts, "But I'm better now."

Those three words extinguish my need to fight better than Fleur's magic. Before the Battle of Ignis, Helena had been devastated by her UnEquipped status, doomed to a life without magic. Now, she has everything she's ever wanted. There are a lot of words I can say, but none that I should. If Helena is happy, who am I to interfere?

"Okay," I say, and it's one of the hardest words of my life.

"Well, now that that's out of the way," Willow says and clicks her tongue, "Laura and Helena are going to check you over to see how well you're healing."

Laura goes first, combing through the void of my aura. She seems more confident than the last time she did this, smiling as she finds whatever it is she's looking for. After she's finished, Helena inspects me physically, observing my scars and my leg. She gives me a few herbs to chew for the pain and clears me for training. The Healers depart, leaving me with Willow, Sabre, and Maverick.

"Don't disappoint me," Willow says though whether that's to me or one of the guys, I'm not sure.

She bids her goodbyes, leaving me with Maverick and Sabre. The air between us feels heavier without her there. Maverick urges Sabre to lead the way to the training field. I try to cling to his side, but he hangs back a few steps in an apparent attempt to get me to bond with Sabre. So I play the middleman, walking halfway between the men the rest of the trip. The walk feels longer than it should, my steps echoing against the muted tension.

When we reach the training field, we form a loose semi-circle, the space between us more like a standoff than a lesson.

Sabre's expression is unreadable. Maverick's is as calm as ever, though I can sense the calculation behind his silver eyes as we discuss mock battle strategies and defensive moves.

"I'm going to give you two some space," Maverick whispers in my ear. "But I won't be far, Lilith. Play nice." He disappears into the shadows around the field as Sabre begins to speak.

I give him a scathing side-eye.

"Aens powers are like breathing," Sabre begins, taking no notice of my visible venom. "Take a breath. In and out. Feel that pressure… that *force* inside you? That's what it's like, but a thousand times more freeing."

My brain splits between a sarcastic comment and obedience. A glint of Maverick's silver eyes reminds me that any disobedience will be noted and reported to Willow. So I swallow my pride and draw a breath, following Sabre's instructions despite the bitterness burning in my chest. Now isn't the time to start another fight. If I'm ever going to earn back Willow's trust, I need to survive this lesson first.

"Relax," Sabre says, noticing the tension in my shoulders.

I open my eyes enough to glare at him. My tension stems from my unease which is *not* such an easy thing to get rid of, but I take in one slow breath after another, washing away my irritation. One more… two, then, I feel it: the slightest wiggle of energy in my core. Earlier, I'd mistaken that flutter for annoyance and thought no more of it. Is it possible that some of my other quirks are new powers trying to manifest themselves, and I simply haven't noticed?

I don't know I'm smiling until Sabre calls me on it. "Feel

it?" he asks, hopeful.

"I do," I say, letting it well inside of me. "Do… I push it out?" I ask. This should be easy to handle from here. Logically speaking, wind power and telekinesis shouldn't be *too* different.

Sabre laughs. "I guess you could if you want to hurt your teammates, too."

"Wait. What happened on the field was *wrong*?"

"Your summoning, no. But your delivery, yes. Wind is a powerful element, but to use it right, you have to learn to manipulate only the air you want to use, not *all* of it. In battle, you would've doomed your team doing something like that. Here, watch me," Sabre says and lifts his hand. His breathing evens out, and he flicks his wrist. A jagged white line appears on the tree at the far end of the field. The product of one of his air knives I've come to know so well. "Like that."

Leo, the Aens Adept, had also formed a ball of energy with his hands the day Crowe and I toured his Coven. At the time, I hadn't given the gesture much thought, but it's the key to properly harnessing this power. I lift my hands in the same way, but pause, feeling awkward. Sheepishly, I ask, "How do I know what shape works best for me?"

"Practice," Sabre says, as if it's the most obvious thing. "Like any other skill. You'll get a feel for it."

Rolling my eyes at the cliché answer, I keep my hands up. *I can do this*, I tell myself. If I could use allegedly inaccessible Ignis powers, I can do this too. Slow and calm, I copy Sabre's breathing, until the wiggle appears. With some effort, I try to push the energy to my hands, but it's a draining process. By the time the power hits my wrists, I'm ready to collapse but manage to remain standing. The energy doesn't quite make it to my fingertips when it shoots ahead, blasting the air around me.

The difference this time? Sabre is prepared.

He blocks it and looks at me for a long time. My mind picks up on him internally contemplating his next words. "You did… *well*," he says finally.

Scathingly, I ask, "Did I?"

"Yes. It'll take time to find your technique and perfect it, but I think you're off to a good start."

"Time's something we don't have right now," I point out.

Sabre shrugs. "There's no way to really rush it."

"You make it sound so easy. Did you know what to do when your powers first developed?"

He draws his lips together. "Yes and no. Of course I knew about air manipulation from my covenmates, but as you've seen, finding what works is a journey only you can take."

"So, why knives?"

Sabre runs his tongue along his teeth. "That's rather personal, Lilith. Why the sudden interest?"

I crinkle my nose in distaste, unsure whether I'm more upset that he won't tell me, or that he's cocky enough to give me an attitude knowing how I already feel about him. "You can either tell me or I can find out from Willow."

Sabre runs a hand though his shaggy blond hair. Rather than be annoyed, he laughs as if I've said something amusing. "Fair enough," he says and looks across the field. "My family has a history of producing UnEquipped children every other generation. I fell on one of them, so my parents made sure to keep me far away from my Equipped family members. But it was my dream to fight in the Aens Army, to protect my Coven. I utilized what weapons I could. A bow and arrow, throwing knives… things of that nature."

"And when you learned you had powers?"

"The skills transferred over," he says, "It saves me time, not having to carry actual weapons."

"Good for you," I say, barely keeping the bitterness out of my voice. Everyone has such fantastic stories of discovering their powers except me. I'm still trying to decide what my real powers *are*.

"Look at it this way. Life may not always go the way we want, but that doesn't mean it's bad."

His words are oddly comforting.

Then a familiar voice calls my name, sharp and urgent. I furrow my brow and spot Helena sprinting across the field like a flash of light.

"What is it?" I ask, steeling my nerve for bad news.

She slows, her expression unreadable as she replies, "Quinn's regained consciousness."

# Chapter Nineteen
## Missing Piece

QUINN IS FULLY awake when we step into his room in the hospital wing. He's propped up in bed, looking around, but even from the doorway, I can tell he's anything but relaxed. The look in his eyes isn't curiosity, it's fear and confusion. Like a trapped animal, he's searching for a way out, an escape, growing desperate with the realization that there *is* none. His broken arm is in a cast, but the other three limbs are held securely in place with restraints. I don't want him to think he's a prisoner or to be treated like one. Glancing around the room, I try to reassure myself that maybe they didn't have a choice. Maybe he already tried to make a break for it and risked further injuring himself, but I see nothing to back up that theory.

"Is this really necessary?" I finally ask Helena.

"He's scared, Lilith," she says simply.

It's probably worse now.

I don't want to think of Quinn as a feral animal in the same way I don't want him to see me as a prison guard, but my slow, cautious steps say it all. His eyes slide from the wall to mine, expression settled somewhere between relief and panic.

His eyes move to my hands as if he's searching for potentially hazardous items. "Lilith, what is this place? Where am I?" he asks, tugging his good arm against the restraints.

He's hoping I'll have the key. I bite my lip, wishing I'd

prepared something to say in advance, but it's too late to back out now. What's his power? I can't remember. If he's a mind reader, all of this is a moot point since he would know everything already anyway. I open my mind to him, trying to find an answer. When that doesn't provide me with results, I stop.

*He's telekinetic*, Grief says.

*Thanks.*

"You're safe," I answer finally, hoping my voice is calm, reassuring. If I were him, the words would piss me off, but I hope he reacts differently.

And he does.

"Where's Tricia?" he asks. There's a tremor when he says her name, the grief of a fresh loss. He still wants to debate what I told him in Mentis, but it's getting harder for him to do.

I glance at Helena for guidance. I have no idea how much he's already been told and how much I can tell him without making him feel any worse.

"Tricia's not here, but it's okay," Helena assures him. "You're okay."

"Is she?" he asks.

Helena and I exchange an uncertain look. There's no way for either of us to know. If a member of the Council has been injured, or captured, I'm sure Willow would waste no time telling the entire Coven and using it to plan our next move.

"Is Tricia okay?" he repeats slowly.

"We don't know," I answer, trying to keep what I hope is a friendly expression on my face, "but you don't need to worry about that right now. You need to focus on getting better. These witches will take care of you."

"How do I know that?"

"They saved your life," I point out. "You were hurt, and instead of leaving you for dead, they treated your wounds and are now offering you a home."

He's anything but pacified when he says, "I'm a prisoner, aren't I?"

"No, no. I promise you're not. You're here under my word of protection." I'm not sure if that's true, but it sounds good, so I keep going. "The restraints are to keep you from moving too fast and reinjuring yourself. As soon as you're well again, you're free to go, if that's what you choose."

I glance at Helena for permission. She gives a nod, and I untie the bond on his unbroken arm.

"They captured you, too, didn't they?" he asks, gazing at me in wonder as the silky band slips to the floor.

I pause, considering the best way to answer. "A while ago," I admit then follow with, "but they didn't do it maliciously. This place, these people… it might be hard to believe, but they're *good*. A lot of them were in our same position at some point. Once you get the hang of things, you'll fit right in." I gesture to Helena. "She's an example. Does she look miserable?"

Quinn looks her over and shakes his head.

I take that as a good sign. He's listening to me, considering my words. No one knows what he's feeling right now better than I do. What he needs now is time to digest his situation and accept that the world as he knew it is gone. Quinn tries to sit up, but lets out a hiss and thumps back against the inclined bed.

"Has he had anything to eat yet?" I ask Helena.

She shakes her head, scattering her flowing red locks, and

disappears from the room. The space feels strangely empty without her. I offer Quinn a friendly smile, but the doubt lingering in his eyes says I'm not quite selling it.

"You'll love the food here," I tell him.

He doesn't look convinced.

When the door creaks open, I expect Helena, but tense when Willow's black eyes appear instead. Her icy gaze lingers on me, as if I've somehow caught *her* off guard. "We need to talk," she says, with no regard to Quinn's presence, and ducks back into the hall.

I mutter curses under my breath. What could I have possibly done wrong this time? I've followed her orders with Sabre and kept my hands to myself.

"Who was that?" Quinn asks, uncertainly stroking the edge of his blanket.

"I'll be back," I say without attempting an explanation, but I'm not sure about that either. Based on the way Willow looked at me, she might murder me in the hallway.

Stepping out of Quinn's room, I find Willow pacing back and forth, her white gown billowing with each measured step. "What's going on?" I ask, though I already know I don't want the answer.

"We looked for Clio," she begins.

My peripheral vision blackens. Out of everything she could've said, I didn't expect this. Did she find something in the aftermath of the battle? If she says the 'D' word, I'll lose my mind. "And?"

Willow's shoulders slump. "We can't find him."

"You can't... *find* him?" I echo, raising my eyebrows. I

can't tell if it's relief or sorrow at the front of my mind. Missing could mean he's still alive. But missing could also mean he's in danger. The idea that she, with all her seemingly infinite knowledge and connections, has *no* idea what happened to him hits me like a fist to the gut.

"He's been gone since the battle," Willow explains. "None of Ignis have seen him. A missing Adept gathers quite a bit of attention, you know."

"How much of it is left?" I ask. Up until now, I'd assumed Ignis had been completely destroyed. If some portion has survived, and is still holding on, it gives me hope.

"I'd say a fourth is holding on strong. Rebuilding, actually."

"But Clio's not there?"

"No."

Never would I have thought one word could be so heavy. "You're sure the Council doesn't have him held captive?"

"Positive. If he'd been captured, we have our ways of knowing." She pauses. "They seem just as stumped on this one."

I roll my bottom lip between my teeth. "What about Fern?"

Willow swipes a lock of brown hair from her eyes. "There's no signs of her either."

"How can the Adept *and* Coven fairy vanish without anyone knowing how or why?" I ask.

"From what I understand, Clio disappeared during the attack on Ignis, but a lot of witches did."

A rock of guilt sinks in my stomach. Whatever happened to him happened because of *me*, because I needed help. Maybe the reason he never came back iss because he needed help too, and no one was there to offer it.

Willow's eyes soften, but her voice doesn't. "Don't take this the wrong way, Lilith, but how do you know he was fighting on our side?"

Heat rushes up my spine, and I shoot her a glare, almost grateful for the anger that shields me from the ache beneath.

"All I'm saying," she presses on, "is you were fighting for *them* when he went missing. How do you know he's not still doing the same under the assumption that you're being held here against your will?"

That's a fair point. If what she told me about Tabitha is true then each word she says makes me feel more and more grim. The only way to win this war is for the remaining Covens to unite with the Elementals, shattering the treaty and overthrowing the Council before the Land of Five is lost forever. But if the Council can control our *thoughts*, what can we do?

After another minute of silence, she adds, "If Clio really is on their side, it's probably better for him to stay missing than to get mixed up in another battle."

Her words come like a slap to the face. "How can you say that? Helena and Clio were *everything* to me growing up."

Willow draws her eyebrows together. "I mean no ill will. I'm simply saying if he's involved on the wrong side of the war, he'll be nothing but a distraction, and you don't need that right now."

I glare at her. "That's easy for you to say. You didn't know him."

A flash of anger illuminates Willow's eyes, then passes,

leaving her looking tired in its wake. "I get it, okay? He was there for you, and I wasn't. You feel some resentment toward me for leaving you to figure this all out on your own. But I was doing what I needed to do to make a place that was safe for witches like me. Witches like *us*. It was the only way to make sure you didn't suffer the same fate as our parents."

"It's funny to hear you arguing in the name of family, seeing as you're the one ripping us apart now," I point out, folding my arms across my chest. "I know I messed up in Mentis, and I can never make it up to you, but how long are you going to hold it over me?"

Willow's face goes blank, her expression hollowing out until there's nothing left behind her eyes. "I'm sorry for lashing out," she says. "I was hurting."

"When *I* was hurting, you told me to get over it."

Willow takes a deep breath in, clearly doing her best to get a hold of her temper. "How did it make you feel when I told you we don't know what happened to Clio?"

The question hangs in the air. At first, I think it's rhetorical until I realize see she's waiting for an answer. "Upset," I spit out. "What's your point?"

"And desperate, right?" Willow presses, ignoring the bite in my tone. "Well, the way you feel for Clio is the way I felt for Larc. Knowing he's dead because of a choice *I* made is something I hope you never have to experience. Maybe it was wrong of me to be angry at you, but if Clio's really dead, I almost guarantee you'll react the same way."

Clio walked into his fate, whatever that may be, solely because he wanted me to be safe. And what had I done? Nothing.

I let him go, possibly to his death.

"Are you okay?" Willow asks, brows creased in concern.

I want to say yes and bury my problems in their usual compartment at the back of my mind, but this is too much weight, and I can't bear it anymore. "No," I whisper.

Willow reaches toward me as if she's about to grab my shoulder, but I don't wait to find out. I spin on my heel and hurry down the corridor to get far away from her.

# Chapter Twenty
## A New Sort of Normal

I DON'T LOOK back to see if Willow follows. By the time I reach my room, a storm is churning in my chest. I shove the door open hard enough to startle Kado from his slumber. He lifts his head, ruffs at me softly, then settles back down as I crawl beneath the blankets.

I cry myself to sleep and dream of Ignis.

At first, it's as I remember it. The houses and dens filled with warmth and love of the witches I've known my entire life. Then it all unravels.

The colors fade, the homes crumble. Shrubs become blackened husks. The earth is gray and cracked beneath my feet. My parents' house appears—what's left of it anyway. A pile of scorched stone, one jagged wall still upright, defiant in its ruin. The grief rises fast, sharp and suffocating, clawing at my chest.

It's gone. *They're* gone. My life I once held dear to my chest is gone.

It fades and Helena's home flickers into view. Somehow, it's still standing. Untouched.

The dream fractures, and I wake in a haze, the ceiling unfamiliar for a moment. Kado shifts at my feet, and I lie there, staring blankly at the wall, unsure what the day expects of me. Doing nothing seems like a valid option until my stomach growls, dragging me reluctantly back to reality.

*Breakfast,* I tell myself. *Food makes everything better.*

Keeping my head down, I make my way to the Community Villa. I don't expect an apology from my sister for our conversation last night, and I don't get one. She's nowhere around, nor are any familiar faces. It's a small mercy. I'm not ready to face Willow yet.

As I force a few bites into my mouth, I look around the room. The groups at the other tables are smaller than they'd been before the battle. Quieter too.

*How many witches did it claim?*

Just like that, I'm not hungry anymore. I toss the rest of my breakfast and head back to my room. Kado greets me with a burst of excitement, but I barely register it as I collapse onto the bed. My eyes slip shut, and what feels like thirty seconds later, a knock sounds at the door.

I tense, heart skipping. Willow?

When I don't move, Kado lets out an impatient yip, urging me to respond.

The door pops open, and Maverick peers in at me. "You alive in here?"

I narrow my eyes, too exhausted to respond.

"Willow's hosting a vigil for Mentis. Thought you might like to come." He disappears into the hall without waiting for my response.

I stare after him, considering. The vigil for Ignis had been rough, but things are different now. A flash of Lavina's body comes to mind, and that's all it takes to get me out of bed.

Kado gives me a questioning look.

"I should go," I tell him.

Willow hadn't mentioned it to me, but I can't help but think this is a test. To see if I participate, without her giving me a nudge in the right direction.

Kado pads quietly at my heels as we wind through the halls and out into the fields of swaying purple plants. Distant voices carry on the breeze, likely from witches on their way to the Community Villa too.

Inside the building, the sounds of dozens of witches echoes down the hall, guiding me toward the room. I stop in the doorway, taking it all in. There had been so many more witches during the Ignis vigil. Is that because they were lost in the fight or did they choose not to attend?

I slink inside, sticking close to the walls as I make my way to Maverick's side.

"Glad you could make it," he says.

I spot Willow across the room, rubbing a crying witch's back. "Of course."

He pats me on the shoulder comfortingly and goes to her. The wall is once again decorated with pictures of the witches lost in battle. The air leaves my lungs as I count them. Larc's picture hangs in the very center. It's larger than the rest and worn around the edges as if Willow's had it for a long time. I hardly recognize him in it. He's younger by at least a decade, serving as a strange reminder that he and Willow are the same age. She stopped aging when she died, but he continued on.

Mentis has never my home, but it has a special place in my heart for the fact that it *almost* was. I didn't know any of the lost witches by name, with the exception of Larc and Lavina, but I recognize a few of the Elementals who had faced me in combat at some point. It's a shame I never actually got to know them as anything other than my enemies, because now I never will.

When I glance at Willow again, her back is to me, and by proxy, the pictures. I should approach her, give my condolences again for what I've done. Or would it be better to not say anything at all?

Before I can decide, a new face slips into the room. Quinn. He moves slowly, keeping his injured arm close to his body. When he spots me, his face lights up and he hurries to my side.

"Good to see you," I tell him.

"I couldn't miss it," he says, but there's a dull look in his eyes that I understand all too well. Pain. A veiled attempt at coping with all he's seen, all he's experienced, all he's *lost*.

"How are you settling in?" I ask, unsure if that's the right question to ask. What *is* the proper thing to say in a conversation like this?

He shrugs. "Well enough, I guess. Ambrossi is very thorough."

That's the truth.

Quinn's gaze stops on the pictures. Tears bubble in the corners of his eyes, and I stay silent, letting him sort through his memories. It's not very often that I can feel someone's exact type of sorrow, but this is one of them. The images from Ignis' vigil will stay branded in my mind.

The tears vanish as quickly as they came. His face drains of color, his gaze distant as if he's just seen a ghost.

Instinctively, I follow his line of sight.

He's staring at the Reanimates.

Or rather, one in particular.

A middle-aged woman with quiet, unassuming features stands a small distance away from the others. Her skin is sallow, lips tinged blue, but there's a trace of softness in her face that death couldn't erase.

"Do you know her?" I ask.

Quinn doesn't answer at first nor does he look away. "She… died in the battle," he manages to say.

"This place is special," I say softly, unsure the best way to tell him that Willow can do *miracles*.

This only serves to double his confusion. He looks from the group of glowing witches to the pictures and back.

"Are they all…"

"They were."

His face loses what little bit of color it maintained as he says, "I'm sorry. I've… got to go lay down."

Concerned, I ask, "Do you want me to walk with you?"

He shakes his head. "No, that's okay." Then he melts into the crowd before I can say anything else.

I begin to follow him, but fingers slip through mine, stopping me. Turning around, I expect to see Willow. It's Helena. "There you are," she breathes, eyes wide with relief. "I haven't seen you all day."

I open my mouth to offer some excuse for my absence, but nothing comes. The truth is too heavy, and the lies feel too thin. So I say nothing.

Her brows pinch slightly. "What did Willow say? Was it bad?"

A new layer of grief crashes down on me when I remember her words about Clio.

Helena picks up snippets of the conversation in my memories. "He's not…"

"Dead?" I finish for her. "Don't know. Willow doesn't either. She can't find him."

Her eyes widen. "He's not in Ignis?"

"Apparently not," I murmur. "Fern's missing too."

Helena frowns, the expression flickering across her face before she pushes it away. "They're alive. They're hiding somewhere."

That's what I want to tell myself. It's the comforting answer, but how true is it? If Clio and Fern are hiding, where are they and who are they hiding from? When are they going to come back? What if they never do?

"Yeah," I say, too emotionally exhausted to add anything else.

"Come on," Helena says.

She gives my hand the smallest squeeze and takes me across the room to meet a few of the Reanimates. I'm proud of her for making friends so quickly, for moving on with her life, and making the best of her situation. I want to follow in her lead, but the past is hard to forget. It haunts me.

This place, once a cage in my mind, is starting to feel like home. The witches who once saw me as a threat now meet my gaze without suspicion. Some even smile. Somehow, I've become one of them. An equal.

Willow's land is far from home. I've moved so much in the past few weeks that the idea of "home" has blurred. Maybe it no longer lives in a place, but in people. With Clio and Fern gone, there isn't much about Ignis I long for. I can hardly remember what my life was like in my UnEquipped days.

Maybe that's not such a bad thing.

Maybe forgetting is the first step to moving forward. Maybe letting go of what holds us back is the only way we ever really begin again.

# Chapter Twenty-One
## Astral Projection

LIFE GOES ON, and a week passes. Most of it, I spend alone, working to master my new Aens powers. I've practiced the breathing techniques Sabre taught me, but controlling the air feels like trying to hold water in my hands. I haven't found a shape or flow that feels right yet. My abilities still surge strongest when I let them burst out all at once wild and uncontrolled. But after seeing how dangerous that can be, I can't afford to make that mistake again.

Lying in bed, I raise my hands, fingers splayed toward the ceiling. Kado, sprawled nearby, lifts his head and watches me with quiet curiosity. I pull my hands closer, focusing every ounce of my energy on the air between them. Slowly, I shape it, coaxing it into a small sphere. For a moment, it crackles with power, swirling rapidly, then, just as quickly, it fades.

With an agitated groan, I give up. I don't understand why others have so much faith in me when I can't summon any in myself. I flip over and Kado laps his tongue over my face. Giggling, I wipe my face. "Gross!" I say, but the moment has successfully lightened my mood. My powers have a long way to go.

But at least I'm making progress in my Coven. Things are almost normal again. Except for Willow. She still avoids me when she can, keeping a stoic expression during meetings and training.

I try not to take it personally.

Everyone grieves in their own way.

*Willow just needs time.* A voice in the back of my mind tries to convince me. She needs support, too, but that's harder.

I'm grateful for Helena and Kado's company to fill the gaps in my days. Afternoons spent with Helena have always been an important part of my life, but that's more true now. I'm glad she's here with me and that she's safe.

*Unlike Clio and Fern,* I remind myself. If neither of them can be found, is it possible they escaped the battle *together* and are hiding out until they find the opportunity to come back? I hold onto that hope. I have to believe they're out there somewhere, and that they're *choosing* to stay away.

Clio's green eyes are the last thing I see when I close my eyes that night and the first when I enter a dream. Not a night goes by anymore that I *don't* dream of him, though this one *feels* different, more lucid. I'm searching for him in the ruins of Ignis. Anticipation fuels my blood, a desperate urge pushing me to keep going with the belief that if I put in the work, he'll appear to me.

But he doesn't, and I don't know why I expect anything different.

I see the border of Ignis as clear as day. Then I'm in the heart of the Coven, in the smooth spiral of stairs surrounding the altar. It's a place I've spent many afternoons. My mentor, Angel, lived near here once. Ambrossi, too. My gaze flicks back and forth from the house on one side and the small dwelling on the other. I wander toward Ambrossi's old place, desperate to see it in my memories. My last glimpse of it was when it was actively being destroyed.

Inside the den, the familiar scent of herbs smacks me in the face, causing me to pause. They're *fresh*. There's a bed tucked into the tiny nook of the bedroom at the back of the Den, and I gasp with familiarity at the witch sleeping on it.

Angel.

"It's safe to say you now have an *Alchemy* power too." Maverick's voice barrels into my head.

My eyes shoot open, and I'm back in my bed in Willow's mansion. I'd been *asleep* or at least I *thought* that was the case.

"Maverick?" I ask, groggy. I struggle to keep my eyes open to see if he's really there or if he's eclipsed into my dreams.

Light streaming through my window highlights his black hair, illuminating lighter streaks of brown. How long has he been here, watching me? Kado lets out a little whine as if he's thinking the same thing.

"What do you mean?" I ask at last.

He ignores the question. "What did you dream about?"

I raise an eyebrow and sit up, confused by the concern. Kado leaps off the bed to stand beside Maverick, but I can't take my eyes off his face. He smirks in the way I've come to learn means he knows something he's not saying. "Why does it matter?"

"I'm curious," he says simply. "Humor me."

Now I'm more suspicious. He's a soldier, not the curious type. "Ignis."

"What *about* Ignis?"

I flare my nostrils and swipe a lock of black hair from my eyes. "Clio. Okay? I was looking for him."

"Well, I hope you found something, because you were really there," he says, the smirk growing into a full-blown grin.

I don't get it. "No, it was a dream, and…"

His grin could split his face in half at this point.

"What? What is it?" I demand, clenching my hand into a fist around my blanket, frustrated.

The grin doesn't fade as he says, "Congratulations, Lilith. You have the power of astral projection."

I want to hit him for lying to me. Even if he's telling the truth, I still wouldn't mind smacking him. "No, I was asleep. It was a dream," I insist.

Maverick raises an eyebrow. "Not to sound like a creep, but I came in here to wake you up. Your eyes were *open* and you were whispering something. Instructions to yourself, I think. Anyway, I didn't know whether I should wake you or not, then there was this loud *whoosh,* a bright streak of light, and your eyes closed."

"Are you sure?"

"How long have you been doing this?"

I think of all the dreams I've had recently. So many of them had been about Ignis. Could I have *really* been there? If so, the devastation I saw is *real.* Those glimpses are an honest snapshot of what's left. Worst of all, my search hasn't yielded a single clue about Clio's whereabouts.

"You don't look happy," Maverick says.

"That's probably because I'm not."

He plops down on the bed. Kado jumps a little to avoid Maverick's swinging feet and comes to rest beside me, eyeing him over my knee, as if he doesn't trust him so close to me. I pat the white fur on the top of his head in reassurance.

"What's on your mind?" Maverick asks.

"I *saw* Ignis. When I thought it was a dream, it was hard to take. But *that*… it's gone, isn't it?"

"Not all of it." I'm sure he says this as a form of comfort, but it doesn't help. "They're rebuilding."

It should make me feel better. The Council hadn't been successful in taking them off the map. Instead, I'm paranoid. How long before they decide to try again? If this is a power, not a fluke, I need to better understand it. Understand what I can *do*. "You said it's an Alchemy power? I thought astral projection came from Mentis."

Maverick shakes his head. "No. They use it to scope for herbs, mostly." The gleam in Maverick's eyes as he explains this makes it clear how excited he is for me. I'm not as upbeat. "That's four out of the five, Lilith. Ignis, Mentis, Aens, and now Alchemy? Willow will be ecstatic to hear this!"

"Yeah… I'm sure." I push myself to my feet so he won't catch the shadow crossing my face.

"I get it." Maverick lifts his palms in mock surrender. "You two still aren't on good terms, but maybe this will fix it."

Not convinced, I say, "Maybe."

Maverick shakes his head and lets out a soft chuckle. "Usually, witches *celebrate* the development of their powers. But you? You'd think someone died."

His attempt at humor falls flat. My voice is sharper than I intend when I answer, "Witches *have* died."

The smile fades from his face. "I get it," he says again and stands.

"I can see that kind of thing with this gift, can't I?"

He pulls his lips tight. "Yeah, I suppose you could, but *all* gifts have downsides. Why would you do that, anyway?"

I glance at Kado. "What else can I do with it?"

"Help us," he says, flatly. "We *always* need people to do surveillance. With your gift? Gods, I can't imagine what we can accomplish."

I close my eyes. That was the answer I feared. I don't want that much responsibility. The kind that will only hurt more witches if I fail. I don't want any more blood on my hands, not when they're already so stained.

"You can see what others *can't*," he adds in a softer tone, as if he suspects my thoughts.

"Yeah."

Maverick briefly glances from me to the door, then back again as if I'm making him uncomfortable. "I came to get you for battle training, but—"

"I'm not up for it today," I say flatly.

"I figured not," he says, holding out his hands. "I'll let Sabre know." He takes a step forward, then pauses to look back at me. "Take a breath, okay? I know you're tired. You're going to be. You *did* just discover your Alchemy power. Willow will *never* force you to do something you don't want to do."

In spite of the tension between my sister and I, I know he's right. Deep down, she cares about me more than anyone else. That was why the thing with Larc had been so devastating for her. His words bring a real smile to my face, and that makes him smile too. He leaves the room, the click of the door announcing his departure.

Kado yips as if he thinks I want to play, but I plop back down on my bed instead. "Astral projection," I mumble, testing the way the words feel in my mouth. I look down at my thumb, at the place I've already managed to pull a few layers of skin free in my sparing bouts of anxiety. I have no idea how the power works or how to control it.

But astral projection will open up the world, and I can't wait to see what it has to show me.

Lying in the middle of the mattress, I fold my hands over my chest and close my eyes. I exhale slowly, and as the breath leaves my lungs, a calm, dreamlike sensation washes over me. I bring to mind the image of Ignis the same way I'd seen it in my vision.

An overwhelming sensation of dissociation washes over me. Eyes wide, I look down at myself. At my clear form then the body on the bed. *Also me.* Fascinated horror gradually gives way to curiosity. I wander through the labyrinthine halls in this form, following Maverick on his journey to deliver today's updates to Sabre. He steps into the purple plants outside, and I stay put, watching him go. With a gasp, I slam back into my body, staring at the ceiling.

"It's real," I tell a very confused and concerned Kado. "He wasn't lying."

The dog yips, jaws parting to reveal a floppy pink tongue. His way of congratulating me. I delve into my new ability, picking up my search for Clio and Fern in the exact same place I left off.

## Chapter Twenty-Two
### Connections

DAY BLEEDS INTO night, then into morning once again. I haven't slept. Haven't eaten. I keep searching. It's easy to lose track of time between the shifting planes of existence, but I can't stay in this place forever. I have obligations I must fulfill.

I force myself out of bed and get dressed, ready for whatever today has in store. Maverick isn't here to pull me to battle training so I make my way to Helena's house and poke my head inside. She's sitting in a rocking chair, a heavy Alchemy tome open in her lap.

"Taking your Healer studies seriously, I see," I say, taking a few steps into the room.

She looks up. "This place has the most amazing library. It'd be a shame to throw away the opportunity. I'm learning about more advanced healing techniques. Ambrossi says I'm a natural at this."

"He does?"

A blush lines her cheeks, and her gaze drops sheepishly to her book. "Well, he hasn't actually *said* it, but he thought it a few times."

I laugh. "Using your powers for evil?"

She shoots me a look of mock innocence, her lips curling into a playful grin. "Not all the time," she says, her expression almost too convincing.

"Helena, if he hasn't bothered to shield his mind from you by now, it's because he *wants* you to read his thoughts."

A guilty grin is plastered to her face as if she's already reached that conclusion. "True. How're your Aens powers coming?"

"They're... so-so," I reply, my voice a little flat. In the wake of my newest discovery, they don't seem as important anymore. "I discovered my Alchemy power."

Helena's face pales, her fingers loosening until she almost drops the book. "You *what?*"

"Astral projection. Apparently, I've had it for a little while," I reply, gritting my teeth as I remember how the ability came to be. "I thought I was dreaming, but Maverick told me what it was."

"Does Willow know?"

I shake my head. "Unless Maverick told her, I don't think she does."

"Well, once again, you should be proud. That's a useful ability."

I shrug, disheartened.

Helena senses the mood shift. "You were searching for Clio, weren't you?" she asks gently, as if she already knows the answer.

My bottom lip trembles, despite my best efforts to bite it back. *Don't cry.*

Helena reads either my blank expression or my churning thoughts, because she sets her book aside and wraps me in one of the tightest hugs I've had in a while. "I... I'm sorry to ask, Li. I miss him, too, you know. I hope he's okay."

It helps, knowing her words are sincere, but it still hurts to think about him. Our purpose, our reason for *being*, is to scour every inch of this planet for that one specific person. The one who can resuscitate us, bring us back from the darkness, and remind us why the light is good.

Clio is that person for me, but if he's gone, so is a part of me I'll never get back.

"I know you do," I reply finally. With her here, I can almost imagine that he is, too, in a sense.

"If anyone can persevere in a tight spot, it's him," she says and makes her way back to her seat.

I murmur a noncommittal, "Yeah," that I can't fully make myself believe.

"Knock, knock!" Maverick calls from the door, saving me from spiraling. "Lilith, you in here?"

"Yep," I reply, wiping my face with the back of my hand. I tell Helena, "I'll be back later."

She looks all too grateful to return to her book. I leave her to it and follow Maverick to the training grounds. With my current mood, some battle training will do me good.

"What did you do yesterday?" he asks, his tone casual but probing.

I keep my eyes fixed ahead, unwilling to dive into the details.

"You seem better today," he comments, though I can't tell what gives him that impression.

I let out a short, bitter laugh. "I don't know what you're basing that on, but you're wrong." I pause, my voice hardening.

"Have you told Willow yet?"

He smirks, an expression that irks me more than usual. "So, you admit it now?" He tilts his head, eyes glinting with mischief. "No, I haven't. I'll leave it to you whether you want to tell her. Seems like you two could use an excuse to talk."

"I appreciate it," I say, my words cold as ice, and then I fall silent, the weight of his insinuation hanging in the air between us.

Maverick tries to bring up Willow again, and I walk faster, *glad* to see Sabre in the distance. I nod at him as we approach, a small sign of respect. I hate to admit it, but Sabre is a good teacher. I've come to trust Maverick's judgement on that. Of a lot actually. He reminds me of myself in a way, and I like the way he looks out for Willow, especially since I've been slacking on that responsibility.

"I'm going to head out," Maverick says after greeting Sabre. "I've got a run to make today, and Willow's expecting me back before sunset."

"Good luck," I tell him.

He glances at Sabre, as if to say he won't need as much luck as my teacher. Sabre meets his gaze, then Maverick walks away. I watch him disappear from the field. This is the first time he, or anyone else, for that matter, has left me entirely alone with Sabre.

Skimming his mind tells me the situation makes him feel as awkward as I do. "So, I don't think I told you how much I like your underwear," he jokes, nudging me with his elbow. I glare at him from the corner of my eye.

Maverick's been a buffer in our previous training sessions,

and I'm feeling his absence now. My skin prickles with agitation as Sabre watches me, waiting for an answer.

"Oh, come on. It was a joke," he adds.

"Jokes are funny."

"All right, I figured it out. It's not the joke. You still haven't gotten over what happened with Helena, have you?"

I let out a very unladylike snort and whirl on him. "Obviously! Helena is a forgiving person, but she also doesn't have to live with the visual of what you did."

"If it helps, I'm sorry," Sabre says. He opens his mouth as if he wants to add more but closes it again, either in frustration or a lack of words.

I flare my nostrils, watching him, waiting for whatever else he might offer. His apology doesn't do much to ease the tension, but I need to find a way to get along with him. It's easier when there's a chaperone keeping me in check, steering me away from doing something stupid. But getting to a place where I don't feel like punching him in the face on my own will be a lot harder.

"Okay," I force myself to say.

*Baby steps,* Grief encourages.

"You feeling okay?" Sabre asks. "You didn't show up to training yesterday."

"I'm fine," I say. The last thing I want to do is open up and tell him about my new power. To tell him how it's getting easier and easier to lose myself to it.

"Are you—"

"I said I'm fine."

"Okay," he says. He sounds as if he doesn't entirely believe me, but he's tired of arguing. We launch into training, but the tension between us doesn't make us good sparring partners. Our moves are off balance or too rough, and neither of us is willing to apologize or back down. Sabre must sense this isn't going well because he calls it quits around lunch, much sooner than the other sessions have ended.

I take my leave without a goodbye, stepping out of the field and into the warmth of the Community Villa. The noise inside is loud enough to drown out my thoughts, yet I still feel strangely alone. I grab a small plate of food more out of habit than hunger and leave the cafeteria in search of solitude. Going back to Helena's isn't an option. I'm not ready to talk about Clio.

So, I wander down the path, letting the sweet scent of the plants fill my senses. I walk until my feet ache, then sink down onto a smooth rock and take a bite of my sandwich, staring up at the sky. The blue contrasts sharply with the purple of the plants, making the view even more striking. This place is beautiful, and I can't help but wonder where it actually is. If Zane transports us to the Land of Five, we could be anywhere. I pluck a leaf from a nearby plant. Its texture is soft and silky, almost like a blanket, unlike the rough foliage of home.

According to legend, The Land of Five was once three times its size. The war that led to the treaty had been so brutal, the land itself was destroyed and deemed uninhabitable. If the Land of New Life lies outside the Land of Five, can it be possible that other livable lands exist beyond the borders with witches we've never met?

"Hey, are you okay?" a small voice prompts.

I jump and work to compose myself when I notice Malcolm peering at me from the plants. His red wings stand out, but other than that, he could've been completely camouflaged. There's no telling how long he's been watching my silent struggle.

"I'm okay," I manage to get out, picking at the sandwich's strip of brown crust.

"You and Willow still haven't made up, huh?" Malcolm asks, landing beside my knee.

I feel myself sneering and rip off the strip of crust to hide my bitterness. "How'd you guess?"

"I'm a fairy. Sensing emotions comes easy," he says, tilting his head in a way that reminds me of Fern. It hurts. "Plus, Willow hasn't seemed herself lately."

"That's the problem," I tell him. "She's still hurting over Larc, and I get it. It's my fault he's gone, but she's taken it to a new level."

Malcolm nods along, big eyes watching me intently.

I continue, "I shouldn't have pushed her. She told me to stay. That was what she wanted, but I put her in a situation she was already uncomfortable with, and it cost her the love of her life. I wouldn't be surprised if she never wants to talk to me again."

"Willow isn't like that. You're her *sister*, and she loves you. She's dealing with a lot right now."

"I know, and that's why I'm letting her be," I reply. I'm not sure whether that or cowardice is the true reason I haven't tried to fix things yet. Probably both. "Has she told you about Fern?"

"Yeah," he says. "I'm not worried, though. My momma's strong. I have faith that she's all right. She has to be."

I wish I could have that much blind faith in something. Especially something *this* important. As much as I want Clio to be okay, I can't fully believe it's true because there's a nagging voice saying, *I'll never see him again.*

"Do you miss her?"

"Every day."

Guilt prickles under my skin. Here's a child, hurting for his mother, and I'm the reason for that too. "I… I'm sorry for taking her away from you."

"Lilith, you didn't *take* anyone away. She *chose* to go, just like Willow *chose* to bring you to Mentis. You can't keep blaming yourself for the decisions others make."

"Right." I want to argue, but it won't do any good. I shift my gaze to the ground. *It sure doesn't stop Willow from blaming me.* "I hope Fern's okay."

"I hope Clio is, too."

Oddly enough the simple statement brings me some comfort, and I bask in it.

"Lilith! Lilith!" Helena's voice rings around the field, interrupting us.

Panic has me on my feet, and Malcolm disappears back into the foliage with a simple swish of his wings. "What's wrong?"

"Quinn's gone!" Helena says, eyes wide. Red marks scour her cheeks as if she's been frantically hollering for the past twenty minutes and no one's heard.

"How did this happen?"

"I…I don't know," she stutters. "Things were fine and dandy. He was in his room this morning. I went to get him breakfast, and when I came back, he was gone."

"And no one's seen him?" I ask, wracking my brain for a possible explanation.

Helena shakes her head, scattering her hair in a blurry rush of orange. "You don't think he went back to Mentis, do you?"

"Mentis? No." But I'm not sure about that answer. He was struggling to come to terms with things, but would he really leave to go back to a Coven reduced to rubble? Another possibility I don't want to consider whispers in my ear. He could go to the source of our problems, the Council themselves, and spill everything to Tricia, including where to find us.

I take off through the purple plants. The battle training with Sabre had been short but fierce, and I'm feeling it now, but force myself to keep moving at a steady pace. There's no way Quinn could get far; he's injured and paranoid. If anything, he'll end up running in circles until he collapses from exhaustion.

As if on cue, a bloodcurdling cry rings out from the direction of Willow's mansion. I hurry toward it. When I burst through the doors and into the foyer, Quinn is backed into a corner by both Kado and one of Willow's undead tigers. When he spots me, Kado wags his tail, but the tiger doesn't lose focus.

"Heel," I tell it.

It lifts the corner of its lip in an exasperated snarl then stalks away.

I rush to his Quinn's side, checking him over for any possible injuries. "Are you okay?" I ask, creating a barrier between him and my dog. Kado whines happily and butts his head into my shoulder, completely oblivious to how uncomfortable he makes Quinn.

"What the fuck is wrong with these animals?" he asks, waving his good hand in Kado's direction.

"They're pets. My sister has the power of resurgence."

Quinn looks at me as if I murdered his mother. "S… who?"

"Willow. She has resurgence." I set my hand on the top of Kado's fuzzy head, hoping the display will show him that, although these animals *look* scary, they're actually sweethearts. Like the Reanimates."

"*The* Willow… the one from the legend?" he whispers.

"The very same."

"Whoa," he says, slumping against the wall. The bit of information seems to have only complicated his crisis.

I sit next to him, giving him a few minutes of silence to process things before I ask, "So, why the escape attempt, Quinn?"

"These people… are evil," he says and glares accusingly at Kado.

"Who? Ambrossi and Helena? They saved your life," I remind him.

He looks away.

I dip my face close to his. "Am I evil, too? I brought you here."

"That's not a fair question."

"But it is. If you're still considering the Council to be the good guys, remember what they did to your Coven. All of us? The ones you're calling *evil?* We've worked nonstop, day and night, to save your life, expecting nothing for the effort but your well-being."

Quinn groans but shifts his gaze to the ground. He wants to argue but knows I have a point. I give him time to search for words. His world is literally collapsing around him, and this is only the beginning. Getting through the Council's conditioning will be the hardest part of his adjustment.

"We'll protect you," I assure him. "They can't hurt you here."

"Why? You're… you're…"

"What?" I ask, drawing my eyebrows together.

"You're supposed to be the enemy," he finishes, his voice strained.

"We're scapegoats," I state dryly. "The Council? *They're* your real enemy."

"Why would Tricia do this?" he asks, tears twinkling in his huge brown eyes. "She didn't even warn me that—" A sob escapes him. "She killed Lavina, and… and for what?"

I don't have any answers for him. I don't know what the Council plans to do or why they're willing to kill innocent witches to pull it off. But I do know one thing: Quinn is spiraling into despair, and I'm the only one who can keep him from drowning in it. Pulling him into my arms, his tears soak through the fabric of my shirt. Holding him tighter, I let him cry it out for both of us.

## Chapter Twenty-Three
### Addiction

I DON'T KNOW how long Quinn and I stay like that, but eventually Willow, Maverick, Sabre, and Katrina stroll into the mansion. Their footsteps echo eerily around the empty foyer, amplified by the fact that none of them are speaking. I watch their approach, but Quinn keeps his face buried in my shoulder as if he's ashamed to let them see him like this.

Willow moves a little closer than the others. In her hand, she grips a long wooden staff, and for a moment, I wonder if she's about to strike me with it. "Lilith, we need you."

I look up at her through my lashes, doing my best to keep my face neutral. She's all business now, as if she's set aside our personal skirmishes for the time being.

I can respect that.

"Go find Helena, okay? She's worried sick," I say to Quinn, moving my shoulder slightly to nudge him off me.

Reluctantly, he obeys, though I can see the effort it costs him, wiping his reddened face with the back of his hand. Rising to his feet, he keeps his gaze fixed on the floor as he pushes past Willow's entourage, making his way toward freedom.

"Go with him," Willow orders the others, never taking her eyes off me. "I need to talk to my sister alone."

The others remain silent, forming a protective barrier around Quinn as he steps out of the foyer. He stiffens but keeps his eyes locked ahead.

I work on standing so I can speak to her at eye level as I ask, "What's going on?" There's something degrading about her literally looking down her nose to speak to me.

"Here," Willow says, passing me the stick.

I purse my lips, hand against the wall for balance. "What the hell is that?"

"It's a walking stick. I had it made for you," she says, inching it toward me. My eyes run down the length of the golden-hued wood, taking in the elegant markings carved into it. There are pictures, a story. I recognize the tale. The birth of Ignis.

In the beginning days of the Land of Five, there were no Covens, no distinctions between the Equipped and the UnEquipped. They all lived together in a society in which the Equipped's very existence was hidden behind the disbelief of the UnEquipped. They were outnumbered and crucified when the truth was revealed. As society eventually collapsed under its own weight, the UnEquipped grew to trust the Equipped, and depended on them for protection and shelter.

Many of the UnEquipped fell to disease, famine, and each other's wrath, but the Equipped held strong, caring for themselves and the UnEquipped under their protection. After the ways of the Old World were forgotten, the survivors remained strong, faithful in the Equipped to whom they had pledged their loyalty.

One day, a young witch named Myalis took control of them. She was Equipped with telekinesis, and she could also manipulate the most logical person into carrying out her will, regardless of the circumstances. For the most part, she was a great leader, except for her one major flaw—an obvious favoritism for witches like herself. Witches with mind powers.

They had the best houses, the best food, and were kept the safest from the threats many others had already succumbed to. Needless to say, not everyone was happy about that. Igneous, a fire-Equipped witch, disliked Myalis and her favoritism. Young and hotheaded, he was convinced he would be a better leader. So he gathered others Equipped with fire conjuring, fire manipulation, and a range of other powers, and incited a battle from which neither faction emerged victorious.

So they decided on a truce. Under it, they agreed that the best way to raise children of a certain ability would be to surround them with other witches of the same aptitudes and similar lifestyles. Myalis took her band of witches to the edge of the ocean, and Igneous, never wanting to see them again, went in the opposite direction to the best environment for his powers, the desert.

There's more to the story after that, but I can't focus on it. I keep comparing the rise of Ignis to the rise of the Elemental Coven. Willow faces a path quite similar to the one Igneous trod in his desperation to care for his people.

"A… walking stick?" I finally ask.

"Yes, and I know you like to reject kindness," Willow replies with a barely repressed roll of her eyes, "but at least use it until you finish healing."

In all the years of dealing with my handicap, I've always balked at the idea of help, with the exception of my telekinesis, of course. But since the Battle of Ignis, my telekinesis has been unpredictable, and when it does come, I don't trust it like I used to. Not in this place with witches who can lock it away like it never existed.

Either out of fleeting sanity or guilt, I take the peace offering. The wood is strong and smooth, perfect for my height, and the tip hardly makes a sound against the floor.

I hug her, realizing how much I've missed her these past few days. "Thank you," I say into her curly brown hair.

"I'd do anything for you, Lily. You're my family."

She tries to pull away, but I hold on a bit tighter. Then I finally let her put some space between us. "Did Maverick tell you about my new power?"

Willow's expression drops. "No, he didn't."

I need to take some time to thank him for being the only honest witch around here. "I can astral project now."

Her eyes spark with something, and she perks up. "Really?"

"I went to Ignis," I say but out of fear of rehashing our last conversation, I don't tell her why.

"Have you tried to travel anywhere else?"

I shake my head. "No. I haven't wanted to *go* anywhere else." I meet her gaze, my voice quieter. "Why?"

Willow tucks her lip between her teeth, her posture more rigid than usual. The way she stands, straight-backed and poised, makes me feel like there's something more to this conversation than just catching up.

"What's going on?" I ask, forcing the calm I've been holding onto into a tight, hidden box at the back of my mind.

She hesitates for a moment, then exhales slowly. "I'm worried about Alchemy," she admits. "I have my suspicions that the Council may go after them next. They, uh… they found a replacement for you."

I feel sick, imagining a witch going through what I did. Or even worse—a witch *wanting* to go through it. "Who is it?"

"His name is Colby. I… don't know what he can do."

The name isn't familiar. "Is he from Ignis?"

"No."

A pit opens in my stomach. Not from Ignis? Why? I'm relieved Clio's not there to fill that space, but it leaves me with more questions. If the Council isn't following their own rules about keeping fair representation for each Coven, what other rules are they willing to break?

"Where *is* he from?"

"I can't answer that either."

"Well, why do you think they're watching Alchemy?"

If they hadn't hurt my Coven already, I'd say *this* is the worst thing the Council could ever do. Healers are peacemakers, lovers. Not warriors. Maybe that's the problem. In this time of war, there's no place for compassion. Traits like that can be costly on the battlefield. Healers are the only witches allowed to cross between Covens, and Alchemy is the only Coven not bound by *all* the laws of the treaty.

The only threat to the Council right now is the one thing they offer: unity.

Willow's jaw clenches when she says, "Hurt the Healers, hurt the chances of your enemy's recovery."

It's true which only makes it more messed up.

Willow puffs her cheeks, and I know what she's going to ask. It's the very thing I feared when Maverick first told me of my abilities. "Can you check on them?"

I swallow, leaning on the walking stick to give me a reason to look away from her hopeful eyes.

"What's wrong?"

I look back sharply. "How can you trust me with something like that? What if I let you down again?"

"You won't," she says firmly, though I can't tell if she really believes it or if it's just something she's saying to push me.

"How will I know what to look for? What if I miss something important?" I ask.

Willow simpers. Not because I said something touching, but because she knows I have a point. "The only failure here would be to sit back and wait until it's too late."

I hate that she's right. Sighing heavily, I meet her gaze. "Okay. I'll do it."

Willow pulls me into her arms again. "Thank you."

I don't answer. She threads her fingers through mine, guiding me back to my room. As soon as we step through the door, Kado trots over, his tail wagging furiously. He's instantly fixated on the walking stick, eyes bright with excitement. The moment I take a step inside, he pounces on it, sinking his teeth into the wood as though he's ready to start a game of tug-of-war.

"No. No, Kado," I say, batting the edge of the stick playfully against his ribs. "Momma needs this to walk."

He yips in excitement but seems to understand my tone is serious. He sniffs the stick one more time, but he doesn't grab it again. I settle on my bed, staring up at the beams above my head. How many more times will I have to do something like this for her benefit?

"Relax," Willow encourages as she settles in at the foot of

the bed.

"Okay," I say, crossing my arms over my chest. A heartbeat later, I'm stepping through the barrier between reality and another realm.

Outside my body, I watch Willow and Kado. I move closer to her, but she's completely unaware of my presence. Confident, I continue through the building. The world around me shimmers, and suddenly, I'm in Alchemy.

Though I've only been to this Coven once before, everything feels strangely familiar. Lazarus is sitting comfortably in front of his fireplace, teaching Flora and a witch I don't recognize how to properly create a purple poultice.

As I travel deeper through the Coven, I pass the Coven altar, a boulder covered in a variety of moss and vines, and peek through windows, occasionally drifting inside homes. The witches are content in their lives, cooking food and talking with their friends and family. None of them look hurt or scared.

With that, I slam back into my body, gasping for air.

Willow launches to her feet. "Are you okay? What'd you see?"

"Everything looks normal," I say, trying to sound calm, even though my heart's still racing.

Willow's shoulders slump. By the look on her face, she expected a different answer. There's something else she wants to ask but she's holding back.

"You want me to spy on the Council now, don't you?" I ask her.

"No, I don't. The information you could obtain would be valuable, but it's too dangerous. I don't want to risk you like that."

"Would they even know?" I raise an eyebrow and think of all the other witches I've already spied on. I hadn't considered that some of them might sense they're being watched.

"I don't know," she admits. "They might." She reaches down to pet Kado. "But don't worry about it, okay? I appreciate what you've done for me today." Her mixed emotions are obvious, but she plasters on a grin that I'm sure is fake and leaves the room.

Kado lets out a little whine when the door closes. I relax back against the bed, lifting my hands to cover my face. Is she proud of me? Or is she disappointed I didn't do more?

What else *can* I do?

*"You could scope out the Council anyway,"* Grief replies, his little voice burrowing into my head.

I don't want to go anywhere *near* the Council, but maybe he's right. If they're planning something against Alchemy, I have the potential to stop it. To save innocent witches.

*"You don't have to do a thing,"* Maverick had said.

He's wrong about that. When you love someone, truly love them, you *have* to do some things you don't want to do. That includes things that make you uncomfortable.

Kado whines again, resting his massive paws on the edge of the mattress, his nose brushing against my cheek. I gently push him away and settle back, sinking into the sheets. A few deep breaths bring me into a meditative state, and with a few more, I slip out of my body. Each time I do this, it gets easier to move between realms. I can only hope that means returning will, too.

Standing on the edge of the Grove, things are as I remember them. Ahead of me looms the shining glass walls of the

Council's Headquarters. It's haunting even in the evening light. I take a few steps forward and stop. My entire body feels sluggish, as if I've been wrapped in a web.

I take a step backward, and the feeling vanishes.

There are wards protecting the Grove. *Which witch can do that?* I take a few steps into the topiary garden, and try again, but it's the same feeling here. Slowly, I work my way around the Grove, trying to find a break in the magic, but it's strong. Unyielding.

An invisible wall.

I walk, working my way around the barrier, until I find myself at Fern's oasis. Seeing the scooped-out Earth that had once been filled with shimmering water twists something in me. The beautiful vegetation that once ringed it is now brittle, fading away as if it was never there. My eyes drift to the lone tree Fern calls home at the north of the depression, but it's dark and empty. I make my way over to it, staring directly into the hole.

*Where are you?*

The chance to sift through any more of those thoughts vanishes when I'm unexpectedly slammed back into my body.

I gasp and open my eyes to stare at the ceiling, confused. At first, I can't remember where I am. My throat is dry, and I smack my lips, desperate for water. That's when I realize I'm not alone. Willow sits beside me on the mattress, a glass of water in her hand.

"Willow?" I ask, and my voice cracks.

"Drink," she says, holding the glass to my lips.

The cool water runs effortlessly down my throat. I take the cup from her, drinking until it's empty then hand it back. Kado stands on the floor by Willow's legs, and when my eyes drift to him, he tilts his head. I wait for Willow to speak, to see *why* she's decided to visit me again, but she doesn't say a word.

"Is something wrong?" I ask.

"Four days," she says, staring at the empty glass.

"Huh?"

"You've been unconscious for *four days*." She drags the black pits of her eyes to meet my gaze.

I knit my eyebrows together. "No, that can't be right… I…" I swallow again, the motion eased by the water. I lift a hand to my forehead and glance around as if something in the room will agree with me. "I took a nap…"

"What did you dream about?" Willow asks softly.

"I did as you asked," I reply. "Or I tried. They have wards. The Council." Willow doesn't look surprised. "Then I… don't know. I wanted to find a way in, but…" It's too embarrassing to say I kept wandering, hoping to find answers to *something*.

"This isn't good," she says, putting a hand on my knee. "What you're doing isn't healthy."

"I was only doing what you *asked*," I remind her.

"All I asked was for a quick trip, sweetheart."

It *felt* like a quick trip. *Four days*, the concern on Willow's face reminds me.

"You went to Ignis, didn't you?" she presses, her eyes narrowing with understanding. "To search for Clio?"

I don't answer, knowing any defense would only make things worse. "What if I did? I'm not bothering anyone. I'm handling my business."

"But you're not, are you?"

My vision blurs, but I don't remember *when* I started crying. She looks so worried, so *disappointed*. I hate myself for causing it. "Nightmares. All I used to have were nightmares. Every… single night," I say. My voice waivers and threatens to break. "About Ignis and Clio and Fern, *everything*. This gives me *peace*. What's so wrong with that?"

Willow's face is drawn so tight that I think she's going to get up and leave. "Do you remember the last thing you ate?"

I don't. Food seems eons away. "Moving is easy," I say softly. "There's no awkwardness, no…" I pause. "I'm *normal*." As odd of an ability astral projection is, it's the only one that leaves me feeling like everyone else, as if I don't *have* a handicap. "I don't need the walking stick there. I don't need *anything.*"

Willow pulls me into a hug. "Oh, dear sister," she says. "You can't keep doing this. You're *losing* yourself. You may think you're minding your own business, but you're wasting away from simple neglect. You think Clio would want you to do this to yourself in his name?"

No. No, he wouldn't. "He's not here!" I snap. "It doesn't matter what he wants!"

"Exactly." She brushes the hair from my forehead. "For all the torture you're putting yourself through, it's not worth it. There's no changing what's been done."

I want to hate her for saying that, but she's right. My eyes glaze over.

"Let's get you something to eat," she says.

I don't object.

# Chapter Twenty-Four
## Battle of Alchemy

THE MEAL WILLOW serves me tastes as good as the water. At first, it's difficult to get more than a bite down, but as my stomach loosens, the hunger finds its way free. I shovel bite after bite into my mouth until I feel like I might burst. Willow seems more than happy to bring me plate after plate, drink after drink, until a pile of dirty dishes rises around me. When I pop the last bite into my mouth, I groan in pleasure, holding my hand over my bloated stomach. I never knew I could eat so much in one sitting. I shift my walking stick, which is across my lap for easy access, and sit back a bit.

As I push the last empty plate away, Maverick strolls into the dining room. "You're awake!" he says with surprising enthusiasm. Has he been the one keeping tabs on me? The one to notice I'd skipped meals and was absent during training?

"Yeah," I say simply, watching him take a glass of water from Willow and sit down beside her.

"Glad to see it," he says. "I worried we lost you there for a minute."

I draw my eyebrows together, but before I can think of a response, he bends toward Willow, whispering something in her ear. Her face transforms from calm to uncertain to horrified. She stands quickly, causing the chair to screech against the floor, and dashes from the room without another word.

Watching the last of her long brown hair disappear through the door, I ask, "What was that about?"

He taps his fingers on the table beside him as if he's unsure of speaking. "One of our informants has some news."

"What about?"

He shakes his head. "I'm not sure Willow wants you involved, at least, not in your current state."

I grit my teeth. That's another concept they don't understand about being in the astral realm. There's no one there to tell me what I can and cannot do, or to assume what I may or may not be capable of. "That doesn't mean I shouldn't know what's going on."

Maverick stares down at the last sip of water in his glass. "From what I understand, the Council is planning their move on Alchemy."

I set my lips into a tight line. Nothing had looked out of place. *Four days.* Willow's voice bounces around my head. A lot can change in that amount of time, and the fact I could barely get past the topiary garden in the Grove still serves suspicion.

"Did you see anything when you were out?" he asks, glancing at me from the corner of his eye.

"Nothing to suspect the Council has been to Alchemy, but I couldn't get close to Headquarters," I admit. "They've got wards all over the Grove."

Maverick bobs his head. "They've been busy."

I try to stand, stumbling as I push the heavy chair backward, and grip the table to right myself. "I can check again."

Maverick's hand flashes out to grasp my wrist, his warm skin cushioned against mine as he helps steady me. "No. Willow wouldn't be happy if you went back again so soon."

"But I can help!"

He shakes his head and lets go of my arm. "Not this time."

I glare at him, but before I can snap out a response, Willow reappears. "Maverick! We have to go!" There's no mistaking the urgency in her voice.

"What's going on?" I demand, wondering if she'll be as open with me as Maverick had been. She flares her nostrils in an attempt to calm her panic. "The Council's finally made their move, haven't they?" I demand.

She continues to avoid my eye, jaw clenching subtly. "Don't worry about it."

I narrow my eyes, pressing tighter into her skin. "Don't *worry* about it? What happened to *needing* me? Remember when you *begged* me to help? You can't cut me out now."

Willow glances at my fingers, then at Maverick, as if she's trying to gauge his reaction to the situation, but he's his usual calm, cool, collected self.

Her black eyes hardened to flint, as if she's battling her own mind to make a decision.

Why is it so hard for her to decide? Things are so much different now than they had been during the Battle of Mentis.

"I can help," I say. "It won't be like last time."

She stares at me, her shoulders tense, then suddenly, with a slow exhale, she slumps, the fight visibly draining from her. "Okay."

That one simple word fills my heart with warmth and confidence. I would be willing to charge into battle for a lot less. She leads the way out of the foyer and through the purple-plant forest with a rejuvenated sense of purpose. Sabre and Katrina meet us by the Community Villa. The only thing on their minds is the fight ahead. I wish I could be so straightforward, but my mind flicks from Willow to my astral journey, to the battle ahead of us, to the witches on the Council.

I ground myself by focusing on my immediate senses and the world around me. Our group grows as we walk through the Land of New Life. Witches seem to materialize from the shadows to join us, many of whom I've only seen a handful of times before this. The group is formidable, though much smaller than the assembly that charged Mentis. Most of those witches hadn't come back. These are *experienced* fighters who know that going in with anything less than complete dedication can prove deadly.

Zane opens a portal, and one by one, we step through it. In the back of my mind, flashes of normalcy from my astral travels linger, sending a chill of dread crawling down my spine. What will I see now?

In Alchemy, I'm prepared for chaos so the silence is the most unsettling thing I've experienced in a while. Has the battle already come and gone, or could Willow's informant be *wrong*?

Fresh air and foliage. No ash, no blood. I glance at Maverick, but his stoic expression gives nothing away. We shuffle a bit closer to the Coven's border, and that's when the smell hits me—death. It's unmistakable.

"We're too late," Katrina says, and judging by my covenmates' scowls, they smell it too.

"Split up and search for survivors!" Willow commands.

The crowd melts into the shadows, and a knot tightens in my stomach. I don't know many Healers, aside from Ambrossi and Helena, but the thought of finding them dead makes my insides churn. My mind quickly shifts to Lazarus. He's a kind, old man, the mentor to nearly every witch in Alchemy. His wisdom is unmatched. To the Council that could make him a target.

I'm paired with Katrina which is a relief. She's smart and quick on her feet. If we get into trouble, I can depend on her to watch my back. The thick foliage of Alchemy presents its own set of challenges for me, though. My walking stick becomes more of a hindrance than a help as I trip over roots and stumble on hidden twigs. Katrina moves fluidly, alternating between helping me along and scouting ahead, her eyes always scanning the shadows.

Starting with the houses by the border, Katrina and I work our way inward. The first house we enter is empty, clean, and silent, as if the occupants have run out to do some errands. But just because there's no sign of a struggle and no blood doesn't mean a thing.

The bad feeling in my gut is never wrong.

Whatever happened here was quiet, but by no means less severe than the other battles. Katrina and I exchange a glance, as if we're thinking the same thing. The sickening thought hits me that the Council sent assassins here to kill the Healers in their sleep. It's senseless, but so were the explosion spells they used against Mentis. They don't care about casualties. They want to win the war and will do anything to achieve it.

As we move through the darkness, a cold knot of dread tightens in my stomach. Not a single Alchemy witch is in sight. There's no one outside, and the houses we've checked are all empty. The fact that we haven't found a body, alive or dead, only makes the silence more unnerving.

Could all the Healers be dead and their bodies destroyed?

If there *are* survivors, are they hiding under the impression that we're here to finish what the Council started? Anger flashes through me when I remember Quinn, huddled against the wall, crying and assuming we're to blame for the carnage he witnessed. No doubt these witches will blame us, too.

*"That treaty, that godforsaken treaty, hurts us all in some way,"* Quinn had said the day I'd met him.

It certainly does, though I never would've imagined it could hurt like this.

The fourth home we check answers our questions. Death hangs heavy in the air, the way it does in Willow's throne room. Except it's worse here.

It's ripe. *Fresh.*

Lying sprawled on the living room carpet are two bodies. Standing in the door, I step out of the house to catch a lungful of clean air, hoping I don't hurl.

"What is it?" Katrina asks from behind me, her voice grim.

I point into the house, and Katrina steps inside. Reluctantly, I watch her kneel beside the nearest body. Her face twists in disgust then settles into a neutral expression. How often has she been in situations like this? The closer I get, the harder it is to look away from the bodies. Once I overcome my initial shock, I realize the body on the left looks *familiar.* Her skin is purpled and swollen in some places, but there's no mistaking the hair and glasses.

"Flora…" I whisper. The Alchemy Adept. She was shy, sweet, and most importantly, *innocent.* "What happened?" I ask, scanning for wounds without focusing on any one part of her body for too long.

Katrina picks up Flora's tiny wrist. Stroking her thumb over the veins visible beneath her pale skin, she says, "She's been poisoned." She lets Flora's arm fall back to the floor with a *thump*.

"H-how can you tell?"

"That sharpness in the air?" she starts with an exaggerated sniff. "That's nightshade."

The other body belongs to a boy about the same age as Flora, but I don't recognize him. "Him, too?"

"Mm-hmm." Katrina gets up and crosses the room to the cubby shelves filled with herbs. She studies each one and says, "Nightshade isn't a plant she kept."

"I don't think *any* of the Healers do," I remind her. What reason would they have to keep such a potent poison lying around?

A soft thump echoes from the back of the house, cutting off whatever Katrina was about to say. We freeze, both of us paralyzed by the sudden thought of another presence here. Is it one of us or the Council coming back to ensure the Healers are really dead?

I brace myself, expecting a fight, but then a grunt breaks the silence. "Lilith?"

My heart skips a beat. Without thinking, I rush toward the sound, all thoughts of possible danger swept from my mind.

It's Lazarus, and he's alive.

# Chapter Twenty-Five
## Take a Number

THE WHITE WALLS of the hospital wing have become a second home to me. Here, I have Ambrossi and Helena. Everything that should make it feel like Ignis. Except Clio of course. Grief finds its way through my heart, and the usual dark cloud of despair that accompanies thoughts of him passes through my mind. My fists clench, but the two Healers at my side don't notice, and neither does Katrina as she steps into the room.

Lazarus lies on the silver slate of a table as if he's already dead. I don't know what I'm supposed to be looking for, but I'm too hesitant to break the silence and ask. His breath is shallow, slowing with each passing second. No Healer training is needed to see that the poison is winning.

But he's a fighter. It's unnerving, seeing a sick Healer, especially one as powerful as he, who's healed half the witches in the Land of Five at some point. Death is inevitable for all of us, but a voice nags at me that this is *wrong*. He should be able to recover; he should be able to *make* himself better.

"Could you make him throw up?" I suggest to end the agonizing silence.

Helena shakes her head.

"His body has already absorbed a good deal of the poison," Ambrossi explains grimly.

He and Helena move in a burst of synchronized motion, but I remain rooted to the spot. It doesn't matter how many cures for illness a person knows. Poison is different. There are some things all the magic in the world can't fix.

Across the room, Katrina sits, her hands steady as she mixes herbs in a bowl on her lap, following Ambrossi's instructions. Nearby, Helena gathers dried leaves from the cubbies in the wall to pass to Katrina. She looks up at me, expectant, silently urging me to recount what happened back in Alchemy. But the words feel like stones in my throat, heavy and stuck.

Flustered, she joins Katrina in sifting through the leaf mixture. Lazarus' eyelids flutter, but he doesn't move. The faint whisper of my name back in Alchemy was the most he's said. It's possible the movement of his eyes is nothing more than an illusion brought on by the falsehood of hope.

Ambrossi studies Katrina's mixture and mutters a string of unintelligible things as he continues pacing. Of all the patients he's ever had, most likely none of them have been closer to Ambrossi's heart than Lazarus, his mentor. There's a good chance he won't make it. Ambrossi knows this, too, of course, and I can only imagine the struggle to accept that fact.

"Is he going to die?" I finally ask. The room goes silent.

Ambrossi stops pacing. One heartbeat, two heartbeats, and finally he says, "I'm not sure."

That's the expected response, but not what I'd hoped to hear.

"I'll do what I can," he continues. "Don't you worry about that."

I'm not worried in the slightest. A quick glance at my leg is enough to remind me that when it comes to never giving up, he's unmatched. My gaze flicks back to Lazarus, still lifeless on the table, before I follow Ambrossi to stand next to Helena.

"It's wrong. Why attack a Coven full of Healers?" she asks. "They don't hurt anyone. It doesn't make sense."

Katrina scoffs. "Isn't it obvious? The Council will gain the upper hand if they have Healers, and we don't."

It's classic war strategy. The Council took the Healers willing to bow to them and killed those who weren't. If they had chosen to slay every Healer in Alchemy, it would have hurt them just as much. It's a good plan, but there are two important factors the Council didn't take into consideration—we have Healers on hand, too, and witches like Helena, always willing to learn in times of need.

The door bursts open, and everyone stops. Quinn stands in the doorway, face red and good hand clutched to the wall to keep his balance. "Is it true?" he asks, eyes darting wildly from witch to witch.

I'm not sure what he means, so I don't respond, and neither do Helena, Ambrossi, or Katrina. My eyes flick to Lazarus, still lying motionless on the table, and that's when Quinn rushes to his side. He doesn't speak, just stands there, staring at Lazarus with the same intense expression Ambrossi has been wearing for the past half hour. The reaction stuns me. It must hit Helena and Katrina the same way based on how they watch the scene. I had no idea there was any connection between him and Lazarus.

"And the whole Coven is like this?" he asks without looking up.

"Or worse," Katrina replies, shooting me a sideways glance as if she thinks I've got the answers.

"I can't believe they would do this." Quinn clenches his free hand into a fist. "Tricia *knew* Lazarus, and…"

It's crumbling again, his world, and I'm clueless as to how I can help. "They aren't going to get away with this," I assure him, placing my hand on his shoulder.

Eyes red-rimmed and watery, Quinn's face twists more in anger than sadness, as if I had slapped him instead of attempting to comfort him. "Are you kidding? Of course they will. Who's going to stop them? They're destroying entire *Covens* at a time, wiping out hundreds of innocent witches at a snap of the Sage's fingers. No one's stupid enough to say no to that. Isn't it obvious what they're trying to tell us?"

Clenching my jaw, I wait for him to finish speaking.

"Join them or die," he says, licking his lips. "They'll take us all out if they have to."

"It's smart," Katrina agrees. "Who would refuse?" She rubs her chin, flicking away a bit of smashed green pulp that escaped the bowl.

I raise an eyebrow and glance between them, my lip curling. "Us," I say, curling my hands into fists. "*We* will refuse or die trying. That's what this whole thing is about, right?"

"Hopefully, Aens and Aquais will feel that way," Helena says.

"You're strong, Lilith, but not everyone is," Quinn reminds me. "At this point, I don't see that they have a choice. Most of them will side with the Council out of fear. That's what they're betting on."

A muscle twitches in Katrina's jaw, but she remains silent. I can see the storm brewing beneath her calm exterior. She wants her people safe, but the idea of them choosing the Council after everything that's happened clearly eats at her.

"Lilith…" a voice rasps, and it takes a minute for me to understand it came from *Lazarus*.

I shoulder past Quinn and lean toward the elderly witch, clutching the silver railing on the side of the bed to get as close to him as possible. "I'm here, Lazarus. What is it?"

"Lynx… his powers…" He gasps, struggling against his own lungs to speak.

My mind fills with static as I try to process his words. Why would he be thinking of someone who isn't here? And an *enemy* at that?

"What about him?"

"His magic is special," he rasps. "It… it can heal… b-but it… comes at… a price." His sentence is followed by an immediate coughing fit.

"A price?"

His glossy gaze focuses, and he opens his mouth, but instead of words, a horrific gurgle echoes up his throat. He collapses back to the table, head lolling to the side.

Helena grasps Lazarus' wrist, probing his skin. Face drawn tight, she says, "He's dead."

## Chapter Twenty-Six
### The Catless Witch

HELENA HAS ALWAYS been smarter than me. This situation gives her another opportunity to prove that fact. As soon as the knowledge of Lazarus' death sinks in, she bolts out the door, leaving the rest of us to stare at each other, dumbfounded. She reappears with Willow at her side a few minutes later, and Maverick trails behind, his face as grim as the rest of ours.

No one speaks, but their thoughts race through the room, a thousand whispers a minute. I wish I could block it all out. Helena guides my sister to Lazarus' body. Willow is the only one who appears calm. She has to be, both for herself and for us. With graceful steps, she moves toward Lazarus' table, her gaze fixed on his face. Her lips are set in a straight line, cold and unreadable, but when I catch the slightest glimpse of her eyes, there's a flicker of sadness. This isn't easy for her. Even with her gift, seeing death still hurts.

"Everyone, step back," Maverick commands, extending his arm as if we'd do anything to disrupt what's happening.

Willow lifts her hands, rubs them together, then places them on Lazarus' chest, as if she's about to press all her weight on him. They stay like that for a long moment.

Nothing happens.

The black pits of her irises flicker purple, burning into the same shade of bright white enveloping her skin. It flows from her core and down her arms. When it connects with Lazarus' chest, a whisper rises, not unlike the rush of voices I couldn't block earlier. Slowly, the light spreads through Lazarus' body, engulfing him in a veil similar to Willow's aura. The light grows brighter and brighter, swelling to engulf them both.

Then it disappears with a *pop*.

Willow doesn't move, so I watch Lazarus. What I'm expecting, I don't know, but I'm disappointed when nothing happens. His body remains pale and still. Willow's lack of response doesn't give away any clues, either, as she hovers over his body. When I finally make the decision to pick Willow's mind for information, Lazarus sits bolt upright as if someone poked him with something sharp.

Willow steps backward, and Lazarus gasps for air with such force, I feel as if he's taking my soul with him. His head swivels from side to side, glazed eyes flickering about the room like he doesn't see any of us. Maybe he *can't*.

Willow takes one more step away, a faint hint of the glow still rising from her skin. When the light fades from her eyes, she collapses in a heap of blue dress and brown hair. Maverick and Helena rush to her side, while Ambrossi whispers soothing words to Lazarus. Katrina and I remain in place, the odd ones out. When Katrina moves toward Lazarus, I take the cue to approach my sister.

"Is she okay?" I ask, dropping to my knees beside Willow.

Maverick wipes a strand of hair from her face and says, "She'll be fine. The process takes a toll on her."

Helena sits back on her haunches, looking relieved. She

stands to check Lazarus, mumbling words of encouragement to him, then approaches me. Her exhaustion is apparent. Willow isn't the only one affected by healing.

"Go get some fresh air, Lilith," she says. "We've got this."

Who am I to argue?

FRESH AIR DOESN'T help much as the minutes pass by gradually stretching into hours with no news. The scene plays on a loop in my head, and I can't make it stop. I'm glad Lazarus will be okay, but I can't stop picturing Willow's crumpled form on the floor. If it's *that* exhausting to save a single life, how long can she possibly manifest her gift? Could it one day end up *killing* her?

*Can someone die if they're already dead?* I ponder this, then pinch the bridge of my nose. I'm in no place to try solving that one.

Resting my chin on my knees, I stare out across the field. I feel restless, but I don't know what to do with myself. I want to go back to the hospital wing to help, but I'd only be in the way. Kado barks excitedly and drops a stick at my feet. Half-heartedly, I toss it again, watching him tear across the field to intercept it. I'm grateful for the zombie dog's company and the fact that I can always count on him to be here for me. It's a shame he can't talk, though. I've tried, more than once, to read his mind, but there's nothing to find.

"Hey, you all right?" Helena calls across the field.

I lift my chin to see her approach. When she sits down beside me, I reply, "I'm fine. How are Willow and Lazarus?"

Helena exhales softly, leaning back as she crosses her legs.

"Willow recovered about an hour ago, and Lazarus is as expected."

I envision several possible meanings of this, but I don't point that out.

"Lazarus will have to be kept in the hospital wing for at least a week now that he's… well, you know."

He has an adjustment to make. Physically and emotionally. Nodding slowly, I ask, "What's it like?"

Helena lets out a small chuckle as if she's surprised by the question. "What? Dying?"

"Yes." I can still picture my parents' deaths. As much as I want to believe that they didn't suffer, I can't be sure.

"It's peaceful," Helena says. I'm not sure if that's the truth, or if she can sense my worry and is pacifying me. "With any luck, Lazarus won't remember it happened."

It's hard to believe anyone could forget their own *death*, but Willow had mentioned a similar phenomenon. Shrugging I say, "Hopefully."

Kado pads toward us, breaking the moment, and drops his stick at my feet. He lets out a joyful yip, tail wagging furiously when he spots Helena.

Her eyes glaze over as she reaches out to pet the fluffy fur on his head. "Seems you too get along well now."

"Yeah. He's great," I say, hardly remembering my initial standoffishness.

"Pets always are," she says thoughtfully as she sits back, folding her hands in her lap. "I miss Lexi." Lexi, Helena's silver and black cat who spent many nights curled up in my lap.

I nod, the ache in her voice making my heart tighten. "I

can't imagine."

Helena tucks a strand of red hair behind her ear, her eyes faraway. "Maybe I can find her one day."

I hesitate. The weight of something unsaid hangs between us. "Helena, you know you can't… go home."

The mask she wore in the hospital wing breaks. "I know. I don't know why I said that. I guess I'm feeling a bit homesick."

"Me too," I admit.

"The survivors… they think I'm dead, don't they?"

I nod stiffly. No need for words here.

She doesn't ask anymore questions, and I don't volunteer the information. Ignis may be rebuilding, but the Coven as we once knew it, is gone. Our classmates, our Elders. So many familiar faces have been lost forever.

Helena and I sit with Kado for a while until Willow eventually summons me. Her black eyes are wide, almost swallowing me whole, as if I could get lost in their depths. "Alchemy is gone," she says, her voice barely a whisper.

I've already guessed as much from the bit Katrina and I scouted, but the confirmation makes it worse. "How many dead?"

"More than those who are missing," she replies.

"How many do you think the Council took?"

"Less than half," she says. "Judging by how many witches are still there."

I grimace.

"Come on." Willow grasps my hand. "I need to hold a Coven meeting."

I follow her, the weight of the news pressing on my shoulders as we head to the conference room. Once inside, she calls her Coven close, her voice steady as she addresses those who love and adore her. When she announces the destruction of another Coven, there's no shock in the Elementals' faces. Only the quiet understanding of those who've seen too much loss. For the witches from Alchemy, their pain is raw and immediate.

"We need to return to Alchemy," she says, after a moment of silence. "Gather any witches we can find."

That brings me a bit of hope for Flora. Maybe they'll find her, revive her, and she can live on as a Reanimate. I let that hope burn bright in my chest, clinging to it like a lifeline through the rest of the night, keeping me warm where otherwise I might've frozen in despair.

WITCHES KNOCKING ON my door in the middle of the night is becoming a regular occurrence. This time, Kado gets up for me. I watch him hop on his hind legs and use the side of his paw to twist the knob.

"Thank you, Kado," I call, using my telekinesis to pull open the door.

Quinn stands in the hallway. He seems confused to find Kado at the threshold instead of a person, then he looks up and sees me. "Lilith."

"Quinn." His sudden appearance is both surprising and somehow overdue. Willow hadn't given me the chance to talk to him earlier, to ask him how he knows Lazarus so I'm glad the opportunity has presented itself. I sit up, gathering my blankets in my lap. "Are you okay?"

"I was at the Coven meeting," he states. By his tone, it's

clear he has no interest in social pleasantries. "Was Alchemy... it was as bad as Willow says, wasn't it?"

I let out a slow breath, not wanting to sugarcoat it. "Probably worse, actually."

Quinn's expression tightens as he shuts the door and leans against the doorframe, eyes shadowed with something hard to place. "Lazarus is pretty hurt by the whole thing."

"Don't tell him too much right now," I say. "Let him heal first."

"Why? He already knows what happened. He was *there*, Lilith," Quinn points out.

He's got me there.

"Still, I don't think reminding him is the best move right now."

"You're probably right," he says and stares at the wall. Emotions flicker over his face, fluctuating between anger and grief as if he can't quite decide which one he feels more. Which one he *should* feel more.

"She's dead to me, you know." When my brow furrows, he continues, "Tricia. I don't know if she did this but... to stand by the people doing this to her friends and family? It's unforgivable. After what happened to Mentis, I tried to talk myself through it. I came up with every excuse to justify what she's done, but there *is* no justifying it. She's a monster. For her to not miss me? To not care whether I'm safe or not? To not care about her *entire* Coven? No other words can describe her."

He's right, but pointing it out won't do either of us any good. I glance at the empty spot on the bed beside me, then back at him. "Need to sit down?"

He nods, his voice quiet. "Yes, thank you." He moves toward me, his footsteps slow, and the bed creaks under his weight.

I watch him settle in before I ask, "How do you know Lazarus so well?"

"Tricia," he says, nearly choking on her name. "Lazarus would bring Lavina whatever herbs she needed every two weeks, and Ray—*she* would escort him."

"I'm sorry, Quinn," I murmur and ball the blanket in my fists, wishing I could come up with something better to say. Really though, nothing I can say will help him work through the ache of betrayal. That's something he's going to have to come to terms with on his own.

"I can't believe my sister could hurt so many witches. Is it…" Quinn's voice falters. "Is it *wrong* that I hope she fails in one of her missions? That she experiences a portion of what she's put everyone else through?"

"Not at all," I assure him.

Quinn's bottom lip trembles, and his gaze drops, like he's teetering on the edge of another breakdown. I can see the battle in his eyes between his beliefs and the anger that's threatening to consume him.

"One day, she'll pay for what she's done," I tell him, almost a promise. If I ever see her again, it won't be pretty. "You can't put that much grief into the world and not expect some of it to find its way back to you."

"Yeah," Quinn says, but there's little conviction in his voice. "But I can't help wishing she'd understand that what she's done is wrong. I guess that's a fool's errand, though. Monsters don't ever see themselves as monsters."

I stay quiet, letting him vent. At this point, it'll help him more than any medicine could.

## Chapter Twenty-Seven
### Special Powers

WILLOW SENDS A new recovery group to Alchemy every day, the previous group almost always unwilling to return after witnessing the carnage firsthand. Only a handful of witches have been brought back so far, and I'm counting the days until Flora is one of them. The Elementals seem to be prioritizing witches with family ties among their ranks. Flora, apart from Lazarus and me, doesn't appear to have anyone here who knows her. So I wait, filling the days with Aens and Alchemy training. Astral trips are limited with Maverick keeping an eye on me.

When Lazarus is cleared from emergency care, Helena informs me that he's been placed in the same room as Quinn. As I enter, both pairs of eyes flick to me in relief, as if they dread the idea of anyone else coming to see them. To Lazarus, I ask, "How are you feeling? We haven't had a chance to talk since…" The rest of the sentence hangs in the air, and I'm unsure of the best way to finish it.

Lazarus holds up a weathered hand. "Lilith, we have a conversation to finish."

I nod anxiously as Lazarus asks Quinn for time alone. Quinn hesitates for a moment, then agrees and steps out. Now it's me and the elderly Healer in the tiny hospital room.

"You mentioned Lynx and his powers," I offer. During

my time on the Council, I hadn't talked to Lynx much, but his background is the one I've been the most invested in. With his ability to heal magical damage, a feat no other witch has done, I have a selfish interest.

Lazarus nods. "When he was my apprentice, he was very quick with his hands and his mind. He could memorize the poultice recipes after one glance at the formula. Originally, I thought that was his power. I believe he thought so, too."

"So how did he figure out what he can really do?"

"There was a fight. A boundary skirmish between Alchemy and Aquais. Some of the witches came into the Coven to steal herbs, I think. Well, Lynx's job has always been his life. He fought to keep every scrap of medicine we had. The attackers fled, but on their way out, they attacked every witch they could. Flora was one of the unfortunate victims."

Hearing Flora's name brings to mind the image of her corpse. "She had to have been—"

"Young?" Lazarus guesses. "She was. Lynx was overwrought. Here was this little girl, surrounded by Healers, yet no one could do a thing to help her because the damage had been done with magic. Lynx. If there's one thing I can say about him, it's that he doesn't give up. He rushed in when no one else would, told her to hold on, to keep breathing. Even *I* was sure she was dead, but then… she wasn't. He *touched* her, and the wound was healed. I couldn't believe it."

I still can't. "That doesn't particularly sound like a fault."

"You didn't let me finish," Lazarus says. "Flora came back, but she lost her powers."

At the Arcane Ceremony, she hadn't shown any signs of

weakness or doubt. Her healing had been flawless, and it's hard for me to grasp that she did all of that completely UnEquipped.

I must look as confused as I feel, because he decides to explain more.

"She used to be able to make plants grow at her command. To *control* them. When Lynx healed her, that ability disappeared."

*Stripped him of his powers,* Willow had said about Larc. Raya had mentioned a similar phenomenon happening to my adopted father, Haze. Had they encountered the same witch or others? How many gifts have the same awful consequences? Does the Sage know about this side effect of Lynx's magic? Is that the real reason for her keeping him on such a strict leash, or is it for more nefarious purposes?

"She was still the Adept," I say in awe.

"She studied hard after it happened. No one had the heart to tell her to stop trying," Lazarus says with fondness. "She was brilliant. Until… well, you know."

Unfortunately, I do. She worked her way up to Alchemy's Adept just to be brutally murdered. "It's not fair."

Lazarus' smile is bitter. "That's the thing about it. Rarely do we actually get the things we deserve or desire. What's the old saying? 'Only the good die young.'"

If that's true, if only the good die young, what does it say about me, the only one of my friends who *hasn't* died yet despite having a massive target on my forehead?

The door opens, revealing Quinn and Helena in the hall. "The recovery team is back," she says. "They've got Flora."

A weight lifts from my shoulders. "I've got to go," I say to Lazarus and follow Helena, hobbling along as fast as I can.

I catch up with her as soon as she reaches the main door of the hospital wing. Inside one of the bigger rooms are five beds and four bodies, but I only recognize two of them—Flora and the boy who's laid out beside her.

Willow comes in behind us, her gaze running over each witch. It's not so easy for me to take my eyes off Flora when I remember all Lazarus had said about her.

"These are the ones from today's search, ma'am," Helena announces.

Willow bobs her head, gaze settling on the boy who died beside Flora.

"Willow," I say and grab the railing of Flora's bed. The girl in it looks so small, as if she's an infant wrapped in swaddling blankets. "Can she be first?"

Willow's face softens. She asks no questions as she takes her place beside me. Purple glows in her eyes, and I take a step back as she circles the bed, standing in front of the shortest rail. She lays her hands on Flora's chest and repeats the steps she did when she brought Lazarus back.

When Willow collapses, I catch her, cradling her a foot off the ground. I glance up at Flora's bed, but from this angle, I don't see any movement. Gently, I lay Willow on the ground and force myself to stand. Flora lies still, head slumped to the side. Her chest doesn't move, and when I place my fingers on her neck, I feel no pulse.

Helena's eyes widen. I hold my breath, staring at Flora, willing her to prove me wrong, to spring to life with a sudden, miraculous movement.

But she doesn't.

A groan comes from the floor, and I drop down to Willow's level. Helena takes a cautious step closer, eyes bouncing between Willow and Flora, as if she's not sure which issue to address first.

"Get Maverick," I order. He needs to be here if for nothing more than to support and comfort Willow.

Helena dashes off to find him.

"Lily," Willow croaks, sounding as if she's just woken up. She sits upright and cradles her head in her hands. Her skull pulses in agony. I can feel it even without trying to tap into her thoughts, and now I understand the resurgence physically *hurts* her.

"It's okay," I whisper and try to help her stand.

She sways for a moment, her hands gripping my upper arms for balance. When her eyes land on Flora, she drops her hands from me to the silver bed railing, squeezing with such force, the tips are an alarming shade of blue. "It didn't work," she whispers, her voice trembling.

I move around the bed, trying to stand between her and Flora, but she doesn't react. "It didn't work!" she shouts, her voice breaking.

I flinch.

"W-why didn't it work?" Her words hit me like a punch, and I'm left staring, utterly dumbfounded.

Helena re-enters, followed by a winded Maverick. Face flushed from exertion, his eyes flick to the confusion on Willow's face, and without a word, he pulls her into his arms. She lets him, but her body stays rigid, her hands outstretched as if ready to grab hold of anything that gets too close.

Maverick's hand gently rests on the side of her head.

"Hey, hey," he murmurs, then looks at me and Flora. *What happened?* he mouths.

I glance quickly from Flora to Willow, and his gaze follows, understanding dawning on him as the gravity of the situation settles in.

"This has never happened before," Willow says, her voice devoid of emotion. She looks at Flora's bed one more time as if she thinks the girl's playing games with her. "Why didn't it work?" she asks in the smallest voice I've ever heard her use. She sounds so helpless, so *defeated.*

They're *all* clueless—Maverick, Helena, and Willow—but I feel an itch in the back of my mind and *hear* the story Lazarus told me. The warning. "There's something I should probably tell you."

All three pairs of eyes turn to me.

"Lazarus shared a secret with me about Flora. She was UnEquipped when I met her, but… not always." Helena pales more than usual, but no one says anything, so I continue. "You've all heard of Lynx's ability to heal magical damage? Well, *she* was the one he saved. When he did, she lost her powers."

"You think that's why—" Maverick stops, choosing to look at Flora's body rather than say the words out loud.

"It's a possibility," Helena offers. "There's no telling what side effects the magic could've had."

Willow wipes her eyes, but the information doesn't seem to make her feel any better. "I suppose that makes sense," she says in an apparent attempt at sounding strong as she pushes away from Maverick. As this Coven's leader, she feels the need to portray strength at all times, but she sounds numb, *lost.* "I think I should be alone for a while," she adds in a voice made of glass and moves toward the door, Maverick on her heels. He'll do what he can to bring her comfort. That brings me some peace.

"Wait!" I call, and Willow pauses to look at me.

Maverick shoots me a bitter glance, as if I'm some sadist who takes pleasure in making my sister suffer.

"Can you try your magic on one more person?"

"Lilith!" Maverick snaps.

I ignore him. "Consider it an experiment."

Willow waves him off. Her expression belies her desperation to see if she still *can* bring anyone back to life. "Let's do it."

I point at the boy. "I'm pretty sure, he died beside Flora. If anyone can help us understand what's happened, it's him."

"Good idea," she says and approaches his bed.

Maverick remains near the door, but his glare feels like a brand, burning into the side of my face. I refuse to let it bother me. If this works, it'll be more cathartic for Willow than whatever he had planned for her. I step back to where Maverick is, giving her space.

He huffs. "You don't know when to quit, do you?"

I tilt my head, meeting his eyes. "When I'm an optimist, you complain. When I'm a pessimist, you complain. How do I win?"

He smirks. "Smartass."

I smirk right back at him as the purple light flares to white in Willow's eyes. The boy glows with it, and a minute later, Willow collapses to the floor. The next thirty seconds drag with unreal slowness. I don't move. Maverick doesn't move. It's like time has frozen, broken only by the sharp intake of air from the boy on the table.

"Get Lazarus," I tell Helena.

Her tiny footsteps hardly make a sound as she dashes from the room.

Willow doesn't rouse herself from her second faint, and Maverick scoops her into his arms. "I'll put her to bed."

"Thank you."

When Maverick exits the room with Willow, Helena enters with Lazarus. He looks frail, tottering behind her, but he doesn't notice my concerned looks as he approaches the boy.

"Alpine," he says.

The boy stares at him as if seeing a ghost. "Lazarus," he manages in a broken whisper.

Lazarus pulls him into a hug, and I recognize that gesture—the same powerful embrace Helena gave me during the vigil for the witches lost in the Battle of Ignis.

When they pull apart, Alpine clings onto Lazarus' robe. "Where am I?"

"You're safe," Lazarus assures him, using my typical, noncommittal approach to such a dangerous question.

Alpine presses his lips together as if he doesn't believe him. "Where's Flora?"

Lazarus is silent. We're *all* silent.

"They're all dead, aren't they?" he ventures.

I step closer. When Alpine looks at me, I find recognition behind his eyes. And why not? Half the Land of Five knows who I am thanks to the Council.

"What happened to Flora?" I ask softly.

His eyes go *darker* if that's possible. "The poison didn't work on her," he chokes out. "So, they… tortured her. Nothing they tried worked until…" The black pools of his eyes glitter as if he's about to cry. If he was still alive, his face would most likely already be soaked in tears. "They used telekinesis to… to keep the air out of her lungs until she…" A sob rises from his throat.

Lazarus sets a strong, reassuring hand on Alpine's shoulder, and Helena approaches, grasping the bed's railing. "Come on," she says to Alpine. "Let's get you to your own room so you can get some rest."

She's careful to block his view of the bodies on the other beds. Lazarus catches on, and I take a few steps to the side to help as they push Alpine into the hall. Alone again, my eyes stray back to Flora. For a fraction of a second, I envy Alpine. I wish there was someone to shield *me* from the carnage, too.

## Chapter Twenty-Eight
### 'Til Death

WHEN NIGHT FALLS, the weight of the day's events makes it hard to rest. I barely get any sleep and wake up to face what's sure to be another difficult day. A gloomy feeling lingers, but it fits with the challenges today will bring.

A funeral. Here. In the Land of New Life.

It's as depressing as it sounds. The entire Coven stands among the purple plants. In the center of the clearing, a small sheet marks the spot where Flora lies. I can't help but stare at it, fighting the urge to picture her wrapped inside, but the way the fabric clings to her leaves little to the imagination.

Willow speaks from her place beside the open hole a few of the Elementals dug this morning. Flora's final resting place though they don't have a graveyard in the normal sense. No tombstones, no rows of markers. Instead, they have a memorial plot where witches leave photos of the ones they've lost. No bodies were buried there though.

Flora is the first.

Willow wears a long, white gown, her dark tangles of hair pulled back into a simple ponytail. She looks neither at the pit nor at the girl beside it. Her back is to me, to *all* of it. I don't have to see her face to know she's still thinking about failing in bringing her back. Most likely it will always haunt her.

"…but Alchemy will not be forgotten and neither will Flora," she says when I tune back in.

Across the field, the Reanimates are gathered. Three new faces have joined the group from Alchemy—Alpine, Cheryl, and Rosyln. I avoid looking Alpine in the eyes. Cheryl is an older woman with a hefty frame, an angular face, and layered red hair, while Rosyln, her opposite, is a petite teenager with a rounded face and sleek, brunette hair. I haven't said a word to either of them, though Willow told me they're both Equipped. Cheryl can control plant growth, like Flora once could, and Rosyln has the ability to talk to animals. I'm impressed by both of them.

I haven't heard what Alpine can do. I'm hesitant to ask for fear of Willow or Helena taking me to speak to him. I've managed to avoid him since Willow brought him back, and life's easier that way. He'll always have a tie to Flora in my mind, and judging by the curious look in some of the other Elementals' eyes, they're filled with the same thoughts.

Before the ceremony, Willow had tried to comfort me by telling me they *have* indeed had funerals in the past, but I don't believe her. Even if I did, this funeral should never have happened. Flora is young, and newly deceased. The formula perfect for reanimation.

When Willow finishes her eulogy, a few Reanimates lower Flora's body into her grave. One at a time, Alchemy witches take a handful of dirt and drop it into the pit, covering the sheet. When the scattered earth has piled too high to make out the human form beneath, I add my own handful. The soil slips through my fingers to join the others in the growing mound.

"I'm sorry, Flora."

## Chapter Twenty-Nine
### The Informant

THE REST OF the day drags on after Flora's funeral, and I'm relieved when it's finally time for bed, eager to leave it all behind. But when I wake up to find Maverick and Helena standing by my bed, I know today won't be any easier. I wipe the sleep from my eyes and sit up quickly. "What's going on?"

"Making sure you're okay," Maverick says.

I translate it to: *Want to make sure you're not going to sleep the day away again.*

"I'm fine," I say, irritated because I *had* considered trying to go to the astral plane to see Alchemy again and count how many witches are left.

"Let's get some breakfast," Helena says, her voice surprisingly upbeat. How does she manage that? After Flora's funeral, even the thought of eating feels like a chore.

"Okay," I agree, too tired to argue, and they help me to my feet.

Helena follows me into the bathroom, and Maverick waits outside with Kado. She helps me dress and brushes my hair, then we all head to the Community Villa, Kado trailing closely behind. Willow is already there, an appetizing breakfast spread out on the table. Helena helps me into a chair and sits beside me. We dig in as Maverick excuses himself and follows Willow out of the room.

"Is something going on?" I ask Helena after swallowing a large mouthful of eggs.

"They're worried about Ignis," she says.

"Why? Ignis has already been hit. Shouldn't they focus on Aens and Aquais?"

"I don't actually know much about their reasons for it. I've only read their fears."

My hands clench into fists, and I stare down at the remaining food on my plate, losing all interest in it. "If the Council knows Ignis is rebuilding, they might want to wipe out those who are left to make a point." It wouldn't surprise me if the Council decided to kick a Coven when they were at their lowest point. "Does she have a way to warn them?" I ask and consider taking the astral trip after all. I don't know how to breach the veil and communicate with witches I see in my non-corporeal form, but I'm willing to try.

Helena bites her lip. "I think so. She sends witches to check in a few times a week."

What would it take to get added to her list?

Helena must see something in my eyes because she says, "If you go back, I want to too."

"Helena," I begin, cautious.

"I know, I know," she interrupts, rolling her eyes. "You're worried, but if we ever get the chance to go back, wouldn't it be good for them to know I'm alive? We don't have to tell them about the reanimation."

Without it, it's still clear something has happened to her. No one would believe otherwise. I've found myself once again in a delicate situation even though I'm no good at handling these.

How does this keep happening? "You can't forget," I say, "some of them saw you die. If we explain how you came back, we'll have to explain everything—Willow, the Elementals. We can't risk that getting into the wrong hands."

Helena runs a hand through her long, red hair, her frustration obvious. "You're right."

I can't bring myself to look at her, to see the emotion behind her eyes. "It's dangerous, anyway."

"How much of Ignis do you think is still standing?"

My astral trips have given me more than enough knowledge to make a guess, but I decide to lie. I'm not sure how much she knows about my ability. "I don't know. I've been gone the same amount of time as you."

The light in her eyes dims, and I take that to mean she believes me. "Do you think my parents survived?" she asks hesitantly, as if she's scared of my answer. "Or Lexi?"

I don't want to break her down, to leave her bleak and cynical like me, but her parents, being UnEquipped, stood as much of a chance in battle as mine had. And I doubt her cat made it out of the battle when most of our fellow witches hadn't.

"Why don't we *see* how bad Ignis is for ourselves?" Willow asks as she strolls into the room, thankfully saving me from answering.

Helena's face draws tight, her eyes squinting slightly. My face probably looks similar to hers.

Willow doesn't look put out by our lack of enthusiasm. "My informant has something we need to hear."

Maverick and Katrina emerge behind her as I ask, "Who's the informant?"

"You'll see in a bit, but we need to move if we're going to make it before sundown," Willow replies.

"Okay," I say and wipe my face. I go to pick up my plate and clean the mess Helena and I made from engorging ourselves when Willow stops me.

"We'll get someone to clean that up. Come on."

I hesitate, side-eyeing Helena. "Is… this such a good idea?"

Helena draws her eyebrows together. "I'm fine with it, Lily. You don't have to worry about me."

It's not her I'm worried about, it's the other witches. "What if someone in Ignis sees her?"

Willow tips her head, looking thoughtful. "It's a risk we've got to take," she says. "I need a Healer on hand, and Ambrossi has too many witches in his care right now so…"

"What about Laura? Can't she tap in?" I ask, increasingly more desperate now that I see the situation is slipping out of my control.

"I can handle it," Helena assures me, less upbeat and more aggravated.

"Come on," Willow says and starts to cross the room. "No time to waste."

My eyes volley from Willow to Helena and back again. I'm outnumbered in my concern. Reluctantly, I say, "Okay," and grab my walking stick, listening to it *thump* against the floor as I stand.

I'm not entirely sold on this trip. Heading out in daylight feels like a mistake. Willow glances over her shoulder, her long brown hair falling in front of her face. When our eyes meet, I can't help but blurt out, "You really think we can all slip into Ignis without being noticed?”

“We’ve done it before.”

That doesn’t make the trip any less dangerous. But she probably has her reasons. As the leader of the Elemental Coven, she knows more about strategy than I ever will.

*Have faith,* I tell myself.

Willow issues commands to Maverick, and I fall back. Helena and I are the only ones new to this, the only ones who don’t know what we’re doing. Maverick and Katrina are reliable. They won’t let us crash and burn. The problem lies with me. I need to learn to trust in a world designed to make that impossible.

“This is huge,” Helena whispers, eyes wide. She seems so small, so *innocent,* as she trots at my side, but she has that way about her. “What do you think they’re going to tell us?”

There’s no telling what news the “informant” could have and why Willow wants *us* of all the Elementals to hear it.

*Does it have to do with Clio?* A small part of me wonders.

Briefly, I prod Helena’s mind. She’s in the process of sorting through her memories of Ignis, both the good and the bad. The battle that killed her seems to be locked away for now.

That leaves me to wonder how *I* should feel.

“No idea,” I say finally, but it’ll be good to be home again. *Or what’s left of it, anyway.*

“Yeah. I can’t wait to see my parents again,” she says, twitching her button nose.

If her parents didn’t make it through the fight, it’ll devastate her. On the other hand, if they *are* alive, it would be in Helena’s interest to stay away. If they know she’s alive, they’ll want her to come home. If she goes back, the Council will capture her for information about the Elementals.

I open my mouth to voice those thoughts, but Helena seems to sense what I'm going to say. "I need to know," she says firmly, her eyes on the path ahead.

*That* I can understand.

Silence falls over our group as we zigzag through the purple plants, lost in our memories. I'm not sure whether Helena read my thoughts of Clio or not, but if she did, she doesn't comment on it. Zane opens the portal, and I follow the others through the strange, wavering air.

On the other side, water burbles from somewhere up ahead, and I recognize the creek leading into Mentis. I almost expect to take the same route Crowe led me down once upon a time, but Willow veers left, heading straight into the heart of Ignis, leaving me once again uncertain.

Beside me, Helena nearly buzzes with excited energy, but I can't match her level. My heart thumps with trepidation. The last time I stood here, it was amidst the chaos of war.

I feel sick every time Clio's face crosses my mind.

After a while of walking, Willow stops and gathers us all with a wave of a hand into a haphazard circle around her. "This isn't going to be easy," she says, "and if we're going to be successful, we'll need to split up."

My stomach twists into a knot. "I'm sorry. Did you say *split up*? I thought you wanted me to hear what your informant had to say," I say, caught somewhere between hurt and disbelief. "You made me come all this way."

"Tarj can't stay away too long. If anyone notices his disappearance, they'll trace it back to us. I can't risk that. Our best chance is to have a crew nearby, ready to swoop in if anything goes wrong. You're here because you're the most trusted witches I've got. If I can't rely on you, then I can't trust anyone."

That's a lot of information to process in thirty seconds. "*Tarj* is our spy?"

Willow's eyes darken as if she's unsure how much more she should say.

"How long?" I ask. Iris. The attack on the Arcane Ceremony. My mind races through everything that's happened, trying to make sense of it all in the light of this revelation.

"Long enough."

"Iris *died*," I say crossly. I'd been such a naïve witch then, living with the impression she was a radical, that she was *crazy*. But she made me rethink the world. Rethink *myself.* "Tarj was the executioner!"

Willow tosses a clump of brown hair over her shoulder. "We don't really have time to talk about this right now."

"Did you bring her back?" I demand, hoping she'll offer a deeper explanation for all that's happened.

"Lilith," Maverick says, trying to distract me.

I wave him away, not taking my eyes off Willow. "Tell me you brought her back."

She lets out a deep breath that seems to come all the way from her belly. "No. I didn't."

"*No?*"

"The plan was for Tarj to let her go during the night, but Iris wanted to do something different. She wanted to leave an impression."

"She *chose* to be *killed?*" I ask, unable to believe what I'm hearing.

"She thought it would have the greatest impact."

"And Tarj was okay with that?"

"No. No, he was not. But that's the nature of the beast. War can make you do some pretty ugly things, and things got out of hand quick."

"You don't say."

"Before you ask, I never meant for you to join the Council," she admits, "but Tarj needed to step down, and after what happened with Iris, he was emotionally shot. To save him, another Ignis representative had to be chosen. We never expected you to jump in the way you did to save him. We hoped someone else would, someone who didn't matter to us as much. Once word of your bravery spread through the Land of Five, we couldn't pull the wool over everyone's eyes and steal you away in the night."

Tears burn in the corners of my eyes. Maybe this time it would've been better if I kept my mouth shut.

"Any more questions?" Willow asks, eyebrow raised, as if daring me to challenge her again.

It won't help anyone to drag this out. The longer we stay here, the more we risk being caught. Clenching my teeth, I say, "No."

It's hard to miss the relief in Willow's eyes. "You and Helena stay close to the portal," she says, dismissing me as if this conversation never happened. "Take note of what you see and keep your senses alert in case we need your help."

# Chapter Thirty
## Everything that Glitters is Not Gold

HELENA LEADS THE way across Ignis' dry, cracked soil. I glance back, watching the distant silhouettes of Willow, Katrina, and Maverick fade into the haze. Despite Willow's reassurances, doubt gnaws at me. The last time I split from someone in Ignis was Clio.

Ignis still bears the signs of battle—scorched trees, and the rubble left from where buildings had once stood.

Helena slows ahead of me, and when I catch up to her, the corners of her lips are pulled down. We see the same corpse of Ignis, but where it fills me with rage, it's left her wary. "This is hard," she whispers, blinking to keep the tears she can never shed at bay. "B-being here… seeing this."

"I know." I resist reminding her that I *warned* her it would be like this. She's going through enough.

We keep walking, and her foot scuffs over a patch of bloody sand. I stare at it, wondering if it came from someone I know. The closer we get to our old stomping grounds, the more Helena starts to slow, eventually coming to a halt.

I face her, confused. "What's wrong?" I ask. She was so sure about coming here, but now she's hesitating.

Her black eyes stare at me, and I know if she could, she'd cry. "Just tell me… are my parents still alive?"

I put my hand on her back. I haven't seen them, but her

house is still standing which is promising. "I think so."

She pulls me into a hug, burying her face in my shoulder. "Thank you," she says. "I don't know what I'd do without you."

My shoulders slump as I stroke her bright red hair. I wish I could take away her pain, but I can hardly get past my own. I don't mention that I need her as much as she needs me.

She sniffles when we pull apart. "I guess we should find somewhere to wait."

"Clio's house is near here," I remind her. As far as I know, it's still standing too. She nods, and we walk in silence for less than a mile before it comes into view. My heart thuds in my chest, a fresh wave of anxiety rising. I'm ready to rip through every inch of his house, searching for any clue of where he might be.

A soft *meow* echoes through the silence, stopping us in our tracks.

"Did you hear that?" I ask, not wanting to say *what* I've heard until I'm one-hundred percent sure I haven't lost my mind. We may be in Ignis, but we're not close to Helena's old house, so it makes no sense to see a familiar, silver-and-black-striped cat running toward us from the shrubs.

"Lexi?" Helena says in disbelief, dropping to her knees to coax her feline forward.

If I'd been physically capable, I probably would do the same. The cat's pace slows, and she lifts a paw, meowing again.

"It's okay," Helena encourages, but the cat doesn't come closer.

She shakes and shimmers, in much the same way as Crowe during a transformation. Helena stumbles backward, eyes wide. By the time she scrambles to her feet, Lexi isn't a cat anymore.

She's a *woman*.

I can't move. I forget how to even breathe. The woman holds up a shaking hand, clearly as upset by the situation as we are. "Please, I mean you no harm," she starts, as if reading my thoughts that designate her as such. When neither Helena nor I speak, she continues, "I'm so sorry to deceive you, Helena, but let me formally introduce myself. I'm not a cat. I'm a witch. My name is Ivy."

"You're a shifter," Helena notes

Ivy nods, scattering her long, curly black hair. "Among other things."

Helena, clueless but always considerate, doesn't hesitate to hand her cloak to the shivering woman, once again proving her ability to think on her feet. Meanwhile, my mind feels like it's stuck in a void, teetering on the edge of shutting down. *Ivy*. My knees give out when I finally put two and two together. I hit the ground, hardly registering the impact.

"Are you okay?" she asks, running to my side. Her hands hover helplessly in the air above me as if she thinks about trying to help me stand but is scared of coming too close.

"No," I choke out, studying her familiar blue eyes. *My eyes.*

"Li, who is this woman?" Helena asks, baffled.

My fingers dig into the dirt, the answer gurgling in my stomach like bile. One look into Ivy's mind offers all the confirmation I need. "She's my mother."

Now *Helena* looks ready to collapse, staggering back as if I've hit her with a blast from one of my abilities. "*What?* Your parents *died*."

"They weren't my real parents," I say, remembering that I never got the chance to tell her that bit. I look at Ivy. "Right? *She* knows the story."

Ivy dips her head in acknowledgement, but I have the feeling it's also to avoid looking at me. "It's not safe to talk here," she says, helping me to my feet. "Follow me, and I'll explain everything."

I don't want to do that. A sensation of danger rumbles in my gut. This could be a trap, but I want answers more than anything. If this woman knows something, *anything*, about me, what choice do we have but to obey? I glance around for Willow, but her group hasn't sent any type of signal. No way to be sure if she's on her way back. Will Willow cross our path in time to see our *mother?*

*Did she know she was here? Is this why she wanted me to come?* I ask myself.

The edge of the Wilderness looms nearby, and Ivy slips into the trees. If it was up to me, I would've suggested heading to Clio's. It's a straight shot to his front door. But maybe Ivy feels the trees are safer, or maybe she just doesn't trust anywhere that could trap her.

Helena shoots me a sideways glance. "Is this a good idea?"

I don't answer. I don't know. Decision-making isn't my strong suit, but if I want answers, I have to take the risk.

Helena and I make our way through the undergrowth. Thin beams of sunlight stream through the branches, onto Ivy, and I take a second to really study her. Midnight-black hair curls midway down her back, swooping across her forehead in a light spread of bangs. My eyes catch hers.

"You've grown into a beautiful young woman, Lilith," she says, reserved, and sets a hand to my cheek.

Now that the shock has worn away, the reality of the situation crafts my mouth into a sneer. "All these years you've been *alive?*"

Helena glances at me, and a glimpse into her mind shows me various memories of her and Lexi. She's questioning the validity of every single one of them.

"You hid from me. You hid from Willow. We *needed* you, and all this time, you were hiding like a coward." Ivy lowers her head in shame, but I'm not done baring my teeth. "Why did you stay with Helena and let her believe you were a *cat?*"

"It was too risky to reveal myself. They would've killed me if they knew. You have to understand. I wanted to tell you. So many times I thought about doing it, but I couldn't step into your house. Raya and Haze knew the truth. If I showed up there… well, they had orders, too."

Every time I think I've untangled my own history, it just knots itself tighter. "Orders… orders! *Everyone* has orders, is that right? No one's capable of thinking for themselves? Life is one big, orchestrated event, and no one chooses their part in it."

She winces. "You have no idea *how* sorry I am."

"Don't. Just don't. How can you think *anything* you did is fine? You left me with the people who crippled me for life. Look at me!" I slam my walking stick against my bad leg. "*They* made me this!"

"They did what they thought was best," Ivy says, though her hand pressed to her temple betrays her false certainty.

I barely register Helena's focus on me. In my anger, I've

forgotten she's with us.

Through my blinding rage, another sound cuts in. A soft rhythm of footsteps where there should be none. Helena's head snaps toward a gap in the trees, and Ivy's eyes go wide just as mine do.

"We've been compromised," she hisses, ducking low to the forest floor.

The undergrowth explodes around us into flying twigs and branches. The Council. There's only enough time for Helena and Ivy to wail before we're surrounded. I try to stay by Helena's side, to keep her safe, but as we try to back away, hopelessness sinks in.

My opponent changes from a faceless surge of enemies to Crowe. My only thought is my promise to Katrina. Even if I want to, I *can't* hurt him.

"Crowe," I say, my voice wavering.

He also seems unable to move, suspended in this moment with me. I don't know how the spell is broken or by whom, but Crowe starts to shift, and I recognize the transformation into his bear form. The scar up my left arm burns, the result of his rough training. The only difference now is that Crowe no longer has a reason to hold back.

Worst of all, he already knows *all* my quirks.

*No. Not* all *of them,* I remind myself.

When Crowe charges, I force my new Aens power out with everything in me. Witches scatter. Some run and others are knocked down. Crowe slips beneath the blast and continues the attack. When he slams me to the ground, it's with his full weight. His jaws drop toward my throat. Tendrils of magic bubble in my chest, but none of it comes out. I squeeze my eyes shut, waiting for the agony of his teeth ripping into my flesh.

It doesn't come.

His weight lifts from me, and I open my eyes to see he's back in his human shape. Face devoid of emotion, he shoves a pair of silver handcuffs around my wrists. I don't realize he's lifted me until the ground shifts beneath me at a strange angle. Then I'm hoisted over his shoulder.

I search for help, but Helena and Ivy are gone. They must've gotten away in the fight. I can't decide whether I should feel angry, ashamed, or just plain *hurt* that I've been left behind.

The handcuffs are tight enough to dig into my wrists. Crowe's way of making a point, reminding me that we're on opposite sides. I'm the one who has everything twisted. He snatches up my walking stick, swinging it from side to side with every step, taunting me with it. My bad leg flares with pain, and all I can focus on is how much I could use that damn stick right now. But he takes another step, pushing it just a little farther out of reach, as if he's heard the thought in my head.

He bends over to set me on the ground, urging me forward. I obey, too defeated to act on any of the spiteful thoughts racing through my head. I used to think life was like a game of chess, each decision cold, calculating, and ultimately leading toward one major goal: our purpose in life, whatever that may be. Now I recognize it for what it truly is—faulty, the odds stacked *against* me rather than in my favor, like a kick to the ribs when I'm already down.

I jerk at the restraints again, despair growing with the knowledge that it'll do no good. They won't come off. These cuffs are meant to hold a witch's magic at bay, no matter how powerful they may be. The Council is treating me exactly as I should have treated them.

Instead, I showed my heart, and it was my downfall.

237

## Chapter Thirty-One
### Friends Turned Enemies

A S WE PASS through the Council's topiary garden, seemingly untouched by the war they incited, I'm surprisingly numb. Maybe that's for the best. Crowe walks silently behind me, guiding me onward. I wish I could tap into his thoughts, but the cuffs prevent it. Does he feel any regret? Anything at all?

*Why did I listen to Katrina?* I torture myself with the thought.

Beside Crowe, Tricia chatters on if things are how they've always been, and the past ten minutes haven't changed any of it. Though I was never particularly close to Tricia, it stings to see her so seemingly happy to have me in custody. She laughs at something, and I look at her in disgust.

Quinn's broken face comes to mind. *"Monsters don't ever see themselves as monsters."*

Crowe hands me off to Hyacinth, still holding my walking stick as he goes. He mutters something about the Sage then disappears into the depths of Headquarters. Hyacinth, usually the most sympathetic of the Council, now wears an expression twisted by a mix of emotions I can't quite read.

*Why would you do this, Lilith? Why leave us?* Her question fills my head. She must be projecting the thoughts for me to pick them up through the handcuff's wards.

*Why stay?* I shoot back. *With every horrible thing you guys are doing how can you think this is right? Witches are hurting, dead, because of you!*

*You want to know why I'm on this side, Lilith? Why I support the Council and the treaty and everything it stands for? I've read their thoughts. All their thoughts. So many witches think violence is the answer. Without the treaty, there would be nothing to stop them. There would be anarchy. Mayhem. Murder. Is that what you want?*

"That's because of *you*, you bitch!" I screech out loud. "Families are being torn apart because of this senseless war!"

Hyacinth flinches, her skin a shade paler than usual, but she doesn't speak again as Crowe reappears from the Sage's room.

"Come on," he says, grabbing the handcuffs to lead me away.

I shoot Hyacinth a fleeting glare, hoping it masks the fear twisting in my gut. She rolls her eyes and strides out of Headquarters, the door slamming shut behind her. That leaves me and Crowe heading to the only grim destination I can imagine. My death. "Where are we going?"

Crowe doesn't answer. He pulls harder on the handcuffs. In my time in the Elemental Coven, I've come to a weird kind of peace with the idea of death. With most of my loved ones being Reanimates, and the knowledge that I'll most likely become one too it's no longer something to be afraid of, but if I die here, I *won't* come back. They'll keep me from Willow and any chance she'll ever have to reanimate me.

I dig my heels into the floor, desperate to buy myself a few more minutes. The handcuffs might block my magic, but they can't stop me from physically fighting back. Crowe halts, sizing me up, trying to figure out how to get me moving again. The

Common Room is empty. No one here to help him. Even if he calls for backup, he'll have to deal with me for a while first before they show up. His hand slides down my arm, but he doesn't pull, not yet. He must know I'll only dig in harder. I've got nothing left to lose after all.

It's been a long day, and my energy is close to running out. I can't fight forever. Maybe he's already guessed that.

I catch the sympathy in his eyes as he says, "I'm sorry, okay? But, uh… the Sage wants me to keep you in the Grove. She wants you in the holding cells."

He turns away after saying those words, hiding his face, and tugs me onward. I give in. If Crowe can't get me to where the Sage wants me to be, she'll send others to do the job, and they won't be as nice.

"Since when does the Council have holding cells?"

Crowe doesn't answer.

Iris was locked in a dog cage the night of her capture. That must have been to humiliate her. If they find me dangerous enough to utilize their cells, there's likely worse in store for me.

"Can't I have a dog cage?" I try to joke.

I expect the jest to fall flat, and it does.

Crowe's eyes dart toward me. His face hardly moves when he says, "Lilith, it's better not to ask questions at this point. Trust me. The Sage will explain everything when she gets here. Until then, maybe we shouldn't speak."

"I don't understand. She wants to *talk* to me? For what?" I ask in a whisper. "Does this mean I won't be executed?"

The corner of his lip twitches as he fights his emotions into submission. "Please don't jump to conclusions," he says, keeping his eyes on the path ahead. "I don't want to say anything to give you false hope. That wouldn't be right."

I clench my jaw. That he could think of *any* of this as right is wrong, but I don't point that out. I dip my head and obey Crowe's direction, though for all the urgency of the situation, he doesn't seem to be in a hurry to bring us *anywhere*. That both surprises and confuses me. If I'm as dangerous as the Sage thinks, I should be locked in their prison by now.

"Why'd you do it?" Crowe asks as the shadows of the topiary garden close in around us.

I draw my eyebrows together, caught off guard by the question. "Huh?"

"The rumors? They're true, aren't they? You joined the Elementals. That's why you were with *Ivy Paradox*, of all people."

I bristle. "How do you know her?"

He doesn't seem to hear me, glossy eyes staring into nothing. When he finally does speak, his voice is so quiet, I have to lean toward him to hear it. "You're one of *them*." The words are confrontational, but his tone isn't. His fight is gone, too.

"Yeah," I say at last, seeing no reason to lie. "They rescued me from the Battle of Ignis when you left me to die."

"That girl. *Chastity*. You *executed* her just to turn around and fulfill her mission?"

Every time I hear her name, the scene from that day hits me like a stab to the chest. The effect is less now that I know I didn't technically light the fire, but the guilt never really fades. "You don't think that thought haunts me every day, Crowe?"

"I don't know anything about you, apparently."

"But you know something about Ivy," I point out.

He looks away. When I think he's about to shut down again, he wipes his mouth and says, "It's a long story." He pauses then adds, "I spent time looking for you after you disappeared, you know. I didn't want to believe you'd abandon us like that. I thought we were friends. I *defended* you and—"

"I'm sorry," I interrupt. That's all I *can* say. I sympathize with who he is but not what he's doing. "But they're right. The Elementals. The Council is going to collapse under the weight of its own power. It's just a matter of time."

He laughs, and my eyebrows shoot up in surprise.

"We're *all* going to collapse," he says, the words almost hollow. "Don't you see that? This war is destroying everything. There will be nothing left when it's done."

I stubbornly shake my head. "No. One side of this war has to win."

"And how do you know it'll be yours?"

That's a good question. I *don't* know. Not really. Intuition deep in my gut that comforts me, telling me I'm doing the right thing and that will have to be enough. "Where's Helena?"

His green eyes are watery pools as he says, "I don't know. Dead?"

My head whirls, trying to figure out what that means. Has Helena died a *second time* or is he simply working from previous information? With any luck, Helena slipped out unnoticed during my capture—Ivy, too, if she succeeded in shifting back to her cat form. Crowe hadn't mentioned seeing Helena in the forest with Ivy and me. Could he simply think she's *still* dead after the Battle of Ignis?

Crowe doesn't offer any clarification. We round a bend in

the topiary garden, following a path toward the Council dormitories. My sadness shifts into confusion. We should be heading in the opposite direction, shouldn't we?

He opens the door to his room and pauses, glancing back at me with an apologetic look. "Sorry. I know water's not really your thing." He steps through the inch of water covering the floor, gesturing me inside. "It was either this or the holding cell."

While the Elemental Coven had treated me kindly in *their* holding cells, the Council won't show me the same courtesy. We both know what it means that I'm in Crowe's room and not already locked up. I've been spared from torture, and he's the one I have to thank for it.

"This is fine, thank you," I say, hugging myself as I watch him close the door. I stay awkwardly beside it. "Though I can't help but think this is because you don't *have* any holding cells."

I didn't spend long living with the Council, but with everything that had happened, I would've heard about them sooner. *And Iris wouldn't have been in a cage.*

"Sure we do. We have interrogation rooms too," he says. There's no hint of a lie in his eyes. His face and tone are all seriousness.

My stomach flops with a new wave of nausea. He's not putting me on. If the Council really has them, where are they?

Crowe sits on his bed, leans back against the wall, and stares up at the ceiling. "We have a lot of things you've never seen. Headquarters are bigger than you think."

"Is that right?"

"What you see in the Grove is only a fraction of what we've got. There's a trapdoor in the Sage's room. It leads to a staircase that stretches for miles beneath the earth. That's where the holding cells are. That's where *everything* is."

"Everything?"

"You can't honestly tell me you never wondered how six witches keep the entire Land of Five supplied with food, water, protection… order?"

My shoulders slump beneath the weight of his words. "No…" Until I joined the Council, my worldview had been very simple. Equipped witches fight, the UnEquipped don't, and the Council keeps us fed. Now everything is jumbled. "Where *does* it all come from?"

Crowe smiles, but it seems more from bitterness than anything else. "The Council is a Coven of its own."

I take a beat to digest those words, but they don't make sense.

"We show the world only one representative of each Coven and the Sage, but the Council has *hundreds* of witches."

*Hundreds?* If I wasn't already nauseous, that would've done it. Hundreds of witches? *That can't be right.* But I've seen them. Sparingly, yes, but I've seen them. Willow told me about them when she mentioned Tabitha. And when I remember back to my Dedication Ceremony, there was a girl who handed out crystals to my covenmates while Tarj was otherwise busy. I never saw her again after that day. "Hundreds?"

Crowe runs his tongue along his teeth. "Yeah."

"Who are they?"

"Whenever a new Coven representative is chosen, the witches they replace get a choice: go home, or stay and work in the chambers. No one wants to go home. It's the biggest demotion there is. So, most of them stay. Another cog in the Council's machine."

When I was brought into the Council, Tarj had disappeared for a while and reappeared once again in Ignis. No one questioned it. At least, not that I know of. Did anyone connect the dots and call him out for being a spy? Or did something else happen? Had he been kicked out of the Council against his will?

"Let me see if I've got this right… you're saying the Council has *hundreds* of witches hiding in a bunker underground?"

"Yep. Some of these witches can do things you'd never dream of. The destruction of Mentis? That was the work of only one of them."

The thought knocks the air from my lungs. *One* witch did that. What can the rest of them do?

"That's why the war keeps going," he says, resting his head against the wall to stare past me. "There are always more witches willing to fight and no one to stop them."

Two Covens still remain for the Council to draw new recruits from, and thanks to Willow's ability, the Elemental Coven will maintain its current number of recruits.

"Crowe, I know you're following orders, but this isn't right. How long are you going to support them? What if they go after Aquais? Who knows? They might wipe out the rest of the Land of Five to make a point. Executing *me* won't make any of this stop."

He takes so long to respond that I think he's fallen asleep when he takes in a big gush of air. "Are either of us truly doing the right thing? We tell ourselves what we're doing is for a good cause, and sometimes, we even believe it, but people are going to die regardless of what *I* do, regardless of what *you* do. It's the nature of the beast."

"It doesn't have to be like that! *I* don't have to die. You can let me go."

Crowe shakes his head, scattering his red locks. "No, I can't, or they'll execute *me*."

I expected that response. "So come with me."

"Let's say I did," he says. "What about my brother? My *mother*? They support the Council. *All* of Aquais supports the Council."

Suddenly, his turmoil makes sense. He's not fighting for the Council, he's in a war of his own, doing what he can to keep himself and his family alive. "Your parents *run* Aquais. They can influence their people any way they choose," I point out. "Why let them put their faith in something that'll destroy them?"

"For that very reason," Crowe says. "They don't want to lose their home, and neither do I."

"We can save it," I say, throwing words into the dark, hoping something will stick. That he'll listen. Maybe I've reached him. "We can end this war, Crowe."

Crowe closes his eyes, pretending he hasn't heard me.

Grim silence falls over the room as I wait for an answer that won't come. I glance between him and the door. If he falls asleep, can I slip out of here without him noticing? What can they do to me that's worse than *death* if I attempt to escape and fail? After a tense few minutes, his eyes don't reopen. I creep toward the door and grab the handle. It doesn't twist.

Magically enhanced.

*I'm doomed,* I think and plop down to the ground, not caring about the water that soaks through my clothes.

In my mind's eye, I see myself on the pyre, tied to the stake. I can almost feel the burning torture of fire melting the skin off my bones, hear the cheers of the onlookers, their celebration of my deepening agony. The only question left is: who will be the one to light the fire?

# Chapter Thirty-Two
## For Life

"I SHOULD'VE TOLD you it was locked," Crowe murmurs.

I look up, startled. "I thought you were asleep," I say, desperately trying to wipe the tears off my face. If I'm doomed to die, I want to do so with dignity.

"I know."

I've got one card left to play. My last, desperate ace. If I can use it right, maybe I can push him over the edge. "I met Katrina."

Crowe sits bolt upright, staring at me with wild eyes as if he's woken from a nightmare. "You…what?"

"I met Katrina," I repeat. "*Your* Katrina."

Crowe jerks forward off the bed, eyes wild in a way that makes me think he might attack me. "She's okay? Where is she?"

I raise my hands and stand shakily to my feet, a bit taken aback by his reaction. "She's an Elemental like you thought."

Crowe recoils. "She… she can't be," he murmurs. "She's…"

"Crowe," I say, reaching out to put a hand on his shoulder. I change my mind when his wild gaze comes back to me.

"What?" he snaps, but the tears that glossed over his eyes have started to leak free, telling me he's feeling everything except for anger right now.

"You remember when we toured the Land of Five, and you couldn't find Katrina?" I start. "You told me she's *smart*, that if she joined the Elementals, she'd have her reasons for doing it. Well, she *does,* but that doesn't mean you have to be enemies. You can be with her again."

Crowe lets out a loud sob and pulls me into a hug. He presses his face to my shoulder and cries. I'm too stunned to move, listening for a long time to his raspy wails. I don't know what to say or do. Mentioning Katrina had seemed like a great plan five minutes ago, but Crowe has always been unstable and hard to predict.

"I don't know what to do," he moans, his wet cheek brushing mine as he pulls back to look at me. "If I leave with you and be with her again, they might hurt my family."

"You don't know that for sure. Your family has an entire Coven standing behind them, determined to keep them safe."

Crowe considers this. "You're right," he says and wipes his face with the back of his hand. He stares across the room for a long time, likely weighing his options before finally croaking, "Let's do it. Let's get out of here."

My heart feels lighter than air with hope, filling it full to bursting, until a sickening lurch grounds me to reality. We're not out yet. This could be a trick. Until we're safely back on the Elemental Coven's terf, I'm still in danger.

Crowe tucks my walking stick under his arm to better guide me out of the dorm. We take two steps outside before he stops. My stomach flips with foreboding. What if he changes his mind?

"Why were you with Ivy?" he asks.

Of all the things he could ask, that's the last one I expect. Why would he care? *What does he know?*

"No one's seen her in years. We thought she was dead," he explains.

Not fully trusting the situation, I keep my silence.

Crowe sighs as if he can sense I'm holding back. "I'm asking because there's a file.

"A… file?" I echo, confused.

"Every witch who's ever lived or died in the land of Five has one. It's the Council's way of keeping tabs on everyone."

"Okay?" I say, forcing patience into my voice, though it's harder than it should be. The longer we stand here, the more I feel our chance to escape slipping away.

"She's your mother, isn't she?" he guesses. "Your birth mother?"

More defensive, I ask, "Why does it matter?"

"Don't you want to know what the file says?"

A file on my mother likely means the truth of my origins, my *accident*, everything I've been searching for, and it's been hidden in the Council's bunker this entire time. "Of course, but wouldn't it be easier for you to just tell me what it says?"

Crowe scoffs. "Of course it would be, but I don't know what it says. I've never had a chance to read any of them. If we're leaving, I think we should take it. Our own files too. The less information they have to use against us, the better." He sets his hand on my elbow to guide me as he had when I was his prisoner, except now, everything is different. We're allies united under the same goal. "Come on."

I go with him until I realize he's leading me back to

Headquarters, and *not* toward freedom. "Wait. Where are we going?"

"To get the files," he says with more determination than I expect.

"It's too dangerous," I tell him. "We need to leave before anyone suspects us."

"It's your decision, but if we leave now, so does the chance of ever seeing what it says."

If there's a detailed history on my *real* mother, I want to read it and learn everything I can. But this may be our only chance to escape, and my gut screams at me to take it.

Crowe doesn't appear to suffer from the same bout of indecision that plagues me. He chooses for me, leading me back through the topiary garden to Headquarters. His fingers dig into my skin as we approach the entrance to the Common Room.

"If anyone asks," he whispers in my ear, "you're my prisoner."

And I'll play that role to perfection.

Crowe falls silent as we take the first echoing steps into the Common Room. Inside, Hyacinth is perched in her favorite chair, and I focus all my energy on trying to lock up my thoughts, to keep the clairvoyant from seeing our plan and getting us *both* arrested. She looks up, and her eyes narrow. She isn't happy to see me again, but that's okay because I'm not happy to see her, either. Letting out a disdainful *hmmph*, she gets up and strolls out of the room, flipping her long, straw-blonde hair over her shoulder as she goes.

"Irritation is better than curiosity," Crowe reminds me.

My eyes dart around, heart thudding in my chest as I wait

for any of the other Council members to appear and ask Crowe what he's doing. Thankfully, none of them do. When we come to the door leading to the Sage's room, I stare at Crowe with wide eyes. "We can't go in there."

"The trap door is the only way to the chambers," Crowe reminds me.

"What if she's *in* there?"

"She wants me to bring you to the holding cells. For all she knows, that's what I'm doing."

Play the game. It makes sense, but I'm more than a little uneasy. What if this whole thing is nothing but a trick—a way to get me into the holding cells without a fight? Swiveling my head, I catch Crowe's eyes and see the fear in them. He's not faking this. He's in this as much as I am. If I go down, he's going down with me. Crowe takes in a deep breath and opens the door, leading the way into the shadows on the other side. Goosebumps of foreboding break out along my arms.

"Breathe," he tells me.

I do. In and out, focusing on the pressure in my chest. Then I hold it again as we emerge into the Sage's room. It's as I remember it, cramped and smelling of a variety of flowers and herbs. The warmth I felt the last time I was here is gone, though I can't decide whether that comes from the lack of a burbling cauldron or from my loss of respect for the Sage.

"She's not here," Crowe says, the relief clear in his voice as he releases my arm. He moves behind the desk, and I stay by the door, watching as he shifts the Sage's chair aside and bends down. A moment later, a loud clang echoes through the room.

Alarmed, I call his name.

He peers over the rim of the desk. "I'm okay, Lilith. Come on."

I'm not sure what exactly eases me onward, but I move one shaking step at a time to see Crowe crouched beside a hole in the floor, the rug rumpled beside it.

"Hundreds of witches live here?" I ask, skeptically pointing at it.

"It widens once you get inside," he says. "You can trust me. I'll prove it."

He tosses my walking stick down the hole, and I watch it disappear. Then Crowe launches himself into the darkness after it. I hear nothing from the shadows, and that brings a new wave of panic. What if he misjudged his jump?

What if he's hurt?

"Crowe!" I hiss into the pit, desperate to catch any glimpse of him.

"Jump! It's safe!" his voice echoes from below.

I could collapse with relief if it weren't for the uncertainty of my imminent future. I edge closer to the hole, judging the drop. There's no way I'll land on my feet, and even if I do, I won't be able to hold it. With the handcuffs, I won't be able to ease myself down, either.

How far is the fall?

"I'll catch you," Crowe promises.

I don't trust him, but again, what choice do I really have? If I don't trust him right now, can I ever really trust anyone? Drawing a deep breath, I sit on the edge, swing my legs over the gap, and let go of the ledge and my fear. Darkness swallows me. Then, with a jolt, I crash into Crowe's arms. He steadies me, helping me to my feet. Even knowing he's right beside me, I can't see him.

"Now what?" I ask.

"Hold onto me," he says, handing me the walking stick and setting a hand on my elbow.

I grasp his arm, and he leads the way as if we're going somewhere formal rather than the mysterious chambers below Headquarters. How can he maneuver so well in the dark? He must've been here before. That thought comes with a myriad of questions. Why would he come down here, and how many times has he made the journey?

"There's a staircase coming up," he says.

I jump at the unexpected sound of his voice. "Okay."

Without my telekinesis, every step down the stairs is a challenge. Crowe does a damn good job of keeping me steady, and I'd give him credit if my mind weren't so preoccupied. The farther we descend, the more light begins to seep through the darkness. When we reach the landing. artificial light fills this place. The same kind that used to light Mentis.

Crowe leans toward me, dark eyes sparkling in the light. "It's popular here, too."

That sentence gives me a fresh understanding of the attack on Mentis. Not only did they destroy the Coven, they took resources from it too.

"I don't know if we'll see anyone or not on the trip down," Crowe admits, "so from here on out, best performance from you, okay?"

Crowe places a hand on my shoulder, positioning himself behind me in the standard guard-with-prisoner stance, though there's one exception—he lets me keep the walking stick. I keep my head bowed, partly to shield my awe at the strange surroundings and partly to feign shame. The first room we pass is wide and airy. Heavy shelves line its walls, filled with a variety of Alchemy tools, ranging from plants to cauldrons and bolines.

"This is Lynx's little workshop," Crowe explains, "though he doesn't like to spend much time down here. He says it's too creepy."

"The *entire* first level?"

"Just about. Favoritism runs deep here."

I snort, but the sarcasm fades quickly when I remember all Lazarus told me about him. About what he can do. A breeze leaves goosebumps down my arm. *He's not a favorite, he's a prisoner too,* I remind myself. A prisoner with a plush cage.

When we reach the next level, we hear the first sounds of movements. Crowe squeezes my shoulder, reminding me of the importance of our act. If one of us fails, we *both* fail. The next floor is bustling with witches, carefully organizing bundles of plants and vegetables.

*This is where the distributors prepare supplies for the covens,* Crowe thinks clearly for my benefit.

"Hi, Crowe!" A slender girl with shoulder-length black hair and purple eyes approaches. "What're you up to?"

"Prisoner lockdown, Sabrina," Crowe says with a laugh that most likely stems from nervousness.

"You're all work and no play." The girl pouts, bending down to scoop a handful of plant bits from the container in front of her.

"You know me!" Crowe calls back in an apparent attempt

to sound playful except I can hear the undercurrent of fear. He shoves me into the hallway as quickly as he can.

"Who was that?" I whisper.

"Sabrina? She's from Ignis, though I doubt you've ever met her. She's been a member of the Council for about ten years now."

"What's her power?"

"She causes earthquakes."

Wonderful.

I realize then why Sabrina looks familiar. She's the one who gave Clio his piercing, the girl who vanished right after the Dedication Ceremony.

"The next floor will be easy," he says. "Kitchens and prep stations, plus dining rooms. Should be empty this time of day."

If there's one thing I remember about the Council, it's the extravagance of their every meal. Of course they had witches slaving away to pull it off.

"Next floor will be the heart of the Coven, if you will. It's got bedrooms and the Coven altar."

"Huh. I thought that would have been in the topiary garden."

He shakes his head. "Too risky for so many old councilmembers to be seen aboveground at once."

"That's what I can't understand. Doesn't their Coven miss them? Or wonder where they've gone?"

Crowe side-eyes me, but I don't need him to answer the question. Tabitha's behind that too.

What else has the Council been controlling?

"The toughest part will be the floor after that," Crowe

says. "It has the files we want, but it also has the holding cells so it's staffed with security. They are the ones who've found the most Elementals out of all of us."

I don't like the sound of that. "If the Council has this, why did the Sage send us around the Land of Five to scope things out?"

"Busywork," he replies, his tone flat, his eyes heavy with exhaustion. "The Sage could have done it all without leaving Headquarters."

I clench my jaw, angry for the naïve me who believed in such a different version of the Sage and the Land of Five. The innocence that I'll never have again.

"Three witches work on this floor, but two in particular worry me," Crowe continues, his voice dropping slightly. Crowe says. "Sable and Caleb. They're twins."

I'm surprised he doesn't mention Tabitha. Maybe he doesn't know she exists. "Do I want to know what they do?"

"Probably not, but it's best to prepare you anyway. Caleb's magic is… *special*," Crowe says uncertainly. We take the first step down the stairs toward the next level.

"Special how?"

"Special in that he can strip *other* witches of their powers. Those handcuffs you're wearing? His creation. They don't bind your powers inside you. They actually absorb them so your powers become too weak to use."

This sounds eerily like what Lazarus told me about Lynx. Could he be related to them? A more sinister question blooms. Could Caleb be the witch responsible for stripping my father's powers and Larc's too? "Isn't that dangerous?" I ask, twisting my wrists so as little of my skin touches the bands as possible.

"It can be."

"Oh, Gods." I glance at him from the corner of my eye. "What does Sable do?"

"Sable? She knows if you're telling the truth."

# Chapter Thirty-Three
## The Plan

"YOU'RE JUST NOW mentioning her?" I snap. Crowe's risking a lot right now for me, for both of us. He isn't foolish. He knows the consequences, but he also must know how easy it would be to change the story completely to absolve himself of any responsibility if we get caught. "She's going to know what we're doing! Why would you expect this plan to work?"

"Don't worry. I've got another plan," he says.

"And what's that?"

"The only way is to take you to the cells," he says. "If I'm really going to take you there, she won't pick up on a lie when we tell her where we're going."

That does it. I can't move another step. His wide green eyes bore into me, searching my face with a battling flicker of emotions behind them. I'm sure all he can see is my suspicion. "This is all a trick, isn't it? I'm still under arrest. You're not going to help me. You're going to put me in that cell and walk away." I almost can't believe my own stupidity for letting him get me this far.

Crowe brings his face close to mine. "You *have* to trust me. Read my mind if that's what it takes, but this is the only way."

I hold the handcuffs up, reminding him. He huffs and grabs them, and I feel the pressure of the magic lessen. I plunge deep into his thoughts, sorting through the mechanics of his plan, and search for anything he may be keeping under lock and key. For the first time since I've met him, he's completely *open*.

He's not hiding a thing.

"Better?" he asks, bringing me back to focus.

Staring into his eyes, I say, "I'm sorry I doubted you."

He turns away. I've offended him, but he's still here, still trying to help me through this, and that's something.

We step onto the next landing and make our way toward the Surveillance Floor. As we reach the top of the stairs, blinding artificial light floods my senses, and my steps falter. It's far brighter here than the other floors. Too bright. The tiles gleam, reflecting the harsh light, making the first stretch of the corridor almost blinding. A few scattered chairs line the hallway, their opulent designs reminding me of the Headquarters' Common Room with their lush, throne-like chairs.

"Where's the file?" I dare to whisper.

"There's a room right beside the holding cells," Crowe informs me.

That's the last thing we can say before we move into the first room. The sound of our footsteps seems unnaturally loud. If anyone else is here, we would've heard them by now. Crowe must think the same, because his pace quickens.

Then, I hear it. Footsteps. Someone rounding the corner behind us. I glance at Crowe, my heart pounding, and see the same alarm in his eyes. We keep moving, but Crowe starts to slow. I push forward, desperate to outrun whoever's coming, but a sick feeling in my gut tells me it's already too late.

They've seen us.

"Crowe," a tired voice calls, echoing off the walls. "What brings you to the Chambers today?"

He tenses. Without asking, I know this is Sable. Crowe gives me a look and slowly pivots, his hand tightening on my shoulder to guide me around with him. Sable looks to be a few years older than Ambrossi, her tousled black hair contrasting her olive skin. Her face is twisted into a sharp, bitter expression. The beginning of crow lines branch from the corners of her eyes, reminding me of my adopted mother more than I care to admit.

"Miss Sable!" Crowe gushes with fake enthusiasm and extends his hand to shake hers. "How good to see you."

"Mm-hmm," she replies with that tight-lipped grin, as if her skin is frozen like that. "I don't believe you answered my question."

"I've got a prisoner here," Crowe says with a sideways glance at me. "At the Sage's request, I'm taking her to the holding cells to await her trial. Unless there's been a change of plans I'm not aware of?" Now *he* seems tight-lipped and bitter. She stares him down, a subtle hint of disgust on her features as if he's nothing more than dirt on her shoe.

I'd hate to see what she thinks of *me*.

"No, Mister Crowe, there hasn't," she says at last, raising her chin. "Carry on."

"Right."

Sable gives me a once-over, her eyes narrowing to slits as she spots my walking stick. Then she goes back in the direction from which she came.

With a long, shuddering sigh, Crowe says, "That was a close one."

"But your plan worked."

"Thankfully. Let's make this quick. I don't have another one."

I don't, either. We pick up our pace, moving through more of the same sterile, lifeless rooms. After a few more minutes, we reach one that's noticeably darker. The door swings open to reveal a row of three identical cells. From where I stand, I can't make out anything inside.

Crowe doesn't slow down. The first cell is empty and I except the others to be as well, but that expectation is shattered when I see someone behind the second iron door.

A very *familiar* witch—Dawn, the Mentis Adept.

She lies motionless on the hospital bed, her body rigid, not reacting to our approach. As I get closer, I understand why. Her arms are wrapped in countless bandages, and the gauze seems to swirl across her torso beneath the loose blue gown she wears. "The bombs," Crowe says by way of explanation.

That's all he needs to say. I imagine the burns and shrapnel wounds that must have destroyed her skin. "Why isn't she with your Healers?"

"She's a prisoner."

"But she's the Mentis Adept."

"She gave that up when she tried to warn witches about the attack rather than follow the instructions she was given." Crowe's voice is stiff as he explains the situation, and I can't figure out how he truly feels about it. "Then she tried to attack a Council witch and that's why the first spell missed. So this is her punishment."

"But she did the right thing by trying to save innocent

witches. She doesn't deserve this," I say. "And she's hurt. You can't leave her here."

Crowe looks away again, as if ignoring her presence will make all of that go away. He doesn't offer more on the subject. Instead, he turns the corner, guiding me to do the same. I keep sending glances over my shoulder at Dawn, but we're running out of time. If I want that file, we can't waste the few minutes we have.

"It's this way," he says.

I'm about to ask where when I spot a slender entrance beyond the cells. Crowe glances subtly over his shoulder to be sure the coast is clear, then he pushes me ahead of him. Books and files line every inch of the three walls. It could take *weeks* to sift through this much paperwork.

"Where do we even start?" I ask, trying not to let the despair seep into my voice.

"There's a section in here dedicated to dead witches," he says. "Let's start there."

"She's not dead."

"I realize that, but until today, everyone believed she was."

"How can you be sure her file's still here? What if they've already taken it?"

"I don't think they've had time," he admits, pulling a stack of files from the shelf. "They're still out looking for her."

That gives me some semblance of hope. If they haven't caught her, maybe they haven't caught Helena either. Maybe they're hiding together. I scoop up a pile of files, reading through both the familiar and unfamiliar names.

"Found it," Crowe announces some time later, holding the file up for me to see.

My heart flutters and plunges right back down into the depths of my stomach. *Footsteps.*

"Crowe?" Sable calls, her voice echoing down the corridor.

"Shit!"

He grabs me by the arm and drags me out of the room. My walking stick clatters to the floor, and he shoves me into the empty cell, slamming the door with a *clang.*

I stumble back and fall to my knees. "Crowe!"

He walks toward Sable, his back to me. I can't hear what she's saying to him, but he doesn't look back. A wave of anger and hurt rises in my chest, and I'm torn between screaming or breaking down. My knees ache from the impact with the cold stone floor, but it's nothing compared to the sting of betrayal. How could I have fallen for such an obvious trick?

Shakily, I remind myself to have faith. I saw his intentions when I searched his thoughts. He hadn't been lying to me. *It's a trick,* I tell myself. *It's all a trick.* He tricked Sable once already, the way he tricks *everyone* when he thinks it's necessary.

Crowe is that he *always* has something up his sleeve.

# Chapter Thirty-Four
## Escape

WHEN SABLE AND Crowe's voices fade in the distance, the first tear falls. I try to convince myself it's a reaction to the pain in my leg, but it's not. I had trusted him, *really* trusted him, to get me out of this.

With a groan, I sink to the floor, my knees screaming as I shift my weight off them. They're already mottled purple and black from the cold stone; ugly bruises that don't matter now, not if an execution's waiting for me anyway. Sniffling, I drag myself toward the bed and haul my trembling body onto it.

I don't think about attempting an escape. It seems pointless. Even if I do somehow manage to slip out of this cell, without Crowe, there's no way I can get past all the witches on the floors above me or traverse the stairs to get there. I curl up atop the white sheets on the stiff, uncomfortable bed, and stare at the gray patterns in the wall.

More tears leak from my eyes, but I don't make a sound. This is it for me, isn't it? I'll never find out what happened to Clio or see how the war ends. Willow will have to go on without me. Staring into the face of death, I find my life suddenly seems so empty, so *meaningless*.

Footsteps echo down the corridor, and I tense.

"Lilith," someone hisses, and my eyes fly open.

Crowe is pressed against the steel bars. His eyes are as

wide as mine, and he gestures for me to be quiet.

I raise an eyebrow, ready to ask him why he'd do this, but he's not alone. The Sage appears with graceful steps belonging to someone much younger. My fingers dig into the silver railing on the side of the bed as I steady myself, looking her over from head to toe. She's taller than I remember. Or maybe that's because the few times I've seen her, she had been sitting in her chair, hunched over her desk. Her opal eyes focus on me. There's no emotion behind them. By the time she stops beside Crowe, he's managed to pull on an impassive mask again, although a flicker of panic lives in his eyes.

"Crowe," the Sage says, as if she can sense us communicating without a word. "Can you give us a minute?"

He swallows, and without any other option, says, "Yes, of course, ma'am." He gives me a quick look then heads down the corridor. When his footsteps fade, I have the Sage's complete attention, and she has mine.

"I never thought I'd see you in here," she says.

I'm not sure how to respond, so I sit a little bit straighter and wait for her to continue.

"It seems as if no matter what side of this war you're on, you're at the center of it," she says, an amused grin tugging at her lips. "How is that?"

I smirk, though I don't find any of her amusement in this situation. "I'm a huge part of it, right? That's why no one wanted me to know the truth about my accident. Just like you didn't want me to know about Willow. Whenever something important happens, the Council makes sure to keep the knowledge away from the general public. All part of the game, right?"

"Perhaps, but there are multiple pieces, some more important than others. But ultimately, *all* are disposable. When you die, this war will continue," she says, "as if you never existed."

"Then let me go if the odds are the same either way."

The Sage's ancient face draws tight, and I know I'm not going to like her next words. "Lilith, you know I can't do that."

I expect that response but it still angers me. If I weren't in these damned cuffs, my magic would already be crackling, destroying the bars with a gust of wind. "But you *support* the Elementals. I'm supposed to replace you! Wasn't that the plan?"

"At one time," she says, "but it seems as if fate had other ideas."

"So that's it? You're going to let them *execute* me like Iris… like Chastity?"

"It's what must be done," she says. "The only way to build something new is to tear it all down first. You've done your part. I'm sorry things have to end like this."

"You're not sorry, or you'd let me go. Chalk it up to faulty handcuffs or pass along the story that I suddenly had a new ability sprout, and it caught you all off guard."

"You and I both know that would never work," the Sage replies. "Now, try to get some rest. Tomorrow's a big day."

"I'll tell," I seethe, teeth grinding as I slide off the bed and stumble toward the bars. "I'll tell *everyone* the truth. What you *really* are."

Her mouth twitches into something like a smile. "Go ahead, my dear. Remember what people thought of Iris? What *you* thought of Iris?"

I do. I thought she'd been a lunatic. But the entire time,

she was telling the truth and no one knew it. The Sage set me up for failure. I'm her scapegoat. Her failsafe. I always have been. Just like Willow was once.

*The family legacy.*

"You'll be remembered as just another radical Elemental."

I open my mouth but close it again. What's the proper reply to news of my imminent demise?

Apparently, that bit of nothing suffices for the Sage. "Things will work out the way they're intended to," she says. "Have faith." Then she leaves, disappearing down the corridor, her hobbling footsteps echoing behind her.

As a person, I've always aired more on the pessimistic side of life, but the despair that washes over me now is a new feeling. Then, I hear a scoff. Crowe steps out of the doorway of the file room, dusting himself off after what looks like a recent transformation. I glance over at him, puzzled, as he pulls his clothes back on.

"I told you I was going to help you out of here," he says, buttoning his shirt, "and I meant it."

"How much did you hear?" I ask quietly, stunned by the act of defiance. After all the time he's spent trying to please the Sage, it's the last thing I ever expect from him.

"I heard enough," he says and digs into his pocket to pull out a set of keys. "You were right about her the whole time." He slides the smallest key into the lock and pulls the door open.

"I'm sorry, Crowe," I murmur, uncertain those are the right words for this situation as he hands me my walking stick.

I don't know how long he's been a member of the Council, but the job had meant a lot to him at one point. This can't be easy for him.

"For so long, I put her on a pedestal," he says, "holding her in the highest regard. I think it was because of how highly I regarded her, that I couldn't see her for what she is. Turns out my admiration only serves the show, the act, the *game* she's playing with all of us. With the entire Land of Five. She's poison masquerading as medicine."

He snags the key hanging from around his neck and undoes the handcuffs binding me. They fall to the floor with a heavy clatter, and I rub the tender skin. For the rest of my life, I'll never be able to make up this debt to him. "Thank you," I tell him.

"Let's get out of here." He puts a guiding hand on my elbow to lead me down the corridor, but I stop when I see Dawn in her cell.

"Come on," Crowe says, confused when I come to a dead halt.

"We can't just leave her here."

"She's wounded," Crowe reminds me. "She'll slow us down."

"They'll kill her if we leave her."

He bites his lip then pulls out the keys again, searching for the right one. As soon as he unlocks her door, I thrust it open. Dawn tries to sit up as I drop to my knees by the edge of her bed.

"Lilith?" she asks in surprise.

I look her over, trying to get an idea of how badly injured she is. "Can you walk?"

Dawn peers down at herself, looking so uncertain that I regret asking. What if she *can't*? What if she's like me? When I examine the bandages, the horrified realization comes that part of her leg is *missing*.

"Crowe," I say, desperate.

"I know," he says, glancing again from Dawn to the empty corridor behind us, "but if I *carry* her, we won't be able to hide what we're up to. We'll never get out of here."

I want to argue with him, but I stop myself. There's nothing to dispute. He's right.

"We can get you out," I tell Dawn, noticing her chest rising and falling in quick, rapid breaths.

"How?" she asks. I recognize the despair in her voice, the desperation that comes with knowing she's no longer capable of doing something that had once come so easily.

"You're going to have to work a bit, and it's gonna hurt," I admit. "The only way to get out of here without drawing attention is for you and me to look like prisoners," I tell her, then look to Crowe for confirmation.

He dips his head once, encouraging me to continue.

"Which means you'll have to try walking." She growls, at that so I add, "You can do it. *Trust me.*"

She holds my gaze and either sees something in me that convinces her or decides she has no other choice. She sits up and leans toward me so I can help her to her feet. With her weight added to my own, I stumble, and Crowe rushes into the cell to steady both of us. Our progress is hard and slow. I lean on Crowe, and Dawn leans on me, but at last, we move. Crowe scoops up my walking stick on the way out of the cell, and I pass it to Dawn.

My leg hurts from the trek, but she needs it much more than I do. We scurry toward the stairs, trying to get off the

Surveillance Floor as quickly as possible. The next three floors of witches are eerily empty. Crowe and I exchange a look.

Something's wrong.

He jumps up first into the Sage's room and pulls Dawn through, then helps me up. I'm grateful to be back on familiar ground, but the relief doesn't last long. Through the window, blips of color light up the night. Magic in the distance. A battle in the Grove.

I piece the situation together. Willow must have escaped from the second attack on Ignis. And she's come back for me.

# Chapter Thirty-Five
## Clio

CROWE, DAWN, AND I hurry down the corridor and out into the Common Room. Beyond the glass wall, a hint of smoke drifts in the air. I can't see any of the battle beyond the topiary garden, but I can hear it.

"I'm going to take her somewhere safe," Crowe says, scooping Dawn into his arms. I don't have time to ask how he plans to do that. He disappears into the night, and I need to figure out what to do next.

This is a lot like the Battle of Ignis—direct, physical, and terrifying. I have a fighting chance now that Crowe took off the handcuffs. I need to make a move, whether it be to fight or run.

Distant cries grow louder, more immediate, laced with terror. The witches around me are unfamiliar. I don't know who to attack or with whom to stand, so I focus my effort instead on rushing across the field, desperate to find Crowe or Willow.

Spells fly everywhere, some aimed at me, but I don't engage. Witches from Aens and Aquais are here. The Council had been ready for the Elementals to attack Headquarters.

I have to find Willow. I need to know if she managed to escape Ignis unscathed or if this fight has been set in motion in case she didn't. Witches part and familiar green eyes catch my attention, petrifying me.

Clio.

It's been so long since I've last seen him that it doesn't feel real. I blink, hoping the mirage will clear, but when I open my eyes, he's still here. *Why* is he here? He can't possibly be part of the Council… can he? Willow told me he hadn't been chosen as my replacement, but he's the most logical choice.

*Please, Gods, don't let it be true.*

He steps toward me. It's Clio, but not as I remember him. His once clear, porcelain skin is now crossed with a variety of long, thick, ugly scars, the worst of which runs across the side of his neck. Battle wounds.

I'm so overwhelmed by his sudden appearance, I dodge Grail's ice attack by pure dumb luck. Reality crashes back down on me. He could have killed me. If I don't get my act together, he *will*.

I pull my gaze from Clio to Grail, ready for his next attack. He's a solid fighter based on his performance at the Arcane Ceremony, but there's a difference between watching and partaking. When he attacks again, it's easy enough to pull up a shield, but his ability isn't his only gift. His energy is out of this world. Each shield I produce is weaker than the last, but his attacks don't slow. His attacks don't slow, and soon, my shield shatters. Ice shards slam through it, plunging into my leg. One, two, three. I watch it happen before I feel it, the sharp, cold creeping in moments later.

The world tilts. When I hit the ground, it briefly registers that I'm lying in a pool of my own blood. The world spins, and the sounds of battle diminish. A blast of fire soars through the air, and Grail lands a few feet away.

"Lilith!" Clio cries. He's at my side, arms wrapped around

me.

His closeness brings me back to simpler times, and all I want to do is bury my face in his chest and wish the world away.

"Lilith, talk to me. Please."

I swallow raggedly and look up at him. "It hurts," I say, but I can't manage a glance down at my legs to see the extent of the damage.

"I know, sweetheart." His voice is low, a little shaky, confirming he's already looked and wishes he hasn't. He blasts away a few witches who stray too close, and I can see he's working up a plan.

The battle is bound to get worse. We need to get out, but in the condition I'm in, I'm not sure how we'll do it. Clio whispers encouraging words in my ear, and somehow gets me up off the ground and kneeling on my bad leg, which is now, inconceivably, more functional than the other.

"We have to go," he says. "Can… can you…"

I'm in far too much pain to do more than this. The sudden weight of my own body makes me cry out, and I collapse again. Clio shields me, his eyes narrowed to attack. I don't look to see who he's fighting this time. The sooner they're out of the picture, the sooner we can get away. He tries to get me up again, but when that doesn't work, he scowls. His magic is getting weaker as the exhaustion gnaws at him. He's not going to be able to keep us safe forever.

"Lilith!" a familiar voice howls.

Crowe.

Clio jolts to attention, ready to launch an attack.

"He's on our side!" I yell, desperately tightening my grip

on Clio's arm. "He freed me."

Clio's hostility eases, and he looks at Crowe with a split-second of gratitude. Then the seriousness of battle hardens his features.

"Aquais is here," Crowe announces.

His thoughts are loud, head in turmoil. He can't fight his loved ones, but he can't hurt us either. Without warning, a blast of fire shoots toward him, but he dodges it, gauging the location of the attacker.

"*Why* is Aquais here? Why is..." His gaze catches on something across the field, and I see her, too—Katrina, cradling the lifeless body of Crowe's mother, Breanne, in her arms. Crowe races away from us.

"Crowe!" I call after him, fighting against my own body to stand.

"Let him go," Clio tells me, wrapping his arm around my shoulders. "We need to get you somewhere safe."

"I can't leave him," I plead, my gaze locked on his emerald eyes. All I can think of is how much Crowe sacrificed for me. I'd be dead without him. "He'll die if he stays here."

Clio's grip tightens, but he doesn't argue. With a low grunt, he scoops me up, pushing through the chaos to reach Katrina. Her tawny eyes are glazed, grief mixed with surprise and horror when she notices Crowe, then the blood pouring from my legs.

"We have to go," Clio urges, one arm still holding me, the other lifting to unleash a burst of fire at a pair of witches closing in.

"Mother!" Crowe sobs, ignoring us all.

Katrina grabs his face, forcing him to look at her. "Crowe, listen to me. She's going to be fine, okay? We just need to get her out of here."

Trembling, Crowe's eyes are glossy. He's in shock. Everything that's happened in the past twenty minutes has been too much for him.

Katrina lifts Breanne into her arms, staggering briefly under the woman's weight. "Come on!" she says and rushes into the darkness.

Crowe takes my outstretched hand, rising to his feet. Snapping back to the present, he follows Katrina, Clio and I a moment behind.

Crowe remains kneeling by the pool of his mother's blood, distant and still. I try to touch his shoulder, but I'm too far away. Just as I think I'll never reach him, he takes my outstretched hand, rising to his feet. For a brief moment, he lingers, weighed down by it all, before snapping back to the present. He follows Katrina, with Clio and me a moment behind.

"Where's Dawn!" I shout at Crowe as soon as I realize she's no longer with him.

"She's safe," he promises. "We'll meet up with her on our way out."

Katrina's bun of blue hair acts like a beacon, making it easy for us to follow her through the horrors of battle toward the spot where we landed in Ignis hours ago. Clio clutches me closer to his body as he runs, but every jostle is agonizing. His clothes are soaked with my blood, and darkness threatens to cloud my vision. My adrenaline keeps it at bay for a while, but when it fades, unconsciousness claims me before we make it to the portal.

# Chapter Thirty-Six
## The Next Wave

THE FIGHT LASTS until the sun rises. Morning light shines across the field, highlighting the aftermath. Bodies and blood. Charred vegetation and despair. Witches who possess any kind of water power rush inside the Council's burning Headquarters to put out the fires and pray the building can be saved.

Every one of the surviving witches carries some sign of the fight whether it be blood, bruises, or the soot that covers the firefighting witches. Their efforts aren't enough. The building groans, vibrating with a low hum as its foundations give way. The massive pane of glass, once a shimmering barrier between the inside and the world outside, shatters. Shards of glass explode outward, raining down into the grass as the building buckles under its own weight. The walls sag and splinter, sending dust and debris spiraling into the air.

A few witches check on the Sage, examining her for injuries, but she's silent as she sits in the grass, watching everything play out. Around her, others break down into hysterics, unsure what to do now that their home has been destroyed. The current members of the Council—Lynx, Tricia, Hyacinth, Grail, and Colby—stare at the wreckage. The last few Elementals seize their chance, darting across the border to vanish into the shelter of the woods beyond.

Tricia moves to follow, to fight to the death, if necessary, but Hyacinth stops her with a gentle hand on her arm.

Hopeless, Tricia asks, "What do we do?"

"Have faith," Hyacinth says and faces the devastated remains of Headquarters as the shadowy figure of a witch emerges from the rubble. "It's in his hands now."

The Sage
(Witch's Ambitions Trilogy Book Three)

The final battle approaches!

After joining the Elemental Coven, young witch Lilith's eyes were opened to the truth that the Council has always been desperate to keep hidden. With only two Covens still standing, Lilith's world is in danger of collapsing… and so is the Elemental Coven. After a mysterious illness begins to infect the Coven, witches are dying, and not even coven leader Willow's power of resurgence is enough to save them.

After the Battle of the Grove destroys Lilith's good leg and her ability to walk, she faces an internal war about her future that consumes her, dragging her further and further into the darkness. Willow is desperate to help Lilith find the light because Lilith isn't just her sister. She's the Elemental Coven's last hope for survival. As the Sage's ex-apprentice, Lilith is the only witch capable of taking down the ancient ruler.

As the war destroys the last of the covens, Lilith knows there is only one way to end the chaos for good—a final showdown against the Sage that only one of them will walk away from.

# About the Author

Raised in Michigan but moved to Texas and has experienced the best and worst of both. Kayla has interests in the dark and macabre. She enjoys '80's music and movies. A little neurotic and a huge lover of Halloween, creepy stories and cats are totally her jam.